BLOOD FOUNTAIN

DAVID J. GATWARD

WEIRDSTONE PUBLISHING

Blood Fountain
by
David J. Gatward

Copyright © 2024 by David J. Gatward
All rights reserved.

No part of this book may be reproduced in any form or by any electronic or mechanical means, including information storage and retrieval systems, without written permission from the author, except for the use of brief quotations in a book review.

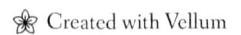

❀ Created with Vellum

To everyone at the Fountain Hotel: Mandy, Angus, Kim, Josh, Jen, Jasmine, Brodie, George, Owen, Di, Diane, Kayley, Darren, Libby, Henry, and the best pub dogs in the world, Hamish and Bonnie

Grimm: nickname for a dour and forbidding individual, from Old High German grim [meaning] 'stern', 'severe'. From a Germanic personal name, Grima, [meaning] 'mask'.
(*www.ancestory.co.uk*)

ONE

Twenty-nine-year-old Ian Lancaster was fairly sure there were better ways to use the school holidays than what he was doing right then. He was knackered to the point of thinking the walk that day had eroded his feet, and now he was just hobbling along on the bleeding stumps of his ankles. Everywhere ached. Even his ears, and he had no idea at all how that was even possible. The wind, probably, he thought, but even so, to come to the end of a walk and find the fleshy lobes in pain, seemed a little much.

He had agreed to the weekend months ago, mainly because he'd had no choice in the matter. A stag do was not something you backed out of, especially if that stag do was for your oldest friend, who had also offered to pay. But that was Mickey through and through, wasn't it? Ever generous, ever enthusiastic and positive and successful and good God, Ian hated the man. Not that he'd ever admit it, because Mickey Lancaster had always been good to him, supported him, kept him going through life's ups and downs, but did he really have to be so nice? Like, all the time?

Everyone liked Mickey. Everyone talked about how great Mickey was, how generous, how kind. And yes, he was all of those things, but that only served to make Ian hate the bastard even more. Yet, here he was, away on the man's stag do, in the Yorkshire Dales, doing outdoor things like walking and mountain biking and pretending to give a shit about scenery and waterfalls, and having to mix with Mickey's awful city friends. Instead, he wished he was home doing not a damned thing, and that Mickey, if not dead, was at the very least on life support after the kind of accident only ever suffered by Wile E. Coyote.

Lying stretched out on his bed, painfully aware of his awful fitness levels, and terrified of moving in case it sent shockwaves of agony through his entire body, Ian tried to work out why he'd said yes to coming along in the first place, and also why the love he'd had for Mickey as a child, had become something quite the opposite over the years.

One thing he knew for sure was that the process had been gradual. They'd attended the same school, the same sixth form, but headed to different universities. Mickey went to a place populated by people with huge brains and equally huge egos, who were all then headhunted on graduation and offered large salaries in high-flying jobs, and Ian to somewhere he'd not even wanted to attend in the first place, but his grades hadn't been up to scratch. So, unable to take the course he wanted at the university he wanted, he had taken anything he could, just to leave home. To add insult to injury, he'd ended up at a teacher training college. He didn't even want to be a teacher! But that's what he'd trained as and that's what he'd ended up doing, because motivation was something he lacked, as was drive, so that was that.

Ian had nothing against teachers. In fact, he admired them enormously. He regarded teaching as the most important job on the planet as well as the most undervalued, but that didn't mean he wanted to do it. He'd stuck with it though, because dropping out would've been the worst of decisions, and anyway, not making a decision was much easier, so he'd stayed on, graduated, and ended up in front of a class of six-year-olds, most of whom couldn't even tie their piss-soaked laces together. On top of all that, he lived in Norfolk, something even he couldn't begin to explain. It had just happened, because a job had come up, he'd got it, and never really thought about moving anywhere else.

Then there was Mickey. Because of course he'd walked into a high-paying job in the city, hadn't he? And of course he'd done really well, earned a fortune, bought a ridiculous car, an exclusive apartment, had far too many unbelievably attractive girlfriends, and in the end found one that he wanted to keep.

And there it was. There was the reason. Mickey, Ian realised, treated everyone around him like possessions. Yes, he was kind and generous and all those other things everyone constantly said about him, like they were a Mickey Fan Club Playlist and set to repeat, but Ian knew the truth. No one was really important to Mickey unless they served a purpose.

This new wife would make him look good. Ian knew that his own purpose in Mickey's life was to contrast and thus highlight the man's meteoric success. He was Mickey's court jester, the one he could show off to his friends, to poke gentle fun at.

This wife Mickey was soon to acquire, whom Ian hadn't even met—what was her name? Nope, couldn't remember, didn't care—their romance had been swift, only months from start to engagement, and the wedding itself had come around just as quickly. They'd booked a country house in Somerset for the event for the kind of money Ian was fairly sure most people would spend on a house rather than a party.

He'd go to that as well, and hate every second of it.

None of these thoughts were helping to improve Ian's state of mind. He wanted to be anywhere other than staying in a bed-

and-breakfast in a place that bore the ridiculous name Hawes. The sad fact was, however, that much like with his decision to stick with teacher training simply because it was the path of least resistance, the one requiring the least amount of thought, he knew he would force himself up and out into the evening to meet Mickey and his friends. Ian had never really been one for going his own way, and as painful as it often was, following the crowd, doing what others wanted him to do, well, it was just easier, wasn't it?

Thus, a couple of hours later, Ian was sitting in a pub, wearing a smile so fake he wondered if he couldn't just peel it off and throw it onto the floor as a chew for one of the many dogs that other punters had brought with them.

They'd finished the food they'd ordered, which had been an unpleasant experience in itself. Not because the food was bad, not by a long shot, but because the loudest in the group, Eddie, had complained there wasn't enough, and even demanded to see the chef. The chef, to his credit, had come to speak with Eddie, his huge beard held back behind a net for the sake of hygiene. Eddie had seen it and burst out laughing, eventually waving the chef away.

Ian took a moment to sweep his eyes around the place, take it all in, to see beyond the circle of unbearable twats he was perched on a stool with. As well as all the walkers still wearing their outdoor gear, there were tourists who'd dressed up a little to sit in a simple, honest pub and eat and drink and chat. The bar was hidden behind a group of men holding pint glasses, a couple of them in wellies, one with a muddy springer spaniel asleep at his feet. In front of the bar, a table was populated by a small group of men and women he assumed were locals, because they all clearly knew each other, and their accents were thick with Yorkshire's twang.

Reaching for the pint of beer sitting on the table in front of him, Ian's mind presented him with the idea of simply pouring it over Mickey's head. That would be a waste of good beer, though, so instead, he sunk the drink in one long, smooth draught, the liquid barely touching the sides of his throat. He didn't even really like beer, not ale, anyway. He was usually one for a bottle or two of cheap red wine from the convenience store rather than beers down at the pub with mates. Though, that might have more to do with not having many mates.

With that god-awful bleak thought smashing through his head like a gorilla armed with a hammer, Ian placed the now-empty glass back on the table, only to be shocked by the sound of applause coming at him from everyone he was sitting with. Then Mickey's hand clapped him hard on the back, knocking him forward.

'Nice one, mate! Where did you learn to do that?'

'College,' Ian replied, wiping his mouth, and whispering, *I'm not your mate ...*

'Can't have been,' said a man called Geoff, who reminded Ian of Beaker from The Muppets. 'No one learns anything at a college.'

That got a roar of laughter from Mickey's friends. Not from Ian, though.

'Another?' Mickey asked, pointing briefly at Ian's empty glass, then giving Ian no chance to respond as he stood up to head to the bar.

'Hey, not your job,' said Chris, who from what Ian could recall was in finance, and had a head that looked a little too much like an egg, so much so that Ian really wanted to find a mallet and crack it open. 'Rule number one: the groom-to-be never buys beer on a stag.' He then pointed a thick, stubby finger at Ian, and added, 'Your round, sir.'

The way Chris had said "sir" made Ian's flesh crawl, built as it was on his attempt to pretend to sound like a child at school talking to a teacher. It was creepy, and made Ian wonder if Chris rather liked to call people "sir," but in private, behind closed doors, and maybe wearing an awful lot of leather, while getting slapped on his amble behind by a horsewhip.

'But I got the last one,' Ian said.

'What did I say about bringing a teacher?' said another of Mickey's friends, this one remaining nameless in Ian's mind, because he'd taken an instant dislike to the way he wore a tiny goatee and kept stroking it.

'How do you mean?' Ian asked.

'Too much holiday, and always expect everyone to buy them drinks,' the goatee said.

'Why?'

'Why what?'

'Why would you think that teachers never buy their own drinks?'

'Can't afford it, can they?' the goatee replied, then burst into laughter and chinked glasses with another from the group sitting beside him.

'But that's not even a joke,' Ian said to himself, but it came out loud enough for everyone to hear.

'Teaching is though, isn't it?' said Chris. 'How the hell you stay sane, mate, I'll never know. You must be mad.'

'Oh, he's not mad, are you, Ian?' Mickey said, resting an arm across Ian's shoulders to give him a playful hug. 'Just likes an easy life, that's all, isn't it?'

'Teaching, an easy life?' Ian replied, his words seasoned with enough scorn to sour milk. 'You should try it for a day and see if you'd last beyond the first break.'

'I'd do anything for all that holiday you get,' said Eddie, who was wearing a shirt that was just tight enough to show off his exceptionally toned body, and who, in addition to complaining about the food and laughing at the chef, had already got off with two women who happened to be in Hawes with friends on a hen do.

'Why don't you, then?' Ian retorted.

Eddie stood up with enough drama to open a West End show, then lifted his arms and flexed his biceps, blowing kisses at them as he did so.

'Can you imagine me in a secondary school? I'd be arrested!'

The laughter that followed that comment, the loudest of which was from Mickey, sickened Ian almost more than the comment itself, though it was a close-run thing.

Eddie sat down, grabbed his glass of beer and went to chug it. The glass slipped from his hand and emptied its contents all over Mickey's pristine white T-shirt, half covering Ian in the process.

TWO

Mickey jumped up from his chair.

'Eddie, mate,' he said, and as Ian stared at the beer-stained areas of his own shirt, heard a hint of irritation in his voice. 'I'm soaked!'

Eddie stared at Mickey, then before anyone could stop him, he stood up and wrestled the T-shirt off him. Mickey tried to resist, but there was little he could do to match Eddie's size or strength.

Mickey stood, half-naked, at the table.

'Now what?' he said.

Everyone in the group except Ian laughed, then a voice cut across the pub from the bar.

'Oi, shirt on, lad, or you're out, you hear?'

The pub fell quiet, everyone stared, and Ian wanted to crawl into a corner and hide.

Mickey gave a shrug, and reached down for his jacket, which was stuffed under the table they were sitting around.

'I'd best nip back to where we're staying, then,' he said. 'Won't be long.'

As he went to leave, Eddie was on his feet again.

'Here,' he said, taking off his own shirt, a red one with black buttons and a chest pocket. 'I'm wearing a T-shirt underneath anyway, so you can have this. Saves you the trip.'

Mickey took Eddie's shirt, slipped it on, and buttoned it up.

'Not sure it fits that well,' he said, holding his arms out, the shirt hanging off him like he'd suddenly lost four stone.

Eddie turned to the bar where the voice had come from.

'There you go!' he shouted. 'As requested, fully dressed again. Better?' He lifted his arms and flexed his biceps, the muscles almost bursting out of his sleeves. 'Of course it is, because you get the gun show, now, too!'

There was no answer from the bar, just the silence of pure disdain.

While Ian, and everyone else in the pub, waited to see what would happen next, the door opened, and someone left. Ian had a sense that whoever they were, they'd been at the door a while, watching perhaps, and no doubt as appalled as he, which is why they had decided to go.

Eddie scratched his chin.

'Maybe you need to make a bit more of an effort to fit in,' he said, and before anyone could stop him, and much to Ian's barely disguised disgust, he strode across the pub to the table by the bar, and whipped a flat cap from off the table.

'This'll make him reet Yorkshire, won't it, like, aye by gum?' he said, then thrust out a hand to introduce himself to the group Ian had, moments ago, been observing.

'I'm Eddie, and it's reet grand to meet thee, by 'eck!' His sudden and clumsy attempt at a Yorkshire accent was like something out of a seventies sitcom.

Ian, stunned but not surprised that no one seemed to care his own shirt had been ruined by Eddie's stupidity, stared, eyes wide, while everyone else at his table roared with laughter.

Eddie, though, clearly wasn't done, and with no one grabbing his hand to shake it, he instead wiggled his fingers in the air and finished with a large bellow of, 'Wensleydale cheese!' before plonking the flat cap he'd taken from the table onto his head, and walking back to sit next to Mickey.

'There, you see?' he said, and took the cap from his head to rest it on Mickey's scalp. 'You fit right in now, don't you? Proper grand! Now, let's see if we can't get you a whippet?'

Smiling, Mickey took the hat off and doffed it at those Eddie had taken it from.

'Suits me, don't you think?' he said.

'You should probably give it back,' Ian suggested.

Eddie stared at Ian across the table.

'Sorry, sir,' he said, that creepiness in his voice again. 'Did we do a bad thing? You're not going to punish us, are you, for taking the man's hat?'

Then he winked, and if it hadn't been for the shadows Ian noticed standing over the table, he would've been on his feet and out the door.

'You'll be returning that hat now,' said one of the figures towering over Eddie, a man with ruddy cheeks and a heavy brow.

'But I like it,' said Eddie. 'And I'm just trying to get myself into character for when I'm up here in my new house. Can I not borrow it for a little bit?'

'No, you can't,' said another of the figures, this one a woman wearing a waxed gilet over a checked shirt that Ian noticed was ironed very well indeed, with sharp creases down the sleeves. 'Best you hand it back, I think, lad.'

Mickey took the cap from his head, went to hand it back, but Eddie took it from him and slapped it back down on his scalp.

'I don't think he can,' Eddie said. 'Seems like it wants to sit there a while longer. And you know what? I reckon it's bestowing upon him some true Yorkshireness, don't you? By 'eck, 'appen, you're reet, eh?'

More silence, this time so thick that Ian found it hard to breathe.

'That'll do, now,' said the third figure, another man, a stare on him that Ian had a feeling could probably cut through steel. 'You've had your fun, so hand it back. And that's not a request, if you take my meaning.'

Ian watched as the man clenched and unclenched his huge hands, heard his knuckles crack.

The woman in the checked shirt snatched the cap from Mickey's head. Eddie tried to grab it back, but in doing so fell across the table, causing everyone to snatch their pints away before he knocked them over, not wanting to end up like Mickey.

The three figures each gave Eddie and Mickey a hard stare, then returned to where they'd been sitting.

Ian waited a moment, wrestled with what he was about to do next, then gave a shrug and stood up.

'That's me done,' he said.

Mickey glanced at his watch, then looked up at him.

'What's the rush? It's still early!'

'Exactly,' Ian replied, and headed straight for the door.

Mickey was there first, barring the way.

'You can't just leave, mate. You can't; it's my stag, remember?'

Ian stared at his old school friend, desperately searching for a sign that the kid he'd grown up with, played with, gone on adventures with, was still in there. But all he saw was someone whose pride was wounded because of what Ian was doing; rejecting him.

'I don't like you, Mickey, not anymore,' Ian said. 'I've tried, I really have. But ...'

He tried to find the right words, couldn't. Mickey interrupted.

'But what? What's the problem?'

Ian wasn't sure how to answer that, what to say. He thought about all the years they'd known each other, how his friend had changed, how they'd grown apart. They'd shared so much as kids, as teenagers; surely that was worth holding on to?

Then he looked at the pairs of eyes all staring at him, was suddenly very aware of how his beer-covered shirt was clinging to his skin, and knew exactly what he had to say.

'You're all wankers,' he said, and taking advantage of Mickey's momentary astonishment, shoved him out of the way, thumped through the door, and walked back out into the marketplace.

Pushing on into what was left of the evening, Ian heard soft footsteps following along behind him, and mixing with it, like drops of milk swirled in clear water, laughter escaping from the pub. All of this only served to make him walk away even faster. He upped his pace, the aches in his body eased by the alcohol. His thoughts were focused on the bed waiting for him where he was staying, which was, by his choice, somewhere different to where Mickey and his friends had booked, and the welcome journey back home, which he would take tomorrow before any of them had even woken up. He could hardly bloody wait.

The night was cool, and his mind suddenly felt open, like someone had just hacked at it with a can opener. Maybe he could delay going to sleep, because right now, what he needed more than anything was to give himself a moment to deal with what he had just done. So, with that decided, he stopped walking, breathed in the chill of the night, exhaled, and took a left, laughing to himself as he went, the word *wankers* at the forefront of his mind.

THREE

Mandy was out with her two white West Highland terriers, and they seemed to be about as interested in the walk as she was herself, which was not at all.

The evening before had been a busy one at the pub. Not just in the bar, but in the function room at the back, there had been an engagement party. She was having trouble focusing on walking so busy was she with the endless yawns.

She knew the walk would do her good though, so she continued on her way, strolling along the flagstone path connecting Hawes to Gayle. The ancient thread of stone and grass and history was quiet in the early hours of the day and wet from early morning rain, which had thankfully eased before she had left the house. The scent of it still lit the air with the intoxicating aroma of the fells in which Hawes was nestled.

Far off, and dancing in the air with the caw of crows, came the bleating of lambs crying for their mothers to give them breakfast. Then the throaty warble of geese swept into the moment, and Mandy spotted at least a dozen of them swooping down to land in the field that dipped its edge into the cheerful waters of Gayle Beck.

Hawes had been home for longer than Mandy cared to remember, and running The Fountain Inn with her husband, Angus, had never been just a job to bring in enough money to pay the bills. She had always been aware of the fact that she was the custodian of somewhere quite special.

The Fountain was a public house that served not only as a draw for tourists, a place where they could rest their feet after a day on the hill, fill up on the many delicious things she insisted the kitchen provide, but a haven for locals, too. She prided herself on the welcome her establishment gave to all, and a key part of that was ensuring that the food was generous and tasty and the beer was worth the journey. Though she was more of a white wine person herself, she was always listening to feedback from punters, happy to hear the comments about the well-poured pints of Gamekeeper and Buttertubs, and whatever guest ales they had on tap.

A chill gust caught Mandy harder than she was prepared for and she stumbled a little as she passed through a stile halfway along the path. The two dogs yapped at each other, playfully dancing around her feet, their tails wagging as another gust swept in, only this time she was prepared for it and kept her footing.

Walking on, Mandy wondered how many times over the years she had trod this path, how many others had passed the same way, what they had been dreaming of or planning, what loves and broken hearts and good times and bad they had been wrestling with as they'd strolled from flagstone to flagstone and sucked in the rich Wensleydale air.

Letting the dogs off the lead for a run, Mandy drank in a draught of the air herself. Its cold, almost metallic tang filled her lungs with rich wonder, and she smiled.

Life was good. She lived in the most beautiful place on the planet, was blessed with the endless love of family and friends, and could think of nothing she could or would add to her life that would make it better. So strong was her feeling about this at that point, as she called for her two dogs and walked on back home, she couldn't think of a single thing that could even put a dint in the wonderful world she occupied. Yes, there were worries, things that bothered her, and not every day was all sunshine and roses, but she couldn't help feeling that whatever the world threw at her, she would be able to deal with it. The fortress of her life was impenetrable, and she really could not believe her own luck in living it.

A few minutes later, after arriving home to get herself together to head to the pub, Mandy's phone pinged. She opened it up to see a message waiting for her from Harry.

The gruff, scarred detective had arrived in Hawes a good while ago now, and had been so obviously weighed down with a hefty sack of his own troubles that no one had expected him to stay. Not least, because he'd been adamant that his role was only temporary, and that he would soon be heading back to the city to crack skulls, or whatever it was he'd done before as a detective in the city of Bristol.

He'd soon softened though, and Mandy had no doubt at all that the smoothing of his rough edges had little to do with his own openness to change, but more with the Dales and its people's relentless weathering of his tough exterior. She doubted very much that back when he'd first moved to the area, he would have expected that he would not only buy a house with someone he'd fallen in love with, but that his brother would have ended up engaged to one of his very own team. It was this engagement which had been celebrated at the pub the night before, with beer flowing, tasty food enjoyed, and the atmosphere seasoned well with the sound of joy and laughter.

Mandy read the message and laughed.

Great night. Much appreciated. Ben and Liz happy. Thanks. Harry.

In typical Harry fashion, it was lacking somewhat in emotion, and very much to the point, but Mandy was able to read between the lines and know that the fact he'd sent it at all was sign enough of how successful the evening had been.

She pinged back a reply, checked she had everything with her that she needed for the day ahead, then headed back out into the day to make her way to the pub. Angus would bring the dogs down later. She was getting in early to be on reception for whoever was staying in the bedrooms they also provided.

The walk into Hawes had Mandy bumping into friends, as well as memories. Early though it still was, the small market town at the top end of the dale was awake, with business owners heading to work, tractors thundering through the town, and various others out for a stroll, walking their dogs, nipping out for milk and a newspaper.

Nods and waves and greetings danced hand in hand with times past, the place changed so little that she could have been tripping along as a teenager, as a twenty-something with her whole life ahead of her, as a young mother in love with the new life she was sharing her world with ...

Stepping into the cosy welcome of the pub, Mandy removed her jacket and sat herself down behind the reception desk, only to stand back up again and have a quick look through at the function room. It had been cleared immediately after Ben and Liz's engagement party the night before, and was now home to a handful of tables set out for breakfast.

She popped her head around into the kitchen, then stopped at the tables already occupied by guests, asking what their plans were for the day ahead, and suggesting excursions when requested. The walk from Hawes to Hardraw Force was always top of the list, the waterfall itself a wonderful sight, but the addition of a pint and a bite to eat at The Green Dragon was something not to be missed. The Dales, and Wensleydale itself, had so much to offer that Mandy often had to stop herself from talking and allow the guests to finish their breakfast.

Heading back through to the reception desk, Mandy found a man with tired eyes and a weary smile waiting for her.

'You look done in, Larry,' she said. 'And it's not even eight in the morning yet!'

The man gave a shrug, stifled a yawn, and scratched his balding head.

'Just struggling with sleep at the moment, that's all,' he said. 'Trying to keep the wolf from the door. You know how it is when the mind's too busy.'

'I do,' Mandy agreed. 'How are you finding this delivery work, then?'

'Early mornings, long days, late nights,' Larry replied, then stretched his back awkwardly. 'That's why it wasn't a late one for me last night. Got to get myself back for some shuteye, and those pints don't help with that, do they?'

Mandy laughed.

'It's a bit different to what I'm used to,' Larry continued. 'My body complains more than it did, and it's getting more vocal, like. You know, sometimes when I get out of bed, my old bones pop and crack like fireworks thrown onto a fire.'

'That what woke you up, then?'

'Worry mainly, but I'm used to it. I ended up downstairs and fell asleep on my sofa trying to finish knitting a scarf. Woke up in a panic covered in wool thinking I was trapped in the web of some huge spider.'

'A scarf?'

'Heard somewhere it was good for my mental health,' Larry sighed. 'Mindfulness or some such bollocks.'

'Well, it doesn't sound pleasant.'

'It wasn't.'

Larry handed over a sheet of paper.

'Van's out the back,' he said. 'Your folk from the kitchen okay to come and collect it all?'

'I'll come and give a hand as well,' Mandy said. 'By which I mean, I'll stand well back and order them about a bit.'

'Very sensible.'

'Always.'

Mandy led Larry through into the function room, quickly dipping into the kitchen to ask for some help, before heading out of the back door and into the car park.

'Looks like you had quite the time of it after I left last night, though,' Larry said, as they approached his van. It was taking up a good amount of the car park, pulled up bumper-close to a car belonging to a visitor who had booked a room at the pub for the weekend. Mandy was always impressed by how he managed to squeeze the vehicle in without so much as a scratch.

'Does it?' asked Mandy, wondering what she'd missed during the tidy-up the night before for the delivery man to notice. There had certainly been no trouble at the party, which was no surprise, really, considering whose it had been. 'Can't think that it was any different than normal.'

Larry opened the side door of his van and reached inside to drag forward his delivery. 'You'll not be leaving him there all day though, will you? He'll catch his death.'

Mandy didn't quite hear what Larry had said at first, but when the words eventually became clear in her mind, the question confused her.

'How do you mean?' she asked. 'Leave whom where, exactly?'

One of the chefs arrived to carry boxes from the van.

Larry pointed in the general direction of the fields out the back of the pub.

'Fast asleep down there,' he said.

Mandy turned to see where Larry was pointing, was momentarily confused, until something clicked.

'The quoits pitch?'

A nod.

'Been down there this morning for a chat with Nancy?'

Larry laughed, shook his head.

'Don't have time for a sit down this early in the day. Saw him when I parked up.'

'And you're sure someone's down there?'

'Best you have a look for yourself.'

Mandy wasn't really listening as worry stabbed at her mind like forked lightning. She was damned sure that no one at the party had been that drunk, and even if they had been, she'd have sent them home before things got out of hand. And as far as she was aware, the same had been the case in the bar that night, with a handful of locals, and a good number of walkers, just enjoying an evening of talking and the sinking of a pint or three of the good stuff. There had been a couple of incidents as there usually were, someone complaining about the food, and a tourist jokingly taking someone's hat or cap or something, but there had been no rowdiness, no drunks being hoofed out the door, no punches thrown. A normal Saturday night, really.

Leaving Larry and the chef to deal with what needed to be carried into the pub, Mandy walked around the back of the van and to the edge of the car park to look down into the fields. There, on a small patch of grass below her, she saw a figure on the quoits pitch.

She'd never played the game, which involved throwing a metal ring about the size of a dinner plate towards a metal stake stuck in the centre of a square of clay, but knew that it had long been a tradition in the Dales. She'd never quite understood it, but folk enjoyed it and that was enough reason for her to support it.

The cost of the rings had shocked her, though, but she'd bought a set for the pub anyway, because again, it wasn't just a business, but a place of deep importance to the community. The pub had its own team, not just for quoits either, but darts as well, with leagues for both up and down the dale throughout the year.

More than a little irritated that someone had got themselves so blotto that their own bed had seemed difficult to find, Mandy made her way down to the pitch to give whoever it was a boot up the arse and a firm talking to. She was also rather concerned; sleeping outside on a cold patch of grass wasn't just foolish, it was dangerous; a chilly Dales' night could easily kill.

From back up at the car park, she heard Larry leaving.

'Right then, you silly sod,' Mandy said, walking past a bench she sat on sometimes just to enjoy the view.

She noticed that the cover to one of the clay pits was off, so pushed it back on with a kick or two.

Coming up to the unconscious figure lying face down on the pitch, she could see it was a man and that he was wearing walking boots, denim trousers, and a waterproof jacket with the hood pulled up. 'Whoever you are, I think it would be best if you—'

Mandy's voice caught in her throat.

Something about this wasn't right, and though she had no idea what, the scene sent a chill through her so sharply that she shuddered.

'Come on, now,' she said, edging closer, telling herself to stop being so daft. 'You can't be lying here all morning, can you? You'll catch your death.'

The man didn't move.

Mandy poked him in the thigh with her toes.

'Stop messing around, now,' she said, doing her best to make her voice sound both annoyed and light enough to imply she was able to see the funny side of what could happen after a few too many. 'Let's have you gone; you're making the place look untidy.'

She went in again with her toe, this time giving the man a hefty shove.

He moved, or at least some of him did.

At first, she couldn't take in what she was seeing, and simply stood there as the man's hood seemed to give birth to something. As it moved, she saw the thin collar of a red shirt reveal itself.

Her first thought was that it was a football, because it absolutely couldn't be anything else, could it? But then what would he be doing with a football under his hood, and how, because there was no way there would be room for it in there with his—

The thing from inside the hood came to a stop a couple of feet away and stared up at Mandy with the deadest eyes she had ever seen, and she screamed.

FOUR

For reasons he couldn't fathom, Harry was out in the early hours and running in the pouring rain. The ever-present encouragement from his detective constable, Jenny Blades, to keep fit was oftentimes a little too much, but then they both knew that without it, he would spend too long sitting on his arse getting a bit lardy.

Harry didn't want to get lardy, not by a long shot. It was just that it was difficult to get going and keep going at his age, compared to his younger days in the Paras. Back then, he'd been fit as a butcher's dog, fitter even, because the only way anyone survived in that regiment was by being almost superhuman. And it wasn't just running fitness that had been important either, but fighting fitness, and mental fitness, too.

Today's run was tough, but Harry's fitness had, to his surprise, improved somewhat. He didn't shout about it, because high on his list of People I Don't Like—and that was a very, very long list some days—were fitness bores, those who did it all, lifted it all, biked and swam and ran it all, then spent the rest of their time telling everyone else all about it, their times, their splits, their nutrition.

Having woken up earlier than he'd wanted or expected to, his head surprisingly clear after Ben and Liz's engagement party the night before, Harry had left Grace in bed with a kiss to her forehead. He grabbed his gear, got ready in the bathroom, and then padded downstairs to find Smudge, his black labrador, waiting for him at the bottom, tail wagging.

Smudge was a big fan of his running, because it meant she got to run as well. Harry had bought himself a specialist lead and belt that allowed her to trot along beside him without the risk of tripping him up, which she'd done on more than one occasion. Once, she'd ended up sending him down the bank and into the river Ure, and he'd had to trudge back home through Hawes looking like a bedraggled rat.

The new house lay just on the outskirts of Hawes, on the road towards Appersett, and up a small lane opposite a caravan site. The driveway was across open fields, giving Harry access to a footpath, which started directly outside the house, taking him across the fields and then up into the fells.

Today, which was bathing itself enthusiastically with heavy rain, he was running up a section of the Pennine Way. It would take him along and into Snaizeholme, with Dodd Fell Hill rising ahead of him, and Wether Fell to his left.

A tree plantation was making its presence known around him, covering the fellside in young growth, which would soon, it was hoped, provide more sanctuary for the red squirrels now living happily in the area. Dave Calvert was very excited about that. Harry smiled at the fact that such a big man was in love with something so small and fluffy. With Dave now on the team as a PCSO, they were all growing used to his talk about the wildlife cameras he had set up around and about, and if it wasn't the cameras and the footage of squirrels and badgers and deer, then it was his goats.

Tramping along through endless puddles, his pace solid but not pushing him to the point of his lungs exploding, Harry pushed on, the path rising, forcing him to dig a little deeper. He enjoyed his time out on the trails, and would do all he could to avoid running on tarmac. Running on a road was faster for sure, but it just wasn't as much fun.

What Harry liked was the sense of adventure he experienced from weaving along thin paths, navigating rocks and streams and fallen trees, saying hello to flocks of sheep that stared at him as he bumbled past. And what he loved more than anything, was running in the rain, which was why he was enjoying himself so much.

Sunshine just wasn't as much fun, and Harry would always end up overheating, but the rain kept him cool. There was more to it than that, though, because being out in the rain gave the Dales a burst of colour and an explosion of smells that Harry knew you only ever experienced if you headed out into it. And the heavier the rain the better, because that meant few if any others would be out in it, too. The occasional farmer perhaps, because bad weather didn't mean they could just jack in what they were doing and head home, or a walker caught out by the storm and desperate to get off the hill and into the warm embrace of a pub. But other than that, it would invariably just be him and Smudge, and she seemed to relish it even more than he did.

Sometimes, Harry would find himself so happy on his rain-drenched runs, that an odd feeling would come over him, and he would notice something strange happening, a pulling of the muscles on his face, a stretching of his scarred skin, and he would realise he was smiling. Another good thing about running in the rain: no one was with him other than Smudge to see the awful grimace on his face, but such was the joy of living with the scars of the professional soldier's life, and getting on the grumpy side of an IED.

Thinking back over the previous evening, and with the path ahead calling him to keep going a while longer before turning around to head back home to Grace's warm embrace, Harry focused on the smile on the face of his brother. It was certainly more pleasant to look at than his own, which wasn't difficult, but that it was there at all was a joy few if any knew better than he.

Ben's life had been tough, thanks to their violent, criminal father, who had surpassed himself in cruelty by murdering their mother in front of Ben when he was a teenager. Harry had arrived home from the Paras, barely recovered from his injuries, to find Ben in a dark house, front door ajar, and their mother lifeless on the kitchen floor. That horrific event had changed both their lives, and that smile Ben had worn the previous evening had Harry leaving the darker memories behind. They had no hold on them now, and Ben's life, which had sent him into a spiral, and the mean, cold arms of prison life, was now transformed.

With his job at the local garage, under the sage guidance of the owner, Mike, he was developing into a gifted mechanic and a valued colleague. Now, with his relationship captured in the glint of the diamond on Liz's ring finger, Harry dared to feel that life couldn't get much better. The Dales were now home, their lives were rich with friendship and love, and he neither missed nor thought of the life he had lived before, except in dreams, or rare moments of quiet when he would grant his mind permission to take a stroll back into darker times, if only to remind himself how far he had travelled since.

The ring on Liz's finger shone in Harry's mind as he hooked himself around on the path and headed back home. Ben hadn't bought it. It had come from Gordy, who had never had the chance to place it on Anna's finger, the love of her life, and the local vicar. Anna was now gone, and the loss haunted the community still. Her funeral was easily one of the most moving, and strangely uplifting, experiences of Harry's life.

That Gordy had wanted the ring to not be locked away and forgotten, and to instead have given it to Harry to pass on to Ben, still made his breath catch in his throat. But that was Gordy, and Anna for that matter, wasn't it? Their love had been a thing rich and full of life, and even in death, it seemed to Harry that their love continued, in Gordy's actions, and also in the impact that her life, and Anna's, had on the community.

The rain was easing, but the going was no less wet, the path a sodden thing of puddle and mud. Smudge, Harry noticed, would seek out the puddles deliberately, almost dancing through them with glee as they made their way back down the fellside. The grey rooftops of Gayle and Hawes were ahead, many of them reaching for the grey clouds above with spirals of smoke from chimneys, beneath which fires were lit to fend off the cold.

Eventually, the path became easier and wider and less populated by the mirrored surfaces of puddles, and after crossing the main road, Harry took the final section of the path back towards home. Again, he noticed the strange sensation of a smile on his face, as he upped his speed and fairly bounced along the narrow path, as it slipped through field and stile to lead him home.

Home!

Harry still couldn't quite believe that such a place was his to call home. But the truth of it was impossible to ignore. He had sold his tiny cottage in Gayle, and Grace hers in Carperby, and they'd bought a property together that neither of them could quite believe they owned.

With an open-plan ground floor heated by an enormous and

somewhat terrifying-looking wood-burning stove, two bathrooms, and four bedrooms spread over the next two floors, plus a large attic space, the house was a dream. The garden looked out from the back of the place and across fields, with nothing overlooking them except tall trees and their resident jackdaws and crows, pigeons and owls, and even the occasional buzzard.

The plan had originally been to live closer to Arthur, Grace's dad, and they had even put an offer on a place that satisfied that aim, but the deal had fallen through. Arthur had been the one who had first spotted the place they now lived in. With his blessing, they had bought it, and now, just a few months into sharing the space and making it their own, Harry still felt like he was living in a dream.

Arriving at last at the front door, Harry went to open it, only to find Grace already doing so. She stood there already dressed for work, in jacket and jeans and wellies, her own dog, Jess, at her side.

Harry went in for a kiss and Grace reciprocated.

'Nowt says romance like the kiss of a sweaty man drenched in rain and half covered in mud,' she said, and gave Smudge a scratch on her head. 'How was it?'

'Wet,' Harry grinned. 'Loved it, didn't we, Smudge?'

The dog wagged her tail and Harry unclipped her from her lead.

'Bed,' he said.

Smudge sauntered off to where her basket lay in front of the stove, which would still hold some heat from it being lit the night before after they'd returned from the pub. They'd not fancied heading to bed straight away, so a fire had been set in the grate, and they'd sunk into the sofa to listen to music and chat.

'Busy day?' Harry asked.

'There's no other kind, is there?' Grace replied. 'Best way to be, though, I think. Dad's been out since goodness knows when dealing with some rabbits. I'm picking up Thomas on my way to meet up with him.'

'How's he doing?' Harry asked. 'Still enjoying the life of an apprentice?'

'He is,' said Gordy. 'And he's turning into a fantastic gamekeeper. He'll do well.'

As the warmth in his body from the run was replaced by a chill from the drenching he'd received from the rain, Harry shuddered.

'Best get myself in the shower before I start to go hypothermic,' he said, then added with a cheeky wink, 'Fancy joining me?'

Grace laughed, kissed him, then stepped back to let him inside the house.

'Yes, but your timing's a bit off, isn't it? Hold that thought for later, though.'

Once out of the rain, Harry turned to pull the door shut, only to see a police vehicle pulling up in front of the house, Jen at the wheel.

'Trained your staff well enough to give you a lift to work now, is that it?' Grace smiled.

Jen climbed out of the car and stared at Harry, and the look in her eyes was enough.

'No,' he said, and waved the constable over.

'Then why's she here?' Grace asked.

'Well, whatever the reason, it won't be a good one,' Harry said, as Jen stepped into the house. 'Will it, Jen?'

The detective constable shook her head, face solemn and run through with faint lines of shock she was doing her best to contain.

'What's happened?' Harry asked.

'You need to get changed, and quickly,' Jen said. 'It's the Fountain ...'

'What is?'

Harry's thoughts went back to the night before, to Ben and Liz's engagement party.

'Mandy's ... Well, she's found something, Harry.'

'What?'

There was then just enough of a pause to make Harry concerned.

'A body,' Jen said. 'There's a body on the quoits pitch.'

Harry's concern evaporated, and before he knew what he was doing, he was following Jen back to her vehicle, Smudge at his heels. He was tempted to send the dog back inside, but something told him that having her around would be useful. Not because she would be any use with whatever police work he was about to be thrown into, but more that, amongst the darkness, she was a furry, soppy, tickle-my-tummy reminder that there was always light.

FIVE

'Well,' said Dave, rubbing his chin between finger and thumb.

Matt gave his head a scratch.

'Indeed,' he said.

Harry wanted to add something, and hopefully have it sound a little bit more eloquent, but he couldn't think of anything, so he just made a sound in the back of his throat, a grumbling, gravelly growl, that was, at best, utterly non-committal, and at worst, horrified and disturbed by what they were looking at.

With Liz away with Ben for the next few days, and Jadyn visiting family down in Bradford and not back till his shift on Sunday evening, the team was down to five. The only one not with them right at that moment was Jim, who was down at the other end of the dale in Middleham. He was originally there to do a walk around, but now he was following up on a report about an abandoned chicken shed.

After a lot of deep thinking and to-and-fro with Harry and his parents about the job and the farm, Jim had decided to cut his time as a PCSO in half. Harry knew that eventually he would go over to the farm full-time, but he understood why he'd not thrown himself in completely. He loved the farm, but he loved the job too, so half and half made sense. He had confided in Harry once that he wasn't sure about working full-time with his parents, especially his dad. Yes, he loved them, but loving your family, living with them, and working with them, too, all the time? That was a lot of pressure.

Harry realised then that he'd never actually given much thought to Jim's somewhat complicated home life. Prior to going half-time with the job, he would still have been spending most, if not all, his free time out on the farm, and Harry found himself wondering just how much time the lad ever actually had off from either the job or the farm. What did he do to relax? What free time did he actually have? And how the hell was he ever going to meet someone if all he ever did was work, work, work?

There was also the thorny issue of meeting someone and then, at some point, wanting to bring them home. That was never easy if that home was a house you shared with your parents. Jim needed a bit of freedom, and also someplace to call his own.

How either of those things would be solved, he hadn't the faintest idea, not now, anyway, but he was thinking, because he cared. Then again, he cared about everyone on his team, didn't he? More than he'd cared about the members of any team he'd ever been responsible for, even when compared to his time all those years ago in the Paras.

Funny how life changes you, he thought.

As to the random abandoned shed, when that report had come in early that morning, Harry had been sure there had been an error. An abandoned shed? For chickens? How was that even possible? Very, apparently.

The shed, a sturdy structure measuring twenty foot by ten foot, and eight feet high, had been found on the side of the road heading into Middleham from the Leyburn side. No one had any idea how it had got there, but its presence was unavoidable, mostly because it blocked half the road.

Jim had already called in to say that he'd had a chat with a couple of farmer friends, and they were working together to try and shift the thing out of the way with a couple of front loaders and some hefty rope, but as to the owner, and the reason for it being there in the first place, the mystery remained.

Staring at the strange and bloody sight on the quoits pitch, Harry glanced at Jen, Matt, and Dave, and immediately found himself missing his former detective inspector, Gordanian Haig. He was also already missing Grace and Smudge, but Grace was busy, and Smudge was best left in Jen's vehicle for now, fast asleep.

As for the team, it wasn't that any of them were bad at their job, quite the opposite actually, or that he desperately needed an extra pair of hands, but more that he just missed Gordy's steading presence and no-nonsense, straight-talking approach to both work and life. She had a way with people that was, as she would say with her lilting, almost tuneful, Scottish twang, 'beyond your ken,' and he'd been lucky enough to learn a great deal from working alongside her for so long.

Building himself up to approach the body and to get on with the next stage of the investigation, Harry briefly wondered how Gordy was getting on down south in Somerset. He was, like the rest of the team, keeping in touch with her, and he'd heard that her first week had been a bit of a birth of fire, with bodies seemingly turning up all over the place, and in various grisly modes of dispatch and display. Harry knew the area well, so was able to envision the places she had mentioned.

None of what he had learned about that first week was just from Gordy's mouth either, but also from two people he used to work with back in Bristol, Detective Chief Inspector Jameson and Detective Superintendent Firbank.

Whereas Firbank was keeping more of a distant eye on things, Jameson had gone for the up close and personal approach, visiting Gordy at her flat, taking her out for a drink or a meal now and again, and really making sure that she was okay. And she was, which was no small task in itself, after the sudden and tragic death of her partner, Anna.

Even so, to have Gordy there now would've been a huge comfort, and he made a mental note to call Detective Superintendent Walker to see if they were ever going to be sent a replacement. Harry had a horrible feeling that he already knew the answer to that question, which was probably why he'd held off on asking.

'Right then,' he said, clapping his hands together loudly enough to send the birds roosting in the trees growing along the old railway line below them, scattering in a chorus of flustered tweets and caws.

'Right then, what?' said Matt, glancing over at Harry. 'Cordon tape and call in the cavalry?'

'Margaret's that all by herself,' Harry replied with a chuckle, thinking of the district surgeon and the way she seemed to approach each day like a general charging into battle on a horse, sword raised. 'But yes, exactly that. I'll go have a nosy first, though. We'll need a list of everyone who stayed overnight, and also as many names as we can get of everyone who was in the pub.'

'Not much, then,' said Matt.

'I know it's pretty much impossible to make the list definitive,' said Harry, 'but I bet you'll be surprised how close we get. There will be locals, and we'll be able to get descriptions of most of the rest, probably even some idea of where they're staying. Hawes is small, and someone somewhere always knows something. That's how this place works, isn't it?'

Harry turned to Dave.

'I want you to get on with cordoning the area off. Jen, set yourself up as Scene Guard, at least until we can get Jim up here with us; give him a call and tell him that this is a wee bit more important than a wayward shed.'

'Will do,' Jen said. 'I'll grab a clipboard from the office.'

'Might be worth putting tape up across the car park entrance, rather than just here at the steps down to the pitch,' he added, 'and then set yourself up there. Otherwise, it'll be too easy for people to come wandering down for a nosy.'

'Word'll get around soon enough, though,' said Dave.

'It will,' Harry agreed, 'but if we can slow it down a bit, keep things quiet for now, that would be helpful.'

'Might get a few walkers going past on the footpaths,' said Matt. 'We could do with someone down there as well, just in case.'

'Dave, that'll be you once you're done with the tape,' Harry said.

'What do you want me to say?'

'Bugger all if you can,' Harry answered. 'Get yourself wrapped up and just keep folk away, say something general like we're following up on reports of a disturbance, that kind of thing.' He turned to Jen. 'Can you also check in on Mandy and make sure she's staying around for me to have a chat with her? With Gordy gone, and all that lovely new family liaison training under your belt, you'll be doing a wee bit more of that. I know it's not strictly that, but I'd still like you to do it, if that's okay.'

'No bother at all,' said Jen. 'I can do that first, if you want? And I'll see what I can do about that list of residents, and names of people at the pub last night.'

Harry gave a nod and Jen turned and jogged back up to the

pub, to head around to the front door and find Mandy. Harry was fairly confident that Jen would find her nursing a large glass of white wine, and he wouldn't blame her for doing so, either. The hour was irrelevant when something like this was thrust into your day.

Harry saw Matt lean close to Dave.

'Whatever you do, don't tell anyone that there's a decapitated body,' he said. 'Doesn't go down too well that kind of news. Tends to make people panic. Not that we've had many decapitations in Hawes, like. In fact, I can't remember one at all, but you know what I mean.'

'Sage counsel there from our DS,' said Harry.

'Probably best to not put that on the tourist brochure, though,' said Dave. 'Welcome to Hawes, where no one's ever been decapitated!'

'Sage goes great with roast chicken,' said Matt.

Harry closed his eyes, shook his head.

'How the hell can you think of food at a time like this?'

'A time like what?' replied Matt. 'I can always think of food.'

'Well, stop thinking about it for a moment,' said Harry. 'Call Margaret, then get a hold of our favourite pathologist and tell her what we've got.'

'She'll be thrilled.'

'How could she be anything else? And when you're done with that, come and join me with our friend down there, okay?'

'Will do,' said Matt, and pulled out his phone.

Leaving the team to crack on, Harry made his way down the steps to the quoits pitch. At the bottom of the steps, he slipped on some disposable covers for his shoes, and gloves for his hands, then took a moment. With his eyes firmly fixed on the unidentified body before him, he took in a deep breath, let it out slowly, then closed the distance between himself and his old friend, death.

SIX

Having come into the Fountain through the entrance used by visitors who had booked a room for a night or two, Jen eventually found Mandy hiding in the public bar, her hands clasped around a large glass of white wine, which looked completely untouched.

The pub was closed, so it was quiet. The lights were off, and Mandy was sitting at a table by the bar, her back to the window, and clothed in enough shadow to be almost invisible. In the far corner, Harry's chair sat silent, like the throne of a king waiting for him and his subjects to arrive.

'Mandy?' Jen said.

Mandy looked up but said not a word.

Jen noticed that Mandy's knuckles were white, much like her face, the shock of what she had discovered clearly still with its claws nice and deep.

'You know what you need?' Jen said, clapping her hands together, as though she was there to chivvy Mandy along a bit, and not talk about the body behind the pub. 'A good brew. Sweet, too; get some sugar in your system. Have you had any chocolate?' She didn't wait for an answer, looked around the bar, found a box of KitKats, and lobbed one over to Mandy.

Mandy caught the chocolate more by instinct than deliberate intent.

'Good catch,' said Jen.

'Not having it knock over my wine,' Mandy replied, a surprisingly playful edge to her voice, which Jen took as a good sign. 'And I don't like sweet tea.'

'Coffee, then,' said Jen.

Mandy gave a shrug.

'I only take my coffee black.'

'Not today, you don't.'

Jen popped out the back of the pub, past the small reading area, and into the larger function room, and instructed the chef to bring through a strong mug of filter coffee, nice and sweet, with extra cream, too.

The function room was now empty of residents eating breakfast, but the delicious smells from the food they'd been served still lingered. Jan wasn't one for a Full English, not unless it was the day after a big race and she desperately needed the calories, but right then, all she could think about was a slice of fried bread dipped into the runny yolk of a fried egg.

Back in the bar, Jen headed over to sit with Mandy, her eyes catching sight of the far corner where Harry would often sit, and sometimes end up almost holding court.

'How are you doing?' she asked. 'I know that's a stupid question, but I have to ask it, not just as a police officer, you understand, but as a friend.'

Mandy gave a nod at her wine.

'I've not touched it,' she said. 'I think that says it all, really, doesn't it?'

'It does,' Jen agreed. 'A mug of sweet coffee and that chocolate will do you a lot more good anyway.'

'I suppose so.'

Jen saw Mandy's hands relax from around the wine glass, so she reached over and moved it out of the way.

Mandy said nothing, just leaned back and sighed.

'I've never seen anything like it in my life,' she said. 'God, it was ... is ... horrible. Do you know who it is? Who would do something like that? You know, cut off ...'

Her voice faded, the memory of what she had seen erasing the words with ease.

Jen heard footsteps and turned to see the chef carrying a tray, on top of which sat two large mugs of coffee.

'Figured you could both do with one,' he said, placing the tray down on the table in front of Jen and Mandy.

Jen saw that there was a small plate with the mugs.

'Cookies,' the chef said. 'Freshly made.' Then he turned around and disappeared again out the back of the pub.

Jen reached for a cookie, but Mandy got in first, grabbed the top one, and dunked it in her coffee.

'That's a good cookie,' she said, taking a bite.

Jen did the same and had to agree.

'I could do with a few of these when I'm running,' she said. 'Sometimes, you just want real food, not gels and nutrition bars and all the other stuff I carry with me. Mini pork pies are good, but these cookies?' She held one up in the air between them. 'Life changing.'

Mandy laughed.

'God, don't tell the chef that. It'll go right to his head, and trust me, it's big enough already!'

For the next minute or so, Jen and Mandy sat quietly, munching the cookies and sipping the creamy, sweet coffee.

Mandy broke the silence.

'You were right,' she said. 'I needed that more than I did the wine. I should put it in the fridge though, really, shouldn't I? Save it for later.'

To save Mandy the trouble, Jen took the glass behind the bar and stowed it in one of the fridges.

'There you go,' she said, sitting back down again.

Mandy thanked Jen, then said, 'At least whoever it was didn't make a mess of the quoits pitch. So, that's something, isn't it? Wasn't cheap having that done. And the rings? If I'd known how expensive they were, I'd have thought twice about it, that's for sure!'

Jen smiled and said, 'Now, if it's okay, Mandy, I'd like to ask you a few questions?'

Mandy's eyes went wide.

'What? You mean I'm a suspect? You can't think I did it! I wouldn't! I mean, why would I?'

Jen held her hands up to calm Mandy down before she turned around and threw herself out of the window to escape.

'They're just questions, Mandy,' Jen said, her voice calm, her eyes relaxed as they held Mandy's own. 'We always have to ask questions. Comes with the job.'

Jen gave Mandy a moment to calm herself a little.

'You okay now?'

'I am,' said Mandy. 'So, what do you want to know?'

Jen took out her little notebook, then got down a few specifics, such as the time Mandy found the body, and where she was when she first saw it.

'It was Larry who spotted him,' Mandy said. 'You'll know him, I'm sure; Laurence Bainbridge? He's working deliveries now for one of our suppliers. Was just dropping a few boxes off for the kitchen.'

Jen asked for Larry's contact details, then asked, 'When you went down to check on the body, did you notice anything unusual?'

'Well, I didn't think it was a body at first,' Mandy said. 'So, I didn't really think it was unusual at all. I just thought it was some daft sod who'd got himself so pissed the night before he couldn't find his way home. Actually, I was annoyed more than anything. That kind of stupid can have you not waking up if the night gets too cold.'

'And what was he wearing?'

'Waterproof jacket, jeans, boots, and he had his hood up,' Mandy said. 'Been messing around with one of the clay pits as well, I think, because I had to put the cover back on. I tried to wake him with my foot, you know, just sort of pushed him a bit. But when he didn't stir, I gave him a proper jab with my toe. That's when ... well, the head sort of just rolled out.'

'Did you see anyone else around at all?'

Mandy shook her head.

'It's just fields out the back, as you know,' she said. 'There's nowt out there for folk to be looking at, is there? You know that as well as I.'

'There are footpaths; I've been running on them enough times.'

'I didn't notice anyone out on them, though, not that I was looking. There might have been someone out walking a dog, but like I said, I didn't notice anything. And it's not summer yet, so there's not so many folk around. Larry thought we'd had a mad night at the pub, but it was nowt out of the normal, like. Just a usual Saturday night, nice and busy, but not too busy, if you know what I mean.'

Jen thought about that for a moment.

'Were you in the pub last night?'

Mandy shook her head.

'Angus was running things. I was out back with the engagement party, as you know.'

'Any trouble at all?'

'Trouble? In my pub? Of course not! What kind of establishment do you think I run?'

Jen back-peddled a little, holding a hand up. 'I wasn't suggesting anything, Mandy, just asking.'

'Well, no, there was no trouble, certainly nothing worth writing home about, anyway. There was a bit of rowdiness, but that's to be expected, isn't it? Folk get a few beers in them, voices get loud, but that's normal. We had no trouble as far as I'm aware, none that's worth writing home about anyway.'

Jen said she would need to chat with everyone who was serving last night, and also that she would need a list of everyone who had stayed at the Fountain. Getting a list of everyone who was in the bar itself would be trickier, but hopefully a few names would lead to others, and the Fountain staff would be able to help with that. Then something Mandy had said floated up to the front of her mind.

'None that's worth writing home about,' Jen said, repeating Mandy's words back at her. 'Don't suppose you could expand on that a little, could you, because that kind of implies something happened?'

Mandy dismissed what Jen was suggesting with a shake of her head.

'Couple of local lads had a bit of a barny,' she said. 'Shoved each other around a bit, got a bit shouty, but they were given a swift talking to by someone else, and that was that.'

'Anything else?'

'A few dogs kicked off, and words were said. I mean, we're a dog-friendly pub, but some people have zero idea about how to look after one, do they? There were a good number of walkers in, holidaymakers, and there was something about a hat, I believe, but that's it.'

'A hat?' asked Jen. 'How do you mean?'

'Buggered if I know,' Mandy replied. 'Angus just said,

"*Something happened with a hat,*" but it was obviously nowt because that's all he said.'

Jen couldn't see how anything involving a hat could lead to a decapitated body finding its way onto the quoits pitch.

Mandy reached for another cookie.

'You're right,' she said, 'these really are very good.' She laughed. 'Could be bigger though, right? Much like all the food we serve; never enough on a plate.'

'Not from my experience,' said Jen.

Mandy pointed to where the chef had gone.

'That was something else Angus told me; someone actually complained last night that the meal they'd been served wasn't generous enough. Can you believe that?'

'No, not really.'

'The chef, bless him, went out to have a chat. Not sure how that went, but he was still muttering about it earlier.'

Jen glanced back through her notes. There was nothing there that jumped out at her, just some locals having a drunken argument, something about a hat, and a complaint about portion size, which in itself was completely ridiculous.

Perhaps whatever had happened to the person outside on the quoits pitch had nothing to do with the previous night at the pub. But then again, why should it? There really wasn't anything in what Mandy had said that made her think someone would get so violent as to cut off someone's head.

Jen slipped her notebook back into her pocket.

'I think that'll do us for now,' she said. 'You going to be okay?'

Mandy wiped a crumb from the side of her mouth.

'I'll be having that wine now,' she said.

'That's a yes, then.'

'It is.'

Jen retrieved Mandy's glass from the fridge and handed it over.

'Mind if I suggest something?' she asked, ready to leave and catch up with the rest of the team.

'Go ahead.'

'Get yourself home. Whatever you're due to be doing in here today, don't. Hand it over to someone else. Your mind won't be on it, so just take it easy, okay?'

'That's very considerate of you,' said Mandy. 'Didn't know the police were so caring.'

Jen smiled.

'Come on, Mandy,' she said. 'We're not like the normal police, are we?'

Mandy smiled, though Jen could see it was born more of relief, than simple happiness.

'No,' she said. 'You're not. And thank God for that, eh?'

'Oh, I do,' replied Jen, heading back behind the bar and out of the pub. Over her shoulder she added, 'And more often than I'd ever dare to admit!'

SEVEN

Over the years, Harry had seen a lot.

A severed head resting in the grass, staring up at him, though? Well, that was a new one, for sure, he thought. Arms, legs, the occasional hand, and on one occasion a foot somehow blown free of both the leg it had been attached to and the boot and sock it had been wearing, but a head? To his own grim surprise, it was a new experience, and one he wasn't relishing.

Harry had seen things done to the human body, which were the stuff of nightmares, and worse. The battlefield was no place for something so fragile, and he knew firsthand what the former could do to the latter. He had seen torsos ripped apart, limbs torn off, men turned into pink mist. He had broken into cellars to find the rawest, bleeding evidence of gang rivalry turned to bloody revenge, heard the echoes of the screams still lingering in the brickwork. This, though? This was just odd.

The head, Harry thought, seemed oddly peaceful. Eyes closed, as if asleep, for a moment it was as though whoever this was had simply dropped into a hole up to their neck, and drifted off. The body just a couple of feet away from it made it obvious that was very much not the case, but still, the scene was oddly serene considering the violence of its creation.

Harry dropped to his heels for a closer look. There was no smell of death yet, and even if there was, the earlier rain would've washed that away. As well as a good amount of evidence, too, Harry thought, grumbling to himself. The weather seemed to never be in a detective's favour; it was always too hot or too wet. Although cold was useful.

As far as Harry could tell, the victim was a man in his mid to late twenties. Short, dark hair, very short at the back, with a face that, though pale now, was clean-shaven and almost porcelain smooth.

Harry lowered his eyes to look at the wound. Whatever had caused it had been sharp, because the cuts to the neck didn't seem to be ragged or many in number. It wouldn't have needed to be razor sharp, though; an axe with enough heft behind it could be absolutely devastating.

The way the body and the head were laid, Harry had a sense that the first blow had been enough to flick off the life switch, dropping the person where they stood. He'd seen that plenty of times, a round to the head stealing life away in a spray of red, the body dropping like liquid, a shell without a soul.

He wondered why this young man had been here in the first place, because there was no real reason to be here at all; the quoits pitch didn't lead anywhere, and the only way in and out were the steep steps.

Harry suspected other blows had been needed to sever the head completely, but he would have to leave it to Rebecca to work all of that out. And he couldn't really see the full extent of the wounds anyway, not with the way the head was sitting in the grass.

Had the blows been rapid? Had they come in a mad flurry? Had the attacker held this young man up as they hacked off his head? Or had they allowed him to fall dead to the ground before carrying on with the onslaught?

Standing back up, Harry turned his attention to the body. Like the head, it was just lying there as though nothing untoward had happened to it. There was no sign of a struggle, or none that Harry could see, which had him thinking that perhaps the attack had caught the victim unawares; a swift hack from behind, severing the spine, would've dropped him where he stood. But again, why the hell had they been here at all? It made no sense. But then these things never did, not at first, anyway. Maybe something would come from the man's mobile phone records, assuming he was carrying one. Harry would leave finding that to the SOC team. It wasn't his job to go rummaging around in a dead man's pockets.

With a scratch of his chin, Harry stepped away from the body and swung his eyes around where he was standing, using them like a searchlight to see if he could find something, anything, which might be of some help. All he saw was a bench, and suddenly weary, he went over to sit down on it, catching sight of a shiny brass plaque fixed to the back and the words 'For my shepherdess' etched into it.

Harry heard footsteps approaching, but he didn't bother to turn, knowing them well enough.

'I know quoits is competitive,' said Matt, coming to stand beside the bench Harry was now sitting on. 'But this is ridiculous. Next thing, we'll have darts players turning up full of holes.'

'I hope not,' said Harry. 'Anyway, I've never played the game, so I wouldn't know. No idea what it actually involves, either.'

Matt pointed at four covered squares in the grass, maybe ten metres away from where they stood, and placed a similar distance apart, like stumps on two cricket pitches.

'Them's the clay pits,' he explained. 'They're covered to protect them from the weather, to stop the clay drying out, or getting too wet. The game's played with teams of eight I think, but I wouldn't quoit me on that.'

Matt laughed. Harry didn't.

'Anyway, all you have to do is throw a quoit, which is a ring of iron, from about where we are now, to a metal stake, or hob, hammered into the middle of the pit. Used to be cast-off horseshoes, and some places still play it like that.'

'Can't see what any of that has to do with our friend here,' said Harry.

'Could the body have been dragged or carried here?' Matt asked.

'Possibly,' said Harry. 'Haven't seen any evidence of that, though; no trace of blood, no marks in the grass and the earth.'

Matt looked up at the sky, still grey and heavy from the earlier rain.

'The weather's been having its wicked way with the ground for a good part of the night, though, so it would be hard to tell, wouldn't it?'

'It would,' Harry agreed. 'We all good with Margaret and Rebecca?'

'They're on their way,' said Matt.

'Best we get back up into the car park then, before they arrive,' said Harry and pushed himself to his feet. 'Margaret will want to chat, and Rebecca and her team won't be best pleased if she finds us down here trampling over everything.'

'Trampling?' said Matt, with a wide-eyed pantomime of shock on his face. 'We never trample, Harry, we tippy-toe, like the light-footed gentlemen that we are.'

Though Matt's quoit joke hadn't made Harry laugh, that certainly did, and still smiling he made his way to the steps, to climb back up to the car park behind the Fountain.

As he approached the steps, he noticed that the quoits pitch was so low he couldn't really see anything other than sky above the top of the steps; the top of the pub, its roof; the handful of vehicles parked behind it only came into view as he climbed. As he was about to reach the top of the steps, he spotted something caught in a gap at the back of one of the steps.

'Something the matter?' Matt asked. 'What've you found?'

Harry leaned into the steps, and with a little bit of scraping and poking with his fingers, managed to pull out a small, thin box.

'Condoms,' said Matt, looking over Harry's shoulder. 'Strange place to keep them, don't you think?'

Harry noticed how the box seemed to stare back at him as though challenging him to try and connect it to the body behind him. It was open, and inside, one of the foil packets was ripped open and empty.

Maybe there is no connection, he thought.

'Someone was planning on getting lucky, maybe,' Matt suggested. 'And if they were, finding that they'd lost those must've been a bit disappointing.'

Had they belonged to the killer, perhaps? And even if they had, why would it matter? There was nothing unusual about condoms. Perhaps whoever they'd belonged to had simply been careful enough to carry protection? It was certainly better than the other option, which was to have nothing to hand should one thing lead to another, as it so often did.

Harry slipped them into an evidence bag and dropped them into a jacket pocket. He was fairly sure that the condoms had nothing to do with what Mandy had discovered behind her pub. Booze and late nights were the simplest of recipes to have folk sneaking off to dark corners for a fumble. And there was no doubt about it, the quoits pitch was a dark corner indeed.

'Probably nothing,' he said, 'but you never know.'

Sometimes, the smallest, most insignificant thing could become the most important evidence in an investigation. He doubted that something *ribbed for extra sensation* would be that, but he wasn't about to ignore it, either.

At the top of the steps, Harry saw Jen coming back around the corner of the pub to take up position at the entrance to the car park.

'How's Mandy?' he asked, as he and Matt walked over to meet her.

'Taking solace in an early glass of wine,' Jen said. 'Can't say I blame her.'

'Anything of importance?'

Jen gave a shrug.

'Sounds like it was just a normal night in the bar. I'll have a chat with the rest of the staff, see if they noticed anything.'

'Anything specific from Mandy, though?'

'Angus was running the bar; Mandy was at the party,' said Jen, which Harry remembered as she said it. 'There was the usual, you know, a couple of locals with a few too many in them having a go at each other, dogs getting out of hand, that kind of thing.'

'Anything else?'

Jen laughed.

'Someone nicked someone's cap, and apparently there was a complaint about the portion size of the food. I think Mandy's just pleased the quoits pitch is okay. I think she spent a bit on it and the rings.'

Harry rolled his eyes.

'It's going to be a bugger tracing everyone who was in there, isn't it? But we'll have to see how we do, see if we can't find out a bit more. Locals should be easy enough. It's the visitors and tourists that'll be hard to trace. Security cameras?'

'Sorry,' said Jen. 'I didn't think to check. Kind of just assumed it was a no.'

'It probably is,' said Harry, at once loving how trusting everyone was in the Dales that security cameras weren't pinned to every wall, gate, and door, simultaneously wishing that folk were a little more welcoming of just how useful it could be. 'I'll go have a chat, you stay here.'

Harry made to leave when a familiar figure walked around the corner of the Fountain.

'I'm supposed to be singing this morning, you know,' said District Surgeon Margaret Shaw, her voice strangely raspy.

'Doesn't sound like you should be,' said Matt.

'I'm needed, though. With Anna gone, we're still in limbo, waiting on news for a new vicar. We've already lost a couple of sopranos. They'll be back, I know they will, mainly because I'll be round their houses dragging them back, but still, if I start missing our Sunday mornings—'

'It's just one Sunday morning,' said Harry. 'It's not like you're taking months off, is it? And anyway, you've got the excuse of being called in to attend a crime scene, haven't you? I'm sure everyone will understand.'

A frown ploughed itself deeply across Margaret's forehead.

'You've not met Garrett, have you?'

'Who's Garrett?'

'Someone who really won't understand,' replied Margaret. 'Now, where am I going?'

Harry pointed across the car park.

'This is going to test you, though,' he said. 'And Rebecca. It's a tough one.'

'Really?'

'Oh, for sure,' agreed Matt. 'Going to take a good while to work out the cause of death.'

Margaret narrowed her eyes.

'Are you pulling my leg?'

Harry had no problem at all keeping a straight face.

'Matt'll take you over,' he said. 'Prepare yourself, though.'

'Why?'

'You might lose your head over it,' said Matt, and with that, guided Margaret over to the steps down to the quoits pitch.

Harry managed to stop himself from laughing at Matt's comment, but only just.

'Mandy, then, to check on those security cams?' Jen asked.

Harry went to say yes, when someone else turned up in front of them.

'Hello, Rebecca,' he said, as the pathologist looked past him to where Margaret was heading. She was already kitted out in her white, disposable, paper overalls, a facemask pulled up on her forehead, the hood of the overalls hanging behind her neck.

'Mum's here, then. Garrett won't be happy.'

'I really must meet this Garrett,' said Harry, a faint laugh nipping at the edge of his words. 'Rest of the team here, then?'

'Five minutes max,' said Rebecca.

Harry looked at Jen.

'Best I stay here,' he said. 'You mind going to chat to Mandy again?'

Jen shook her head.

'Not a problem; she'll be sat where I left her, no doubt.'

From the quoits pitch, Harry heard swearing.

'Must be quite something for my mum to do that,' said Rebecca.

'Oh, just you wait,' said Harry, as a van pulled up behind the pathologist.

Rebecca gave it a cursory glance.

'Don't think I will,' she said. 'Care to join me?'

EIGHT

Three things told Ian that he had not, as planned, woken up early enough to set off back home before Mickey and his friends woke up to their own Sunday morning of white-hot hangovers and blurry regrets.

The first was the sunlight blasting through the gap in the curtains of his room, blinding him as he tried to open his eyes, aware then of both a banging headache and a stomach that was making it very clear to him it needed to eject its contents rather urgently.

Sitting up, his head swam, which made him so dizzy that, as he swung his legs out of the bed to race to the ensuite, he misjudged it completely, and catapulted himself out onto the floor in a painful heap.

A cry leapt from Ian's mouth only to be cut off by the explosive stream of vomit, which thrust itself out of his stomach and directly into his open suitcase. The retching doubled him over, the violence of it so abrupt that his head crashed into the suitcase as well, dunking his face into the growing pool of hot spew escaping from his very upset insides.

The second thing happened as Ian tried to recover some sense of dignity by sitting up to try and wipe his face free of the hot, acrid, lumpy liquid now covering it. The only thing immediately to hand was the hoody he had worn the night before, so he grabbed it, and still retching, tried to scrape the contents of his stomach out of his eyes. Then he caught sight of the bedside clock lying just in front of him on the floor, and the time it flashed up at him burned his retinas with the reality of a morning already more than half gone, and knocking at the door of lunchtime.

Just what the hell happened? he thought, fighting to control the waves of nausea, ignoring as best he could the rancid swill that had just ruined everything that he'd brought with him.

He'd had a few beers, that was true, but certainly not enough to cause this kind of reaction. Was it food poisoning then? Was that it? But from what? They'd all eaten at the pub, and Ian had gone for something very simple, just a steak and kidney pie, with chips and peas. Not that the menu had been littered with the exotic anyway, the most out-there dish on it being lasagna. And for that, he was thankful. He liked to stick with what he knew, something safe. The most adventurous thing he had ever eaten was a chicken korma, and that had been more than enough to tell him life was safer if he stuck to the basics.

The third thing was actually a combination of two things, but Ian didn't really care, so confused was he already by the inexplicable events he'd just woken up to.

Managing to moan and groan himself up and onto his feet, though only with considerable help from the edge of the bed, Ian made a beeline for the bathroom. On the way, mid-agonising sprint, he hammered his toe into an empty bottle of wine that was lying on the floor. It rolled into another, which was also empty, and he remembered then bringing them with him just in case. Clearly, something had happened the night before, and he had sunk them both, which explained the ferocious hangover and projectile vomit. Not that this conclusion made him any happier or more clear-headed.

The shock of pain that raced through him from his toes caused Ian to stumble. Arms whirling like Daffy Duck slipping on a banana skin, he fell through the bathroom door, slipped on the floor, went flying, and crashed headfirst into the toilet. Then he heard the dull, heavy thud of someone thumping their fists hard against his bedroom door.

'Ian? Ian! We've lost Mickey! We need to find him! Ian!'

There was a pause, the sound of moaning, then another voice joined in.

'Ian? We heard you, mate. Come on, get your shit together, come help us find Mickey. Don't go pretending you've a hangover either; you left well early last night, you bastard, but we can talk about all that once we've got Mickey safe.'

Ian recognised the voice, but couldn't put a name to it, and didn't want to. He didn't care where Mickey was, and he certainly wasn't interested in helping his other friends to find him. Sod that. If he'd got drunk and ended up in someone's bed, that was his shit to deal with alone.

The banging came again.

'Ian? Ian! Don't be a dick! Why the hell didn't you stay with the rest of us anyway? You're so weird.'

Ian wanted to shout back that he wasn't being a dick, that whatever Mickey was doing, and wherever he'd ended up, it was his shit to be dealing with alone. But instead, he was back up on his feet, trying to force his body to act and feel human, as the churning of his stomach threatened to have him back down on the floor again.

Grabbing the sink to steady himself, Ian braced his arms as his stomach twisted, sent shooting pain to every corner of his body, contracted itself in readiness to eject what could only be stomach acid, and—

Ian looked at his reflection in the mirrored cabinet hung over the sink, unable to take it in. This couldn't be his reflection, it just couldn't. There was just no way.

Staring back at Ian was his own haggard, drawn face, pale as skimmed milk, and that in itself was bad enough, but it was not this aspect of his reflection to which he was drawn. No. Because, impossible though it seemed, there was something considerably worse, something so god-awful he just couldn't comprehend it.

Ian heard another angry rat-a-tat-thump at his door, like there was a pissed-off drummer on the other side trying to get in. But it had no chance of drawing his attention away from this, no chance at all.

His torso, which was clothed in the same khaki T-shirt he had worn to the pub the night before, a T-shirt he was very proud of, a T-shirt that had the word Nostromo printed on it referencing Alien, one of his all-time favourite movies, was covered in blood. Though covered was underselling it, Ian thought, in an odd moment of cold, hard observation, because drenched was perhaps a better word.

He looked down at himself, touched the surface of the T-shirt with the tips of his fingers, felt how some of the blood was dry, some of it still damp, noticed that it clung to his body, didn't move when he did.

Ian screamed, something he'd never done in his life, because he'd never been involved in any kind of activity or event that would involve him doing anything of the kind. But this, it absolutely warranted a scream, the kind that had hooks pricked into his lungs so that when it came out, it threatened to bring them with it.

With the thought that at any moment he was about to cough

up his own lungs and see them leap from his mouth to end up as spongey lumps of squishy organs on the bathroom floor, Ian, still screaming, backed away from the mirror at such speed that he thunked into the toilet and ended up dropping his arse into it. Then instinct took over and he was pulling at the T-shirt, desperately peeling it away from his skin, heaving it over his head, the seams ripping as he did so. He threw it hard, and it slapped into the mirror, before dropping into the sink below, leaving a dark, red smudge behind it, like the trail left behind by a dying animal hit by a truck.

Another barrage of thumps from the bedroom door, a muffled, 'Screw you, Ian ...' then silence.

Ian stayed statue still, his eyes on where the T-shirt had hit the mirror. Then he was on his feet, had the T-shirt in his hands, and was in the shower, washing it, and himself with every last squirt of shower gel he could force from the bottle, which was when the pain hit.

With a primal scream that ripped his chest in two, Ian was out of the shower and slipping all over the floor, on the water, the blood, the soap. His back was on fire. It felt as though someone had gone to work on it with a craft knife and a blowtorch. What the hell had happened?

Gingerly, Ian turned himself around, so that his back was facing the mirror, and he could see what the problem was by looking over his shoulder.

He saw cuts, a good number of them, too. Some looked deep, but most of them looked barely large enough to be classed as a scratch. He grabbed his T-shirt from the shower, took a closer look, and saw that the back was a haphazard of zigzag cuts.

Ian looked again at his back, knew that he still wasn't clean, so climbed back into the shower. The water hit, and he gritted his teeth and hissed through them, then dumped shampoo on his head, and allowed the suds to run down. The pain was excruciating, but it soon subsided. As it did, his mind was back on the blood, the quantity of it, the fact that it was his.

Eyes closed, hot water streaming over him, and his back turning numb with the heat and the soap, flashbacks slammed into Ian hard and fast.

He remembered leaving the pub, just getting the hell away from Mickey and his other friends. He remembered walking back to where he was staying, then deciding to go for a little walk. He remembered footsteps, someone rushing towards him. He'd turned around, seen a blur of movement, felt the hard shove, tried to steady himself, then ...

Then came the pain, a shocking memory of losing his balance, toppling backwards, the sound of breaking glass, then his back was on fire.

Squeezing out his T-shirt, Ian had no doubt in his mind who was responsible for the mess he was in. The footsteps, the shouting ... He had no idea which of the group it had been, and frankly, he didn't care. One of them had come after him, pushed him, and now he was a latticework of cuts. Worst of all, one of his favourite T-shirts was ruined.

Watching the water at last start to run clear, and squeezing the T-shirt out as best he could, Ian was already formulating a plan that would show every single one of the bastards just how unfunny it all was.

NINE

Jen found Mandy as she had left her, sitting in the same place, in the dark, though the glass of wine in front of her was somewhat depleted.

'You're here again already?' Mandy said, looking up as Jen approached. 'Thought you'd be too busy with what's just happened.'

'Security cameras,' Jen said.

'What about them?'

'Do you have any?'

Jen watched Mandy's expression change from mild surprise at seeing her, to something akin to a teenager trying desperately to think of an excuse for not doing their homework.

'Yes ... and no.'

Now that's confusing, thought Jen.

'Surely you either have them or you don't,' she said.

Mandy rubbed her temples.

'Probably best if I show you,' she said, and eased herself out from around the side of the table, to lead behind the bar to the reception area for the rooms above.

Following Mandy, Jen found herself staring at a computer screen decorated with various notes containing telephone numbers and reminders.

'Just give me a minute,' said Mandy, resting her wine glass on the desk.

A full five minutes went by before she spoke again.

'Here we are,' she said.

Jen looked at the screen to see that it was now split into four sections, three of which were blank, the fourth showing a fuzzy view of the door to the public bar.

'What am I looking at?' she asked.

'Well, like I said, when you asked if we had any security cameras, this is what I meant when I said yes and no.'

'I can only see one camera,' said Jen.

'We have four,' Mandy explained, pointing at each of the four squares on the screen, her long fingernails tapping against the glass.

'But those other three are just black,' said Jen. 'They're not showing anything.'

'Exactly.'

'Exactly what?'

'We don't always remember to switch them on, Jen, that's exactly what,' Mandy said. 'Have you ever run a pub that's also a hotel and a restaurant and an entertainment venue?'

Jen shook her head, not that Mandy was taking any notice because she was still speaking.

'There's so much to do, so much to remember. I've staff to sort out, food to order, punters to deal with, breweries to support, two dogs to walk, darts competitions, the quoits stuff, quizzes, entertainment, bedrooms to clean, guests to welcome and make sure are comfortable; security cameras aren't always top of my must-get-done-immediately list. And anyway, this is Hawes, lass, isn't it? We trust each other up here. That's the way it works. Nowt happens without someone somewhere noticing!'

Jen gave Mandy a moment to gather herself, the sudden outburst causing the well-loved pub owner to slump in her chair a little.

'It must be hard doing all of that,' she said, once Mandy seemed a little calmer. 'You do it well, though, don't you? This place is a haven for locals and visitors alike. But that doesn't mean you shouldn't take security seriously.'

'We do take it seriously!' Mandy replied, eyes wide. 'Why do you think we had those cameras fitted in the first place? I mean, obviously there's the small factor that they were a bargain, but regardless, we only put them in because we thought it was the right thing to do. It's just that we don't always remember to have them running.'

'Is there not a way of setting up some kind of timer or something?' Jen asked. 'Actually, can't you just have them running all the time? Most systems I know of allow that, and any footage is kept for a certain number of days before being deleted, or just left in the cloud, so storage shouldn't be an issue either.'

Mandy folded her arms and stared up at Jen, a wry smile on her lips.

'Well, listen to you and whatever that was you just said. Very technical, aren't you?'

Jen laughed.

'It's not technical, Mandy,' she said. 'It's just how stuff like this works. Want me to have a look?'

A look of relief fell across Mandy's face.

'You have no idea how happy I am that you asked.'

Mandy stood up and Jen took her place on the chair.

A couple of minutes later, Jen had worked out how everything worked, and a minute or so after that, had all the cameras working, and the system set up to run when Mandy thought it would be best for the cameras to be on.

'So, let's see what we've got for last night, then,' Jen said, once Mandy was happy with everything. She clicked on a file and started to look through footage from the previous evening. A problem was immediately apparent.

'Mandy,' Jen said, pointing at the screen, 'do you see anything wrong with this?'

Mandy leaned over from behind Jen.

'No,' she said. 'Why? That's the door to the public bar, isn't it? And you can see folk going in and out. Isn't that what the security camera's supposed to do?'

'It is, yes,' said Jen, deciding not to mention how dreadful the quality of the footage was, but to focus on something else, something much more apparent. 'And you're right, it really is showing people going in and out.' Jen paused, then said, 'Mandy, can I ask you, when was the last time the cameras were checked? You know, when was the last time someone made sure that they were pointing at something useful?'

Mandy frowned, confusion in her eyes.

'Something useful? How do you mean? That one there, it's useful, isn't it? It's showing folk coming and going.'

'It is, yes,' said Jen. 'But I think the camera may have, over time, come a bit loose ...'

'Why?'

'Because,' said Jen, 'all it's showing us is their feet. It's pointing at the ground, Mandy. All we can see is shoes and boots and wellies, and with the quality of what's been recorded, it's not very clear who's wearing what, not that we know who anyone is.'

Mandy scratched her chin.

'You think I should check it, then?'

'I think they should all be checked,' said Jen, then pointed out what was wrong with the other three cameras, one of which was providing them with a very good view of a pigeon asleep on a windowsill.

'Can you not use it, then?' Mandy asked.

Jen wasn't sure what to say, and leaned in closer to the screen to see if what she was looking at could be at all useful.

'Right now, I don't know,' she said. 'However, what I'll do, is send everything from last night to the office email. That way I can go through it in my own time rather than on here.'

'Can't someone, you know, clean it up?' Mandy asked, waving her hand at the screen as though shooing away a fly. 'That's what people can do, isn't it? Clean things up, make them clearer?'

'Like in the movies, you mean?' asked Jen.

'Yes, exactly like in the movies,' replied Mandy.

'This isn't the movies,' said Jen. 'It's the Yorkshire Dales, and you don't get much more Yorkshire than Wensleydale, now, do you?'

'Yes, but even so ...'

Jen spent a few moments sorting out the footage to be sent. Once done, she pushed herself up and out of the chair.

'Tell you what,' she said. 'I'll check the other cameras for you now. How's that sound? Then at least we'll know they're all pointing at something that needs pointing at.'

'Not a pigeon, then?'

'No,' said Jen. 'Definitely not a pigeon.'

Jen was about to head off to the camera at the door to the public bar when a teenager walked into the reception, a dog on a lead at his heel. He looked about fifteen, maybe sixteen, Jen thought, his hair sitting on his head like a frozen explosion, his clothes very much fashioned to be effective against all weathers, rather than attracting the opposite sex.

The dog sat down and stared up at Jen, its head cocked to one side.

'Now then,' the teenager said. 'Saw you were in. You busy?'

'Who do you mean?' Mandy asked. 'Me, or Jen, here?'

'That'll be you, like,' the teenager said, nodding at Jen. 'There's a window out, just down the cobbles.'

'You mean Main Street?' Jen asked.

'I do.'

'What window? Where?'

'One to the right of the old Methodist Church. Used to be that shop, remember?'

Jen had to think for a moment.

'You mean the one that used to be the old hardware shop?'

'That's the one,' the teenager said. 'Used to pop in there to get firelighters and pegs and that kind of thing for my folks, before it changed, like. They had lollipops on the counter. I used to love those. Catapults, they sold those, too, didn't they, and penknives?'

'Used to be a right little Aladdin's cave,' said Mandy. 'Still is, I suppose, if you've a fat wallet and no taste.'

Ignoring Mandy's comment, and keen to get to the bottom of what she was being told, Jen said, 'So, you're saying that there's a window smashed, is that it?'

'It's a right mess, like,' the teenager said. 'Reckon someone's got pissed up and put their arse through it.'

Jen turned to Mandy.

'Best I go and have a look,' she said. 'The owner might not even know what's happened. I'll check those cameras later, if that's okay?'

'It is,' said Mandy. 'Not like they're going anywhere, is it? And I can always have a look myself, can't I?'

Jen gave Mandy just enough of a look to have the woman laugh.

'No, you're right,' Mandy said. 'There's no chance of me doing that; I'd only bugger things up even more, wouldn't I?'

'I'll be back as soon as I can,' said Jen, deciding it was best not to comment on what Mandy had just said. Then she followed the teenager outside onto the marketplace and on towards the cobbles.

Just a few steps away from the pub, however, she doubled back, asked Mandy to see if she could ask around and start a list of everyone who had been in the bar that night, then chased after the teenager again, catching up with him as he reached the cobbles.

TEN

Having followed the pathologist to the steps down to the quoits pitch, Harry had decided against going any further for two reasons. One, he'd seen enough of the crime scene to know that it was best to keep out of the way, and he'd explained enough to Sowerby as they'd strolled across the car park to give her a good idea of what they knew so far, which was precious little. And two, they'd met Margaret coming the other way, with Matt at her heels. Sowerby had stepped back to allow her mother past, before heading down to where she had just come from, pulling the face mask down and the hood up as she went. The rest of her team had followed soon after, laden down with various bits of gear.

'Well, that was a bloody awful way to start the day, so thank you for that,' Margaret said, throwing an overly dramatic glare at Harry with the precision of someone using a red dot sight on a pistol. 'You didn't think of warning me, then?'

'I did warn you,' said Harry. 'I told you to prepare yourself. I was quite clear about that.'

'He's right, he did,' Matt agreed. 'I was there.'

Margaret turned the heat of her glare on Matt.

'And as for your comment about not losing my head ...'

Harry added his own glare to Margaret's.

'Yes, that's a terrible example you're setting,' he said. 'I expect better from someone with your experience and standing in the force.'

Harry watched Matt's face contort itself into all manner of expressions as he tried to work out if either was being serious.

A smile finally cracked through Margaret's fierceness.

'You're a right pair of sods, you know that, don't you?' Matt said, shaking his head. 'For a moment there, I almost thought you were serious.'

'But we are serious,' said Harry. 'Aren't we, Margaret?'

Matt went to say something when a call came in and he stepped away from Harry and Margaret to take it.

'What do you think, then?' Harry asked, as Matt spoke to whoever it was on the other end of the line.

'I'm not sure what to think,' said Margaret. 'Definitely dead, though, I'm sure.'

'That we can agree on.'

'I know quoits can get competitive, but this?' Margaret shook her head. 'Surely not.'

Harry had to agree.

'I've had the game explained to me, but I'd be hard pushed to see any pub league or competition get so ferocious that folk will kill to win. Still, you never know ...'

Margaret rested a hand on Harry's arm, then gave it a squeeze, hard enough for him to look down into her narrowed, staring eyes.

'The hows and wherefores we can leave to Rebecca, can't we? And as for the whys? Well, that's down to your lot, isn't it?'

'Then why are you staring at me?' Harry asked.

Margaret leaned a little closer.

'Because there's something considerably more important I want to talk about ...'

'There is?'

Harry had no idea what Margaret could be talking about. How could anything be more important than the singular reason they were all there together on a Sunday morning?

'Yes, there is,' said Margaret. 'You.'

Harry rolled his eyes, smiled.

'I'm fine, Margaret,' he said. 'Better than, as I'm sure you know. Grace and I are all moved in and comfortable, even if I do say so myself.'

Margaret poked a finger into Harry's chest with surprising force.

'And that's what I want to talk about,' she said. 'You and Grace.'

'You do?' Harry asked. 'Why?'

'Because, after last night, and what happened here, I think someone needs to have a very strong word with you, and possibly give you a hard slap across the back of that thick skull of yours!'

Harry was immediately confused. Last night? How could talking to him about him and Grace have anything to do with a decapitated body? What was Margaret talking about?

'Not sure I understand,' he said. 'Grace and I, we're—'

'Yes, I know you are,' said Margaret, speaking over Harry. 'Which is why—'

'Boss,' said Matt, interrupting whatever it was Margaret was about to say.

'What is it?'

'There's been a break-in. Jen's there now. It's a shop just down Main Street, past Cockett's if you go from this end, by the Methodist Church.'

Harry could tell there was more that Matt needed to say,

and with a nod at Margaret, led the detective sergeant to one side.

Margaret mouthed, *We still need to talk*, and headed off home, her job done.

'What is it?' Harry asked, and pointed at Matt's face. 'Because that look you're giving me says there's more to this than just a break-in. And Jen's supposed to be back here as Scene Guard.'

'It's not just a break-in,' said Matt.

'In what sense?' Harry asked.

'Blood,' answered Matt.

'Can you be more specific? Whereabouts is it?'

'Jen just said it was everywhere,' Matt said. 'She doesn't think the owner's going to be happy.'

'Well, no one wants blood all over their shop, do they?' said Harry.

'You've not met Mr Willis, have you?' Matt asked.

Harry quickly traced back through everyone he knew well in the Dales, then through everyone he knew of. The name Willis had never cropped up.

'Can't say that I have,' he said. 'Why?'

'Oh, you'd remember if you had, believe you me,' said Matt.

'Why?'

'Probably best I leave you to be the judge of that.'

Harry didn't like mysteries at the best of times. At least in the police, he was trained to solve them, and paid to do so. But random little puzzlers gifted to him by friends and colleagues? Not so much.

'Can't you just tell me?' he said.

'I'm afraid I can't,' said Matt.

'Why?' Harry asked, his voice a frustrated grumble.

'It's my job,' Matt answered. 'By which I mean, my job as your friendly neighbourhood git.'

And with that, he turned on his heel, ducked under the cordon tape, and headed into the marketplace.

Harry followed.

By the time he'd caught up, Matt, who had headed off at a surprising pace, was already across the cobbles and heading down Main Street.

Harry caught up with Matt outside Cockett's.

'Not stopping for a pie?' Harry asked.

'No need,' said Matt. 'Bought myself a couple earlier. Ah, there we are ...' He pointed ahead and Harry saw Jen give them both a wave.

Crossing the cobbles, Harry followed Matt over to the younger detective.

'So, what've we got, then?' he asked, as they came up to Jen, who was standing outside a window, or what was left of one, anyway.

Out of the space where a window had been, Harry saw shards of glass spilling out like the shattered remnants of a frozen waterfall. They caught the light of the day, reflecting it back in broken, razor-edged relief.

'Not sure,' Jen said. 'It's a mess, like. Figured it was best to call you down first before I did anything. I've given the owner a ring, though, so that we can actually get inside and have a look around, see if we're dealing with a break-in. A Mr—'

'Willis,' said Harry, finishing Jen's sentence for her.

'You've met him, then?'

Harry shook his head.

'No, but I've already been warned.'

Harry saw Jen stare back at him with a frown.

'Warned? Of what? Mr Willis is—'

'An experience,' said Matt. 'Wouldn't you say, Jen?'

Harry watched Jen's eyes flicker between him and Matt.

'Are we talking about the same Mr Willis?' she asked.

'Well, there's only one that I know of who owns this place,' said Matt.

Harry wasn't interested in getting involved in whatever weirdness Matt was trying to spin around this Mr Willis, and stepped back from the shop front to have a better look at what it was.

'Pique Antiques,' he said, reading the words etched above the window in flamboyant, gold lettering. 'Clever.'

'Is it?' said Matt, stepping back himself to look at the shop sign.

Harry was about to explain, when a cry of shock shot down the cobbled street. He turned to where it had come from and saw, racing towards them from the direction of the bridge at the other end of the lane, a man in a waxed jacket, a flat cap, and the greenest Wellington boots he had ever seen. Running alongside him, clipped to a lead, was a grey-haired dog Harry could easily have mistaken for a small horse.

The man skidded to a halt beside Harry.

'The shop!' he said, staring at the mess of a window now open to the elements. 'What happened?'

'Mr Willis?' Harry said, but the man ignored him as he started to remove various items from a jacket pocket.

'Who would do something like this?' he said, his question cast into the air like a fly on the end of a line, his accent so heavily from the Welsh valleys that Harry was fairly sure he could hear, far off, the echo of male voice choirs.

'I'm Detective Chief Inspector Grimm,' Harry said, trying to get the man's attention. 'Perhaps we could have a quick chat, Mr Willis? I'm assuming you've brought your—'

'Here we are!' the man said, removing a set of keys on a fob in the shape of a highly detailed miniature banjo from his pocket.

He headed towards the door to the shop.

'Mr Willis,' Harry said, following him, 'if we could just have a moment?'

The man turned on his heel.

'You do know he can't understand a word you're saying, don't you?' he said.

'Pardon?' said Harry.

'What you're saying,' the man said. 'He doesn't understand.'

'Who doesn't?' Harry asked, wondering why on earth the man was seemingly talking about himself in the third person.

'Mr Willis,' the man said.

'But you're Mr Willis,' said Harry.

The man laughed.

'Do I look like the kind of person mad enough to open an antiques shop with zero experience of buying and selling antiques?'

Harry looked the man up and down, not entirely sure how to answer the question.

'Then where's Mr Willis, if you're not him?' he asked.

Without any warning at all, the huge dog stood on its hind legs and rested its front paws on Harry's shoulders, its enormous head directly in front of his face.

Harry was too shocked to do anything else beyond saying, 'Hello, there ...'

'Harry,' Matt said, leaning in, 'meet Mr Willis.'

Before Harry could understand what Matt had just told him, the man at the door turned the key in the lock, the dog dropped from his shoulders, and Jen's laughter danced in the air.

ELEVEN

Harry only just managed to prevent the man he had thought was Mr Willis from entering the shop, stopping him in his tracks with a gruff call for him to wait up and let the police in first.

'He won't be happy about that at all,' the man said, before turning to the dog and adding, 'Will you, Mr Willis?'

'You'll forgive me if I don't take my orders from a dog,' Harry said. 'What we've got right now is a smashed window, evidence of blood, and not a clue what's happened inside. Could be vandalism, could be accidental, could be a break-in; it's down to us to check, rather than your frankly gigantic pet.'

The man's eyes went wide.

'Pet? Mr Willis is no pet, are you, lad?' He clapped his hands over the dog's ears. 'Don't you listen, lad, he just doesn't understand you, that's all.'

The dog wagged its tail, and Harry made sure he was nowhere near where it was swinging, fairly sure the thing could, at the very least, leave a bruise, if not knock his legs out from under him and send him to the ground like a felled tree.

'Perhaps you could give us your name as well?' he asked.

'Griffiths,' the man said, his accent thicker and more musical as he said it. 'Owen Griffiths. I'm from the Gower originally, born and bred in Rhossili.'

'And now you own an antiques shop in the Yorkshire Dales,' said Harry.

Owen shook his head.

'I don't, Mr Willis does, as I've said.'

Harry took a deep breath in an attempt to regain some composure, but as he exhaled, he felt no palpable sense of calm as he said, 'I know I may regret asking this, but how or why does a dog own an antiques shop?'

The look on Owen's face was one of disbelief at being asked such a question.

'Because he likes antiques, that's why!' he said. 'I thought that would be more than obvious?'

'But he's a dog,' said Harry.

'Ah,' said Owen, 'but you see, he's not just any normal kind of dog.'

Harry really wanted Owen to get to the point, but could already see there was little chance of that.

'No, I can see that; he's the size of a horse.'

'That's not what I mean.'

'Then what do you mean?'

'I mean,' said Owen, 'that he's a divvie.'

Harry flicked a look at both Jen and Matt, who were standing together, staring at him, and smiling.

'Divvie?' said Harry, wondering if Owen was now edging into very dodgy territory and using words which came with the wonderful experience of ending you up in front of a judge.

'I think it's from diviner,' said Owen. 'I don't mean as is godlike or anything like that. He divines things, you see?'

'No, I don't,' said Harry, relieved that was all the word meant.

Owen stepped closer to Harry.

'He's got a knack,' he said, his voice quieter now, conspiratorial, as he tapped the side of his nose with a finger. 'It's like he has a special power ...' He rested his finger on Mr Willis' black, wet nose. 'You see that there? Most dogs use it to sniff out prey, don't they? But Mr Willis here, he can smell a genuine antique, a bargain, at a hundred paces. I know you don't believe me, but I'm telling you, it's the absolute truth; nearly every item in this shop was found by Mr Willis here. That's why the shop's his. I'm simply the man who works for him and sells it on.'

Harry was starting to get a headache.

'Perhaps,' he said, 'you could stay outside the shop for a minute or two while we take a look inside? There could be broken glass all over the floor, and that wouldn't be good for Mr Willis' paws, now would it?'

Owen took a moment to ponder what Harry had said, then agreed, and let him past.

Matt and Jen came into the shop after him and when they were alone, he pinned them both to the floor with a narrow-eyed scowl.

'Mr Willis is a dog?' he said. 'How the hell has this passed me by? I've lived in Hawes long enough to know something like that, surely? I mean, just look at him! An animal like that, everyone should be talking about him, and probably queuing up in the marketplace for rides!'

'They've only been here a few months,' said Matt. 'Mr Griffiths lives in West Burton. Has a bit of money, like, that's more than obvious. Opened this place not that long ago.'

'And you're sure he's not pulling my leg about the dog?'

'Not at all,' said Jen. 'He tells everyone that story, given the chance. Has the dog insured for a fortune, apparently. Swears by his nose.'

'They visit flea markets all over the country,' continued

Matt. 'Close the shop once a month for a week to go travelling, then turn up with loads of new stuff for the shop.'

Harry glanced around and saw everything from furniture to ornaments to vintage enamelled wall signs, framed pieces of art, and jewellery.

'Well, best we see if there's any evidence of anyone being in the shop first of all,' he said. 'Matt? Could you ask Owen if he can get us a full inventory? We'll need someone to go through it with him to check to see if anything's missing.'

'He'll have one for insurance purposes, surely,' said Jen.

'You'd like to think so,' Harry agreed, 'but a place like this, their stock can be a very movable feast.'

Matt left the shop to chat with Owen, leaving Harry with Jen.

'Did you get anything from the security cameras at the Fountain?' he asked, as they both had a careful look around the shop.

'Feet,' said Jen. 'Lots and lots of feet, all different sizes, too.'

'Feet?'

Jen shook her head.

'Four security cameras, only one of them switched on. And it was pointing at people's feet as they entered the public bar.'

'Useful.'

'Very.'

'Nothing else at all?'

'I'll look through the footage later, but I'm not hopeful. Not unless whoever did it was in the bar and decided to walk in and out of the pub on their hands.'

'Quite the long shot.'

'Isn't it just?'

Matt came back inside.

'Owen and Mr Willis are heading back down the dale to get the list of everything they have in stock,' he said. 'He says it's on the computer system here, but that he added some new items last week and hasn't yet had the chance to add them to the list.' He then gestured towards the window. 'So, what do you think, then?'

Harry said, 'I've not seen any evidence of anyone being in the shop,' he said. 'No one came in through the door, because if they did, why smash the window?'

'You don't think they did a smash and grab?' Matt asked.

'There's not much in the window,' said Harry, 'and what is, is covered in smashed glass. Plus, there's a hole in the window from whatever or whoever hammered into it, but it's not big enough for anyone to climb through, I don't think.'

'And the blood?'

'I've had a closer look,' said Jen, 'and I can't see any inside. Might be worth getting Sowerby and her team down here, though, to have a closer look just to make sure.'

'Which leads me to think this is accidental or vandalism; either someone fell into the window or was pushed, or it was smashed on purpose.'

'Why smash it on purpose if you're not going to nick something?' Jen asked. 'Makes no sense.'

'We don't know that they didn't nick something,' said Harry. 'I know I said there's not much in the window, but there might have been something small that caught someone's eye. Maybe they'd had a few, saw something shiny, and decided it needed to be in their pocket. Next thing, they've smashed the window, cut themselves to buggery by doing it, and headed home with something worth a bob or two.'

'Or they were pissed, and either stumbled or tripped into it, or there was a scuffle and things got out of hand.'

Harry didn't want to put money on any of those options, as they were all equally possible.

'Might be worth asking around to see if anyone heard

anything,' he said, waving a hand at the buildings and houses around them. 'If there was a fight or an argument, someone might have heard something, and that would give us a time to tie it to.'

'Whoever's blood it is, they might visit the doctor or hospital to get their injuries looked at,' Jen suggested. 'I can have a look at that.'

'Do that,' agreed Harry. 'And check in with Jim as well, get him to hurry up. Matt? You stay here and wait for our friends, Mr Griffiths and Mr Willis, to return. I'm going to head back up into town to speak with Sowerby.'

As Harry headed off, Jen said, 'I fixed the rest of the cameras for Mandy, and I asked her to try and start getting a list together of everyone who was in the pub last night. Don't know how far she'll have got, and I can't see us ever getting a complete list, but she might have something for us to get started with.'

'I'll ask,' said Harry, and with nothing left to say, gave Matt and Jen a nod, and continued on his way back up into the marketplace, his mind still unable to comprehend the notion of a dog that could sniff out antiques.

TWELVE

When Harry marched back into the car park behind the Fountain, and over to where a white tent had been erected over where the body had been found. People in white suits were milling around the area carrying out various jobs, analysing the crime scene, looking for evidence. It was a strangely clinical scene, considering what had happened, the murder something brutal and bloody, the white tent and white overalls of the SOC team so clean and bright.

The weather, Harry was pleased to note, was still holding. He had no idea how much damage the rain had caused, but at least for now, it was staying away. He could still smell it in the air, though, a cool, metallic scent which brought with it the rich aroma of peat and heather and moss from the fells and fields around Hawes. There was another note behind it, too, the odour of animals, and Harry heard on the wind the distant bleat of sheep, and behind that, the low moan of cattle calling to each other.

Harry saw one of the white-clothed figures emerge from the tent to glance up at him and raise a hand in a wave, before making their way towards the steps. Once at the top, they removed their facemask.

'How's it going, then?' Harry asked, as Rebecca stretched her neck from side to side.

'God, I'm tired, Harry,' she said, not answering his question.

Then she yawned, so deeply that Harry was surprised he wasn't sucked in with it.

'Late night?'

'No,' Sowerby said. 'I'm not a late-night person; usually to bed around ten, head up with a good book, asleep for half past. But I'm just not sleeping through.'

Sowerby stifled another yawn, but it won through regardless.

'Then I'm just awake, you know? Gave up in the end, headed downstairs, made myself a hot milk and honey, would you believe?'

'I would,' said Harry. 'Because I've done the same myself at times. The work we do, it's more of a shock we get any sleep at all.'

'It's not even the job,' Sowerby said. 'It's ...'

Harry waited for her to finish what she was going to say, but no words came.

'Something else bothering you, then?'

Sowerby still offered nothing, but Harry could see something behind her eyes that was answer enough. It was, however, not his place to pry, so he decided it was best to leave that alone for now and move on.

'How's things down there?' he asked, gesturing towards the tent and the white figures scurrying around it.

'Bloody,' said Sowerby. 'I'm sure you noticed when you had a look yourself that there wasn't much, but that's because of the rain. The ground around the body is soaked with the stuff. A wound like that, the body loses a couple of litres very quickly, before everything slows down, closes up, starts to, you know ...' She yawned again. 'Never seen a quoits pitch before, have you? Seems an odd game. And, if our victim is anything to go by, a little too competitive.'

Harry thought about that final point for all of two seconds.

'Hard to see how throwing a ring of steel at a stake rammed in some mud would lead to this.' He saw Sowerby yawn once again, and added, 'Reckon you should be in bed, not here.'

'So do I,' replied Sowerby. 'No chance of that though, is there? Instead, I'll be drinking a lot of caffeine. And on that subject, fancy grabbing me one?'

Harry laughed.

'You do know I'm not a member of your team, don't you?'

'All I know is that I need something to stop me falling over and slamming my face into the ground.'

'How do you take it?'

'Flat white, two sugars,' Sowerby said. 'Don't usually have the sugar, but I think I need it right now.'

Harry said, 'I'll be five minutes,' then turned to pop back into the marketplace, but Sowerby caught his arm.

Harry turned back around to see the pathologist staring up at him.

'One thing,' she said. 'The body ...'

'What about it?'

'Something isn't quite right about it.'

'Other than the fact its head has been detached?'

'Ignoring the obvious,' said Sowerby, 'and the fact we've found no ID, no wallet, no phone, what we have found is a condom.'

Harry remembered what he had in his pocket and pulled out the small evidence bag to show Sowerby the contents.

'Snap,' he said.

Sowerby narrowed her eyes at the bag, then at Harry.

'Where did you find them?'

'On the steps, between the quoits pitch and the car park,' he said.

'Well, the one we've found has been used,' said Sowerby. 'Someone obviously likes to be prepared, don't they? Clearly not a fan of running short.'

Harry thought about the body, how it had been lying on the ground.

'He's fully clothed, though,' he said. 'Unzipped round the front then, yes?'

'Classy, right?'

'Whoever said romance is dead?'

That got a laugh from Sowerby, though Harry saw it fighting with another yawn.

'Best I get you that coffee,' he said.

'Yes, please,' Sowerby replied, and she sat down on the wall, leaning forward, elbows on her knees. 'I'll tell you the rest of it when you get back.'

'The rest of what?'

Sowerby didn't answer, and instead just yawned and waved Harry away.

Harry headed off, leaving the car park to make his way to a café, only to remember as he did so that it was a Sunday, and nothing would be open. He thought about popping into the Fountain, but decided it was best to leave Mandy alone for now as she had enough to be dealing with. So, instead, he popped into the community centre to the office to make Sowerby's coffee.

Opening the office door, Harry was met by the tail end of an excited border collie.

'Now then, Fly,' he said, looking across the room to see Jim over in the small kitchen area.

'Alright, Harry?' Jim said. 'Just got in, so making a brew.

Was actually about to pop over and ask if you fancied one yourself, as I saw you talking to Sowerby when I arrived.'

'I'll have one,' Harry instructed. 'Sowerby wants a flat white with two sugars.'

'A flat white?' said Jim. 'What's she think this is, a bistro?'

Harry laughed.

'Do your best,' he said. 'All good with the chicken shed?'

'You want a report on it now or later?'

'Later,' Harry replied. 'By which I mean, maybe never, but let's see how the week goes, shall we?'

A few minutes later, Harry and Jim were walking side by side, ducking under the cordon tape to approach Sowerby. They'd left Fly back in the office curled up under a table in one of the two dog beds situated there permanently.

'Glad you were able to get here so quickly,' Harry said to Jim, as Sowerby came over to meet them, her steps slow and deliberate, as though her feet were made of stone and it was all she could do to drag them along. 'Jen and Matt are dealing with something on the cobbles, and Dave is just making sure we don't get too many folk being nosy with what's going on here. I'll need you to be the Scene Guard.'

'No bother,' said Jim. 'I saw Jen and Matt as I drove through anyway. Had a quick chat. They told me that was what I was on with, so I've already sorted the clipboard.'

'Do you know about Mr Willis?' Harry asked.

'About? How do you mean?'

'That he's a dog.'

'Of course I do,' said Jim. 'Everyone does.'

'Everyone except me, it seems.'

Jim shrugged.

'You've been busy,' he said.

'Everyone's busy,' said Harry.

BLOOD FOUNTAIN   83

Sowerby arrived and Jim handed her the mug of coffee. She clasped it between her hands and took a sip.

'Perfect,' she said. 'Where did you get it?'

'Café Jacques,' said Jim.

Harry did a double take as Sowerby said, 'Not heard of that one, has it just opened?'

'Didn't know you spoke French?' Harry said, still staring at Jim.

'I don't,' said Jim. 'French teacher at school was called James, but he always wrote it as Jacques. That's how I know.'

'I'm confused,' said Sowerby, through the steam rising from her mug.

'I made it,' Jim explained.

'It's a Sunday,' added Harry. 'Nowt's open.'

Sowerby took a longer slug of the coffee.

'Well, it's bloody good,' she said.

'The finest instant coffee you'll ever taste,' Jim smiled. 'Anyway, I'll get on with getting down everyone's names, shall I? Then I'll set myself up at the cordon tape, just in case we've anyone else turning up.'

'Everyone's here who should be,' said Sowerby. 'The photographer's already been and gone, though.'

Harry said, 'Still need you there, Jim. Sowerby's right, but having you there as a police presence will give anyone thinking of goose-necking pause for thought.'

Jim left them, and Harry walked with Sowerby back over to the steps down to the quoits pitch.

'Feeling better?' he asked.

'Slightly more human, yes.'

'So, what's this rest of it you wanted to tell me, then?' he asked.

Sowerby drained the coffee and handed Harry the mug.

'First, we found a phone. It's dead, mainly because it's been almost cut in two, but it's a phone. We'll see if we can get something off it, but I can't promise anything.'

'Cut in two? How? And where was it?'

'In some long grass over by the wall, like it had been kicked or thrown, not sure. As to how it was damaged, hard to say, but my guess is that whatever the killer used on the victim, they also used on the phone.'

'That's odd.'

'As to the other stuff I wanted to tell you? Well, we think there were three people on the pitch when it happened,' said Sowerby.

Harry said nothing, just waited for her to continue.

'The victim was on his knees when he was struck; we can tell that because of the indentations in the soil. If he'd been standing when he was attacked, there would be more disturbance, evidence of the body falling. But all we've got is heavy indentations where his knees were, and his feet, or toes anyway. Looks like he rolled to his left, or slumped, but really gently, like he stopped halfway. Then afterwards, maybe when the next strike to his neck came, to finish the job I guess, he was pushed back to where he had been before.'

Harry gave the scars on his chin a scratch; they always itched more when he was thinking through problems, especially those associated with a crime scene.

'How could he stop halfway?' he asked. 'That doesn't make sense.'

'Well, it does if you think about what he was doing,' said Sowerby. 'If he's having a quickie with someone, and they're down there on the grass, and he's ... well, they're doing it doggy style ...'

Harry almost choked on his tea.

'Doggy style?'

Sowerby gave a shrug.

'Can't say I was expecting you to say that.'

'Well, that's what it looks like.' Sowerby sighed, somehow managing to quash another yawn. 'And there's no other way to say it, really, is there? I could've said from behind, maybe?'

'But you didn't.'

'No, I didn't. Seems too polite for what we're looking at down there. Anyway, whoever he was with, that's what they were doing, or that's what it looks like, because we've found other indentations in the ground that make it fairly obvious with regards to body positions, that kind of thing. But, in simple terms, they were having sex, he was struck across the back of the neck, and that strike killed him instantly as the spinal cord was severed. He slumped forward onto whoever he was having sex with, was struck again, the second blow probably severing the head completely. Which means you have someone else involved, someone who was there when it happened.'

'Then where the hell are they now?' Harry asked, frustration crushing his words between his teeth.

'There's no evidence of anyone else being attacked,' said Sowerby. 'So, wherever they are, they're not here. We've got footprints, obvs, and we've taken impressions of those. But they're just showing that some people were tramping around down here. They're too messy to be of much use.'

'None of what you've just said means they're not dead, though.'

'Doesn't mean they are, either.'

Harry was baffled and gave himself a moment to think about what Sowerby had just told him.

'So the killer either just let them go, which doesn't make any sense at all, or chased them down,' he said. 'And that means we've either got another body somewhere still to be found, or someone who managed to escape, hasn't come to the police, and will probably be traumatised for the rest of their lives. All of which means we either have another victim, or a witness.'

'A witness who was covered in our victim's blood,' said Sowerby. 'And you're right about the trauma. It'll be horrendous.'

The itch in Harry's scars grew, but he ignored it as something else crossed his mind, something tomb-dark and haunted by a scream.

'There's always the chance the killer took the witness with them.'

Sowerby's eyes went wide.

'Kidnapped them?'

'Just a thought.'

'Is this where I wish I hadn't asked you the following question?'

'What question?'

'Why?'

Harry's itch became too much to ignore and he gave it a scratch, his fingernails tracing the lines carved out by shards of metal so long ago now he could barely remember it. He could remember enough, though.

'Hostage, maybe. Guilt?'

That word caused Sowerby's eyebrows to try and meet in the middle.

'Guilt?'

'Just because the death was brutal doesn't mean the person who did it doesn't have remorse,' Harry explained, or tried to, anyway. Sometimes he didn't always understand what he was thinking himself, and saying it out loud was what he needed to do to try and work it out.

'Still don't see why they'd kidnap them.'

Harry held up both his and Sowerby's mugs, as behind them he heard the ambulance arrive for the body.

'Personally, I'm baffled why they did it here of all places; it was raining last night, wasn't it? There are more pleasant places to have a fumble.'

'Not all night,' said Sowerby, then she pointed to some trees hanging over the quoits pitch. 'And those would offer a good amount of protection. Plus, down there, it's out of sight, isn't it? Sort of private. Ish.'

'Why not find a bed somewhere, though? Why do it out in the open?'

'To keep it a secret?' Sowerby suggested. 'Maybe to add a little sense of adventure to what they were doing? Who knows? People like having sex in the funniest of places and in all weathers.'

That throw-away statement caught Harry's attention more than it should have done.

'Do they, now?'

'I had sex on a patio once. That doesn't sound very weird now that I've said it out loud, but at the time, it certainly felt it. We had to hurry, as we didn't want the sausages to burn on the barbeque. Oh, and it was raining.'

'You were barbequing in the rain?'

'In this country, you're always barbequing in the rain.'

Harry decided to avoid asking any further questions about Sowerby's sexual exploits, and instead gave the mugs he was holding a bit of a wiggle in midair.

'Best I get these back to the office,' he said.

'Priorities, right?' said Sowerby. 'And I suppose I should get back to the team. I'll keep you posted on what's happening here. If you or one of your team needs to come to the mortuary, I'll let you know, but it might not be necessary. I'll get a report to you as soon as I can.'

With a farewell said to Sowerby, Harry thought about everything he'd just learned. With this crime scene, and what had happened on the cobbles, it was turning into the kind of Sunday he would rather forget. Lunchtime had also passed him by, he realised, but perhaps he would be able to solve that with a trip into the Fountain to chat with Mandy. It was worth a shot.

First, though, he would get Smudge from Jen's vehicle because she could do with a walk, and he could do with the same, if only to help him think. So he popped back down to the antiques shop, grabbed Jen's keys, then collected the dog. That done, he left the keys in the office and strolled back around to the main door to the Fountain's public bar. He was not there for a pint, so he would focus on chatting to Mandy to see how she was doing with the list, and also to see if the kitchen couldn't rustle him up something to stop his stomach from grumbling.

Nothing too big, he thought, pushing in through the door. Well, maybe some lasagne ...

THIRTEEN

By the time the crime scene had been dealt with, the day had already started to draw itself to a close. Though the sky had brightened at points, the clouds had never really gone away, and come the late afternoon, they'd only grown thicker, giving the later hours of the day a deep gloom, which matched Harry's mood.

He'd sent the team home, aware that Jadyn would be arriving soon to be on call. As for the two crime scenes they'd worked that day, they'd somehow managed to join forces in his mind, with the sole intent of making his brain feel like it was going to leak out of his ears.

The smashed window of the antiques shop seemed to be nothing more than that for now. Mr Griffiths had returned with a stock list, and everything had checked out; no items missing, nothing stolen. There were no reports from anyone of shouting or arguing or a disturbance of any kind in the area. So, on the face of it, Harry found it hard to see that the smashed window was anything other than drunken clumsiness. Whoever had fallen into the window and cut themselves badly enough to leave blood all over the place was proving to be very elusive, with no evidence of someone either contacting or attending any local medical services.

The crime scene behind the Fountain, however, was an entirely different beast. They had a decapitated body. They had a killer. And they had someone else at the scene who was either lying low, had been murdered themselves, their now-lifeless body stashed somewhere, waiting for someone to discover it, or the killer had kidnapped them, for reasons unknown.

They had the start of a list of everyone who was at the pub that night, and had expanded it by visiting or calling the various hotels, pubs, and bed and breakfasts in Hawes to get their own guest lists. There were so many questions about what had happened that Harry had trouble grabbing onto any one of them to try and answer it.

He knew that sleeping on it would help, and checking his watch, saw that Jadyn would be at the office soon, and he, therefore, would be able to head home. That thought was enough to cut a beam of sunlight through the gloom, because Harry could think of nothing that beat an evening with Grace and their dogs, just relaxing in their new home. With those thoughts calming the storm in his mind, and with Smudge fast asleep at his feet, he closed his eyes.

A few minutes later, Harry woke with a start. Whatever dream he'd been in the middle of was blasted apart by the sound of rapid gunfire. Eyes wide open, heart racing, he was, for the briefest moment, in the middle of a firefight, but then reality swept in and the office came into focus.

Smudge was sitting up, staring at him, a paw on his knee.

Harry reached out, gave the dog a pat on the head and a good chin scratch, then a rapid knock came at the office door.

Pushing himself out of the chair, Harry went to answer, when the door opened and in walked Jadyn.

'Boss?' he said. 'Didn't expect to see you here.'

'And I'm fairly sure that you know you don't have to knock to enter your own workplace,' Harry replied, yawning and stretching as he spoke. 'Woke me up, though, which is good. How was the family?'

'Good,' said Jadyn. 'But I didn't knock; there's someone outside who wants to see you. Well, not you, specifically; I mean, they didn't ask for you by name, just the police, but you know what I mean.'

'Who?' Harry asked. 'And what about?'

'There's a group of them. Said one of their friends is missing and also that their cars have been vandalised.'

Harry was at the door in a heartbeat.

'Boss? What's going on? What's happened?'

Yanking the door open, Harry found himself staring at the faces of a group of four men he guessed to be in their twenties, early thirties. They all looked tired and stressed.

Harry didn't even bother introducing himself.

'This way,' he said, and led the group up a small hallway to the interview room.

Holding the door for everyone to squeeze in, Harry dashed back to the office to grab a notepad and a pen, and have Jadyn sort them out drinks, and then he was back.

'Sorry there's not enough chairs,' he said. 'Constable Okri says you've a missing person to report?'

'Two, actually,' said one of the men whose face was decorated with a goatee beard so small and thin, Harry wondered why he'd even bothered to grow it. The hairs sprouted from his face like sporadic stalks of wheat on a small, pale hillock.

'Well, Ian's not missing, is he?' said another, this one considerably more thickset than the other three, a torso built in a gym. 'He's just buggered off after what he did, that's all. The bastard. I tell you, when I get my hands on him, I'm going to ...'

The group then descended into calls for whoever this Ian was to not only be found, but given a good kicking, and that was something Harry wasn't going to stand for.

'Right then, you lot, shut it!' he said, his voice loud and commanding, making it damned clear they were to shut up and listen.

He waited for them all to turn and face him, which took a little longer than he would have preferred.

'I need you all to wind your necks in, calm down, and then perhaps we can work out what it is you're here to report, and what we can do about it.'

'But he's smashed my wing mirrors and covered my bonnet in—'

Harry glared at the astonishingly thin man who had spoken, shutting him down immediately.

'Good,' he said, and dropped the notepad and pen on the table. 'That's better. Now, first of all, names, contact details.'

In silence, each of the group jotted down their details. Harry then introduced himself, before having them all do the same, to help him direct his questioning if he needed to.

'Let's start with the missing person, rather than the one you say has buggered off,' he said, thinking of the body found that morning behind the Fountain.

'Mickey,' said the thin member of the group called Geoff. 'Michael "Mickey" Hadley. Mickey's his nickname. We've not seen him since last night.'

Harry heard his own teeth grind at that statement.

'And you only thought of reporting this now?' He checked his watch, not to look at the time, but to emphasise how stunned he was by how long they had left it to report their missing friend. 'Why?'

'Because we were pissed, that's why,' said Chris, whose

head wasn't just bald, but shiny as a snooker ball. 'This is the first time I've been out all day.'

'We're here for his stag weekend,' said Eddie, the one with the muscles. 'Mickey's, I mean. We've done some walking, a bit of mountain biking, and last night was spent in the pub, so we drank, because that's what you do on a stag do, isn't it, drink? And we kept drinking when we got back to where we were staying.'

Harry turned his eyes back on Geoff.

'What time last night?'

'What time what?'

Harry sucked in a breath through his nose, and exhaled hard.

'What time was it when you last saw Mickey? I'm assuming you were in the bar till closing?'

'We were,' said Geoff. 'Got booted out of the place by the owner.'

Harry could well imagine Mandy doing that, but said nothing, and waited for Geoff to continue.

'Then we wandered around Hawes for a bit. We all had hip flasks, so we had a nice little stroll.'

'In the rain?'

'That was half the fun of it,' said Eddie. 'We ended up at the playground. Amazed we didn't injure ourselves. Roundabouts are fast, aren't they?'

Geoff laughed, the sound a thin thing, like the screech of a violin played by a six-year-old. 'Your face when you came off!'

'Yeah, that was piss funny,' agreed Chris, smirking.

Harry could see the conversation was about to get off course, so pulled it back to why they were there.

'Mickey, then,' he said, directing the question at Henry, the only one who hadn't spoken, and who was stroking his goatee somewhat nervously, Harry noticed. 'He was with you at the playground?'

'What?'

'Mickey, he was at the playground?' Harry repeated.

Henry gave a shallow nod.

'You seem unsure,' Harry said.

'No, he was there,' said Henry. 'I'm sure he was.'

The rest of the group murmured in agreement, then Henry said, 'And then he wasn't.'

'What do you mean, and then he wasn't? You must've seen him leave. Where did he go? Was he with anyone?'

Harry realised then that he hadn't actually asked for a description of Mickey, having been distracted by the group's lack of urgency in reporting their missing friend. He was about to ask for exactly that when Eddie said something that shut everyone up.

'He went off with a girl,' he said.

FOURTEEN

Eddie's words were so abrupt, so matter of fact, that Harry didn't quite know how to take it. There was no warmth, no emotion, in Eddie's voice, and as he mulled them over, it struck him that Eddie was maybe saying more with those words than he was letting on. What, though, he wasn't entirely sure. Not yet, anyway.

'Do you know who she was?' Harry asked. 'Was she a local lass, someone he met in the pub?'

Eddie said nothing as the others chipped in.

'I don't remember seeing her at the pub,' said Chris.

'Neither do I,' said Geoff. 'But she must've been there, right, otherwise how did she know where we were?'

'Must've followed us,' said Chris. 'Was she part of that hen do, Eddie? You'd know, seeing as you got off with two of them!'

A titter of laughter, but not from Eddie, Harry noticed.

'Why would she follow us from the pub, in the rain, on the off chance of getting off with one of us?' said Henry. 'That doesn't make much sense, does it?'

Geoff then added, 'She had an umbrella. I remember that, because her and Mickey ran off together under it, didn't they? Giggling as well. Like kids.'

'Oh, yeah, that's right,' said Chris, and Harry saw the man's eyes widen with the memory. 'But where did she come from? We'd have remembered if she was in the pub, wouldn't we? Of course we would.'

Harry noticed that after his initial statement about the girl, Eddie was still very quiet, so he turned his eyes on him and gave him a verbal prod.

'Eddie?'

Eddie looked at Harry.

'What?'

There was an edge in his voice, Harry noticed; something clearly wasn't right. But what?

'You brought this girl up, but then you shut down. Why?'

'Well, everyone else was talking, weren't they? I didn't want to interrupt.'

'You sure it's not something else?' Harry asked, unconvinced by Eddie's attempt at trying to convince him of his politeness.

Eddie shook his head.

'Nothing else?'

'Why would there be? She was just a girl, wasn't she? That's all. It was no big deal.'

Harry cocked his head, Eddie's words jarring, his tone off. And that final sentence, *It was no big deal* ... He decided to go straight for the jugular.

'Do you know her, Eddie?'

Geoff, Chris, and Henry all did a double-take at Harry, before turning to stare at Eddie.

'What? You knew her?' said Chris. 'You can't be serious!'

'I didn't I don't, I mean,' Eddie spluttered. 'Look, I don't know her, okay? I don't.'

'Who the hell is she, then?' Geoff asked.

Eddie shook his head, gave a shrug.

'I don't know her, not personally, anyway. She's just this girl, that's all. What's the big deal?'

And there it was, thought Harry, so he pushed harder.

'Who is she, Eddie? Where's she from? And what do you mean, you don't know her personally? You know her professionally, then? Is that it?'

Eddie opened his mouth, shut it again.

Geoff swore. 'What the hell have you done, Eddie?' his voice quiet, trembling with a rage that Harry was surprised the man could actually muster, because surely any extreme emotion would snap him in two.

Eddie turned to the other three.

'It was just a bit of fun!' he said, raising his hands in the air with a shrug. 'It's his last night, after all, isn't it, know what I mean? Thought I'd get someone in, that's all.'

Harry shook his head in abject despair.

'You paid for an escort, Eddie? That's it, isn't it? That's what you did.'

It was a statement of fact, rather than a question.

'She wasn't cheap, either,' said Eddie, a look on his face that made Harry think that the idiot was now trying to paint the whole episode as something they should be thanking him for, praising him for his generosity. 'Not like I asked for anyone to chip in, is it? Did it myself, out of the kindness of my heart.'

There was the briefest of moments of quiet then, and that should've been warning enough for Harry, but he was tired. He wasn't alert enough to react when Chris threw himself at Eddie like an Exocet missile, sending them both to the floor.

'You mad bastard! You hired an escort? What the hell is wrong with you? And now Mickey's disappeared! This is your fault, all of it, you know that, don't you? Nobody else's; yours!'

Harry was out of his chair and dragging Chris off Eddie, as the man landed punch after punch. They weren't exactly powerful, and not one of them was aimed with any precision, but the shock of the attack was vividly painted in the wild terror in Eddie's eyes.

'All I did was pay for her to give Mickey a bit of last-night fun!' Eddie said, staying down, as Chris struggled to get free of Harry's grip. 'I thought I was doing him a favour, that's all. No harm in that, is there? And I was sensible, too; gave him condoms, because I figured he wouldn't be carrying any, would he?'

'A favour?' Chris exclaimed. 'No harm? What the hell are you on? Can you hear yourself? A favour? He's getting married, you twat! Married! You do know what that means, don't you?'

Harry thought about the condoms he'd found at the crime scene and the one Rebecca had found; there was a good chance they were the ones from Eddie. He wondered about the empty condom packet, about Mickey's last moments, but then Eddie was shouting again, his back against the wall, eyes flicking between the faces of his friends. Though, Harry wondered just how long they would all remain friends.

'Of course I know what it means! It means shagging just one person for the rest of your life, and who wants that?'

With the foul stench of that statement floating in the air, Harry was tempted to let Chris throw himself at Eddie again, and then possibly join in himself. Sense prevailed, though, but only just.

'I can't believe he just went off with her,' said Geoff, and Harry heard genuine shock in the man's voice. 'I mean, who the hell does that? Who? He's getting married! Doesn't that mean anything to him? To anyone?'

'Obviously not,' said Chris.

'Maybe I've done everyone a favour then, have you thought

about that?' said Eddie, with a surprising amount of bravado in his tone. 'Shows he's not ready for commitment, and shouldn't be getting married, doesn't it?'

Chris threw himself at Eddie once again, but this time, Henry held him back. Chris struggled, but gave in eventually, not that it seemed to make much difference to Eddie.

'Anyway, what about Ian?' he demanded, in what Harry viewed as a very clear and clumsy attempt to deflect the anger coming his way. 'What about that mad twat? Where's he now, then, eh? He left the pub early, didn't he? And it's him who's messed around with our vehicles, because it sure as hell isn't anyone else, is it? Maybe he knows where Mickey is. That's why we went round there earlier, isn't it, to ask him? But he just stayed in his room, and next thing we know, our cars have been done over and he's sodded off home! Not answering his phone either, is he? What about him? What about Ian?'

In the moment of silence following Eddie's shouting, Harry realised something.

'Ian?' he said, looking at Chris, Geoff, and Henry. 'Just who the hell is Ian?'

'He was the sixth member of the group,' said Geoff. 'Mickey's oldest friend. Had a strop and left the pub early. No idea what was up with him. He'd been weird all day.'

Harry remembered then that the group had mentioned two missing persons, and not just one.

'A strop? What about?'

'He's jealous, that's all,' said Eddie. 'We're all doing well, and he's just a teacher. Doesn't like having the piss taken out of him, that's all. Too sensitive. Can't take a joke.'

Harry narrowed his eyes at Eddie.

'First,' he said, 'get your arse off the floor. And second, there's no such thing as just a teacher. Is that understood?'

Harry knew that statement wasn't entirely true, because

sure, there were plenty of teachers out there who weren't great, didn't like the job, didn't like the kids they worked with. But he knew full well that there were plenty of others who were, and he wasn't about to let Eddie the weasel paint them all with the same brush of condescension.

He was about to ask what joke it was that had caused Ian to leave early and do whatever it was he'd done to their cars, when Eddie suddenly got to his feet, his size giving him the threatening bearing of a nightclub bouncer.

'I admit it,' he said. 'I hired an escort. But I don't see what that has to do with Mickey disappearing. I even booked her into a bed and breakfast for the night. Not that she used it; I checked this morning, thought I'd thank her, you know? I called, but there was no answer.'

'Do you know where she's from?' Harry asked.

'Leyburn,' said Eddie. 'She was hard to find as well; Leyburn's not exactly a big, is it? Hardly spoiled for choice in that area.'

'Contact details?'

'I can give you her number, but I've not got an address. Called herself Candy, so my guess is that's not her real name.'

'You don't say,' said Harry, tapping the notebook for Eddie to write down Candy's number. Then he said, 'I need a description of Mickey. But my guess is that you can all do better than that and provide me with photographs, correct?'

'I've been official photographer for the stag,' said Henry, and he pulled out his phone, tapped the screen. 'Here, this is Mickey.'

Harry took the offered phone from Henry, and turned the screen around to see the photograph. He recognised the face staring back at him immediately, though the last time he'd seen it, it had been a cold, lifeless thing, staring up at him from the grass.

'What's wrong?' Henry asked, as Harry handed the phone back to him.

So, Harry told them.

FIFTEEN

When morning broke, Harry had no interest in getting up to face it, or the rain he could hear falling outside. Instead, all he really wanted to do was to scooch across the mattress, wrap his arms around Grace's waist, pull her in close, and just *be*. He wanted the night to continue so that he could exist in a world where he was both asleep and awake, drowning in the intoxicating aroma of the woman he'd fallen in love with, fully aware of the moment, yet also fully at rest. Unfortunately, the wet, black nose nudging at his left hand as it dangled off the side of the bed had other ideas.

'Morning, Smudge,' he said, the words stretched out by a yawn so deep it made his jaw lock for a moment. 'You do know you're not supposed to be up here, don't you?'

Smudge answered by lifting a paw onto the mattress and stuffing her nose right up close to Harry's own.

'You really don't care, do you?'

Harry heard the soft thud of Smudge's tail on the carpet.

'Grace?'

When Grace answered, her voice bounced up the stairs to

Harry, an echo to it born of the thick, stone walls of the old house in which they now lived.

'You getting up, then?'

'No.'

'I've just done us some bacon, if that'll help persuade you.'

Harry caught the scent of it.

'That's cheating.'

'That's love,' Grace replied. 'Egg? Toast?'

'Yes, please,' Harry answered, and sat up, swinging his legs off of the bed.

Smudge trotted out of the bedroom and back downstairs. Harry had a sneaking suspicion she had been sent up by Grace in the first place.

Heading through to the shower, Harry squeezed his eyes shut and rubbed them hard with the heels of his hands. Stars flashed, and in each spark he saw images of the day before flicker past, ending with the faces of the victim's friends when he'd told them that Mickey had been killed. He'd kept the finer details to himself, because no one needed to hear that.

Then, when they'd finally headed on their way, having been told someone would be in touch with them the following day, and with Mickey's parent's contact details given to him by Eddie of all people, he'd sorted out officers from the Metropolitan Police to do the one job that was always bottom of the list; telling the family. They were on their way this morning, travelling up to identify the body, and that meant he would have to send someone over to be with them. Who, though, he wasn't sure. Jen most likely, but for this, he would probably want to go with her.

With those thoughts racing around in his head, Harry attempted to get the water to the right temperature. He still hadn't quite got the knack of it, and he had a horrible suspicion that the first major expense in the house was to replace the shower unit. If that meant tiling, he would be very unhappy indeed. DIY was not a strong point. When he did finally manage to find the sweet spot between scalding and freezing, he had little time to enjoy it, as a call from downstairs informed him that his breakfast was soon to be plated up and on the table.

A few minutes later, Harry slumped down at the table. Smudge was sitting over on the rug in front of the wood burner, which still smouldered from the night before. Grace's dog, Jess, was not so much lying *with* her as *on* her, and to Harry's amusement, they were both snoring.

'You didn't need to do this,' he said, 'but thank you.'

'You made breakfast a couple of mornings ago,' Grace replied, as she went to sit down opposite. 'You didn't need to do it then, either, did you?' She leaned over, and they shared a minty fresh kiss. 'Love's a funny thing, isn't it?'

Harry smiled, and tucked into his plate of food, none of which lasted long, and sent it all on its way with great mouthfuls of strong tea.

'I needed that,' he said, leaning back in his chair. 'Yesterday was something else. And there's so much to be getting on with today because of it. Don't really know where to start.'

'With just one thing,' Grace said, as she filled her fork. 'That's always Dad's advice. You can't do everything at once, and if you try to, or even just attempt to think of it all, you'll go mad. Best thing is to just break it down into manageable chunks. So, like I said, just do one thing. Then, when it's done, do the next thing. Anyway, I don't know why either of us are even bothering to worry; it's not like you don't what you're doing, is it?'

Harry reached for a slice of toast and set to with the butter, then the marmalade, which was a jar of Arthur's homemade and had a real bite to it that Harry had become a little addicted to. Breakfast just didn't taste the same without it.

'Fair,' he said, 'but I was hoping that at some point it would feel easier and not so overwhelming, if that makes sense.'

'Why is it overwhelming?'

'I can't really say too much,' Harry replied. 'You know what it's like with this kind of thing.'

'I do, but I also know you've never described anything that you do as overwhelming. Certainly not to me, anyway.'

'Or anyone, actually,' said Harry, baffled then by his own words. 'Did I really say that?'

'You did. But you don't need to look so worried, you know? It's okay.'

'It is?'

Harry wasn't so sure. That he'd said something like that so openly, without any thought at all, was a bit of a shock.

Grace put down her knife and fork, then reached over to hold Harry's hands.

'The whole point of this, by which I mean you and me and us having this place together and a future together, is that we're honest, right? We're each other's safe place, Harry. I know it feels alien to you, but it's okay to lean on other people. With me, though? It's beyond that; it's expected. That's what I'm here for, and while we're talking about it, I hope that's what you're here for, too.'

Grace gave his hands a squeeze, and though hers were dwarfed by his, he felt a strength in them that could match his own.

'You're much better with words than I am,' he said, returning the squeeze.

'You're getting better,' Grace smiled, returning to her food. 'Just don't be afraid of them, okay? Or me. I mean, it's not like I'm going anywhere now, is it, know what I mean?'

There was something in the way Grace said those last words that sparked something in Harry. He wasn't entirely sure what it was, but something told him that it was important, perhaps the most important thing in the world.

'I do,' he said.

Grace gave him a wink.

'You'll be fine today,' she said. 'Like I just said, it's okay to lean on other people, and that's what your team is for, isn't it? Don't try and do everything on your own, think about everything on your own; share it around a bit.'

'Have you just swallowed The Little Book of Wisdom or something?' Harry asked, finishing off his toast.

They both laughed, and then, with breakfast finished, were soon into their own routines of getting ready. Both dogs, sensing that the day was getting underway, trotted around excitedly, their claws tapping on the flagstone floor.

When it was time for him to go, Harry gave a whistle and Smudge ran to the door and sat down expectantly, her lead clamped in her jaws.

'Well, your deputy's ready,' said Grace. 'Go get 'em, Sheriff!'

As ways to start the day went, right then, Harry couldn't think of one better. And with a final kiss and a squeeze with Grace, he clipped the lead on Smudge, opened the door, and got hammered in the face by thick rain throwing itself at the house with the power of a fire hose.

'Looks like we're swimming to work.' He laughed, and stepped outside.

SIXTEEN

The journey to work was short. Smudge had needed a few minutes out in the rain, and he'd obliged, up to the point where she'd done what she needed to do. Then she'd looked at him with eyes that told him she was enjoying it as much as he, which was not at all, so they'd climbed into his Rav and headed up into Hawes.

Parking up in the marketplace, Harry caught sight of the cordon tape still across the entrance to the car park behind the Fountain. With no reason for it still to be up, he quickly took it all down, wrapping it all up into a ball, before dashing through the rain to the Community Centre and stepping inside.

Harry opened the door to the office to be met by the rest of the team. With Liz still away with Ben, and a replacement for Gordy still suspiciously elusive, the office seemed larger.

'Brew?' Matt called over, though obviously didn't expect an answer, as he then strode across the floor with a steaming mug in his hand. 'Lovely day, isn't it?'

'Not really, no,' said Harry, letting Smudge off the lead to go say hello to Fly. 'Drove here just to make sure I didn't drown on the way.'

He hung up his jacket, then took the mug from Matt, throwing the screwed-up cordon tape into the bin.

'How is everyone?'

'Keen to get going,' Matt answered.

Harry saw that Jadyn was in.

'He should be heading home,' he said, his voice quiet so that only Matt could hear. 'And shouldn't you be there as well? You're working tonight, aren't you?'

'We've a couple of Uniforms being sent over,' Matt said. 'They'll be helping us out for a while, what with our numbers down, and this new investigation.'

Harry frowned.

'And why is it that you know this, and I don't?'

He heard the office door swinging shut and glanced over his shoulder to see someone very unexpected standing there looking at him from beneath a slightly raised eyebrow.

'Because I told him, that's why.'

Detective Superintendent Walker closed the distance between them and held out her hand. Harry noticed immediately that she wasn't in uniform.

'Good morning, ma'am,' he said, taking her hand.

'You look surprised to see me.'

'That's because I am.'

'Good,' Walker smiled. 'I do love a surprise!'

Harry wasn't sure what to say, and glanced then at Matt, a very obvious, unspoken question in his eyes, but Matt was given no time to answer.

'Thought I'd pop by,' Walker said. 'By which I mean, I'm going to be around for a few days, if that's okay? The answer's yes, by the way, in case you're wondering.'

'You'll forgive me for asking why,' said Harry.

'I'd expect you to,' said Walker. 'My job, it's very much based in the office. And that gets a bit dull. So, what I'm doing is paying a few unexpected visits to various teams around the region, see how they're doing, get involved in whatever they're busy with, that kind of thing. Otherwise, how can I do my job effectively, if I don't actually know what everyone needs support with?'

'Well, you know what we need, don't you?' said Harry, his blunt manner unashamedly front and centre.

'A new DI?'

'We're a small team as it is. With Gordy gone, as soon as any of us are on leave, like PCSO Coates is this week, then it can get a bit desperate. Even more so if something big happens.'

'Which is why I've already arranged for additional support for you this week,' Walker explained. 'Should help you tackle what you're on with.' She looked at Matt and added, 'And you've me here now, so make use of me, yes?'

Harry frowned, suspicious. Not that he didn't trust the DSupt, but more that he'd had investigations in the past taken from him by those above him who were hungry for a bit of glory, both in the military and in the police.

'In what capacity?'

'In whatever capacity you require,' Walker answered. 'I'm not here to take over. This is your investigation, not mine.'

Harry digested those words for a moment, sipping his tea as he did so.

'Let's get cracking, then,' he said. 'Jadyn?'

The constable, who was standing talking to Jen, snapped to attention at the sound of his name.

'Boss?'

'You're not supposed to be here.'

'I know. I'm okay, though, honest. Wide awake!' He smiled, but Harry could see that it was slightly forced, his eyes a little bloodshot. 'Thought you might need an extra hand, for a while, anyway?'

'Well, I'm not about to write stuff on the board, am I?' Harry replied. 'But as soon as we're done with that, I want you gone. You'll be no bloody use to me if you fall asleep halfway through an interview.'

Jadyn drained his own drink, and was at the board, pen in hand, before Harry had even had a chance to get the rest of the team gathered. Not that he needed to, as they all took their places and turned to Harry expectantly.

Harry half expected Walker to want to lead things, but she had already sat herself down beside Dave, and had Smudge leaning against her leg for a head scratch.

'Right then,' he said, placing his now-empty mug on a table. 'Let's quickly run through where we are with what happened yesterday, and see if we can't get some plan together for how we're going to deal with it all. Matt, can you give us a quick recap?'

Matt stood up, took centre stage, and Harry stepped back, allowing him to lead, with Jadyn jotting notes on the board as he spoke. He was justifiably impressed. He caught a look in Walker's eye, too, as they all listened to the detective sergeant run through everything that had happened the previous day. As good and as detailed as it was, it didn't actually make Harry feel any better about things. Something told him that the discovery of the body was the start of something. He just wasn't sure what.

Matt finished speaking, then with a nod to Harry, sat back down.

'So, that's where we are,' said Harry. 'We've the body of Michael 'Mickey' Hadley, who was decapitated in the very early hours of Sunday morning behind the Fountain, by a weapon we have, as yet, not found. And to make things easier, I suggest we stick with calling him Mickey, so that we all know who we're talking about, and don't get confused when talking to witnesses. We know there was a witness to what happened, but our only way of contacting her is a phone number, which she isn't answering. Unsurprisingly, considering her line of business, it's a burner, so we can't access any data to help us track her down. We have no idea why Mickey was attacked, or by whom. We do not know if the woman he was with is safe, so finding her is a priority. In addition, we have a number of badly vandalised vehicles, all belonging to Mickey's friends who were in Hawes on his stag do, one of whom has seemingly gone AWOL. Oh, and an antiques shop owned by a dog had its window smashed in on the same night.'

'I'm sorry, what?'

Walker's question actually brought a smile to Harry's face.

'Not a lie,' he said. 'So, where do we want to start?'

Walker raised a hand, and on seeing it, Harry's gut twisted. Was this where she stepped in?

'Yes?' he said.

'Ignoring my urge to find out more about the dog and the antiques shop, I'm assuming Mickey's family will be on their way to identify the body?'

'They're travelling from London this morning, yes,' said Harry. 'Family liaison from the Met headed there last night, once I got the positive ID from his friends.'

'Then you'll need someone this side of things to meet them, be there when they see their son. I think maybe the best use of me right now is to do that, if that's okay with everyone else?'

Harry watched as Walker directed her question to the rest of the team.

No one objected.

'Jen?' Harry said, looking over at the detective constable, thinking back to what he had been pondering while wrestling with the shower earlier that morning.

'I'd like to go along as well, if that's okay?' Jen said. 'Maybe we could do this together? And it's often sensible to have two officers available, isn't it, for something like this?'

'It is, yes,' said Walker. 'But if you're needed here, then I'm happy to—'

'She is, yes,' said Harry, 'but I take Jen's point; it would be sensible for you both to go. And, while you're there, you might be able to pop in and see Sowerby; worth giving her a call, see if it's worth your while. It usually is.'

'Will do,' said Jen.

Harry moved the conversation on.

'We've a lot of door-knocking to do,' he said. 'We've managed to get a fairly decent list of names of everyone who was at the Fountain on the night in question. We don't know that the killer was there that night, but we need to be sure; something could've happened that caused things to escalate. And believe me, I know that's an understatement.'

'Dave and I can crack on with that,' said Jim.

'Good,' said Harry. 'My advice, narrow it down to only the incidents that we know of. From what I recall, there was a bit of an argument between a couple of locals, no idea what about, though; someone complained about the quantity of food they were served, which is again, something I just can't see turning into what we're now investigating, but you never know.'

'Some people have a very short fuse,' said Matt.

'There's short fuse and there's lopping someone's head off,' said Jen.

Harry said, 'There was also something about someone taking someone else's cap, and that's all we've got.'

'None of those events sound in any way, shape, or form the kind of thing that would lead to murder,' said Walker.

'Can't say as I disagree with you,' replied Harry. 'But like Matt just pointed out, some people really do have a very short fuse, dangerously so. Add a few drinks into the mix, and you've got the reason behind every single fight outside a nightclub on the planet, a good number of which involve weapons, be that a glass, a bottle, or a knife.'

'Why a quoits pitch, though?' asked Jim.

Harry remembered his conversation with Sowerby the day before.

'On that,' he said, 'and even though I don't think this has anything at all to do with it, we should get the names of everyone on the quoits team. The victim isn't local, but maybe—and this is the thinnest of maybes I can think of—maybe they're a little too protective of their pitch and didn't take too kindly to it being used for a bit of slap and tickle.'

A muffled laugh rolled its way around the team at hearing that turn of phrase, and Harry allowed it its moment to shine, unsure where on earth he'd dragged it from himself.

Jen raised her hand.

'Mandy mentioned that the cover to one of the clay pits was off.'

'Not when I went down there, it wasn't,' said Harry.

'She pushed it back on before trying to wake up Mickey.'

'I'll go have a look after this, then,' said Harry. 'Might be nothing, might be something.'

'There's also the small issue of the missing murder weapon,' said Matt, and Harry was happy to let the DS speak for a moment. 'Something tells me, though, that we're not looking at an attack where it was just thrown away after the fact.'

'Why?' asked Harry, deciding to poke Matt a little, get him to think.

'It's too brutal, and dare I say, too strange even, if that makes sense? Someone went out to commit murder, and they had the weapon to do it; I just can't see them throwing it away after. Why would they?'

'Which leads to another terrifying thought,' said Harry. 'What if this is just the beginning of something?' He saw the look of shock on the faces of his team, but continued on anyway. 'We always need to be aware of just such a possibility. Yes, at first, this may look like a one-off event, a killing that came out of nowhere, but there's a lot here that doesn't stack up, not least the manner of the killing.'

'You don't think we should maybe even look for it, then?' Jen asked.

Harry took the question on board, and decided to put it at the feet of their newest team member. He turned to look at Walker.

'What do you think, ma'am?'

Walker smiled.

'First, I think you should never, ever, call me ma'am again. And I get that you won't be happy with using my first name either, so just go with Walker. You okay with that?'

'I am,' said Harry, a small smile punctuating that two-word answer.

'As to the weapon, I'm inclined to agree. A stabbing, I'd have had us out there combing every field in the area for the weapon, checking the river, but this?' She shook her head. 'Whatever was used to do this, I don't think it's something that the killer can just throw away. And also, maybe they don't even want to. So, I agree, Harry; I don't think we should call in dozens of volunteers and additional officers to go tramping through fields and gardens, or get in a dive team to check out the river, on the off chance of finding something that may or may not be what we're looking for, especially as, right now, we don't actually know what we're looking for.'

'Great minds, then,' said Harry with a nod. 'A bit of common sense goes a long way, I think. If the killer kept the weapon, either to use again, or just because it means something to them, then our best course of action is to see if we can find them first. Another point is that there may be a connection between the killer and the victim. That's for you and Jen to see if you can find out, but go gentle, obviously.'

'What about the victim's stuff?' Jadyn asked. 'His belongings, that kind of thing? If he was here on a stag, he'd have a suitcase, wouldn't he? Maybe that has something in it? And what about a phone?'

'SOC team is on with that,' said Harry. 'Waiting to hear back. And we should get photographs, too, at some point. But I wouldn't count on anything from the phone being useful; it was badly damaged, nearly cut in half, actually.'

'What? How?'

Harry decided to not answer that question, and instead said, 'We've two people we really need to get hold of. First, is the woman who was with the victim when he was killed. Ascertaining that she is safe is paramount. But as all we have is a number of a burner phone, finding her isn't going to be easy. Then there's the missing member of the stag party, Mr Ian Lancaster. He left the pub early the night Mickey Hadley was killed. It's clear there's animosity there between Mr Lancaster and the rest of the group, perhaps even Mickey, but I've no idea why. They're all fairly sure that it was Ian who damaged their cars. I need someone to contact them this morning to look into what kind of damage we're talking about here. We've Ian's contact details, so wherever he is, I want him found, and I want him questioned.'

'That just leaves Mr Willis, then,' said Jen.

'Not really,' said Harry. 'Give him a call, check that he's had the window boarded up, and that he's absolutely sure nothing was stolen, then I think we're done with that for—'

'You mean give Mr Griffiths a call,' said Matt. 'Not Mr Willis. Seeing as he's a dog.'

Harry very nearly rolled his eyes.

'I'll just leave you to deal with it,' he said. 'But make it quick, because our focus is the missing escort, and Mickey's friend, Ian.'

'On that,' said Dave, raising a hand.

'On what?' Harry asked.

'The escort ... The bloke who contacted her, he must've found her number somewhere, like on a website or something, right? Might be that there's other escorts on the website who know her. Maybe they keep in touch, for safety or something? I don't know, not really my area of expertise ...'

Harry mentally kicked himself for not asking that the night before when he had met with Mickey's friends.

'Matt? You and I, we'll be on with that, okay? As soon as we're done here, we'll go and chat with Eddie and the others. We'll also try Ian again, and if he's still not answering his phone, I'll maybe give an old friend of mine a call to go and pay him a visit.'

'That sounds a bit terrifying,' said Walker.

'It is, trust me,' said Harry. 'Especially if he turns up with his daughters in tow; no one gets out of that alive ... Or certainly not without being dressed up like a horse, or having their nails done. Any questions?'

No one raised a hand, said a word, but just stared at Harry, keen-eyed, ready to be let loose.

'Then let's get on with it,' Harry said, and with a thunderous clap of his hands, brought the meeting to a close.

SEVENTEEN

Meeting over, Harry led Matt out of the community centre and back down to the quoits pitch. Now that it was all back to normal, he found it hard to imagine the awful crime that had been committed here not even two days ago.

'It's actually a lovely spot, isn't it?' said Matt, standing still and staring at the fells before them. 'Love how the air smells, that dampness you get on the edge of it, the tang of the heather and the peat.'

'Very poetic.' Harry nodded in agreement, appreciating it himself, then shivering a little against the cold. 'One thing I always notice round here is the smell of coal; not something I was used to down south. Where I lived and worked, it was all smokeless fuel and wood, no coal.'

'Makes me think of the railway that used to run through here,' Matt said. 'Imagine what it must've been like to have that, eh? To see the trains rolling through the Dales, great plumes of steam puffing out.'

Harry walked over to the covered clay pits on the quoits pitch.

'Forgot to ask Jen which one Mandy had to recover,' he said, lifting the first he came to.

Matt came over and stood beside him.

The clay was smooth, damp, but looked undisturbed.

'My guess is not that one,' Matt said.

Harry pulled the cover back over, checked another.

'Not this one either,' he said, finding the clay undisturbed.

Pulling the cover off the third, Harry spotted the difference immediately, and dropped down to his heels for a closer look.

'Matt?'

The DS stared over Harry's shoulder at the clay pit.

'Now, that is odd,' he said.

The clay was churned up, cut through with lines as though something thin had been dropped into it.

'What's been going on here, then?' Harry asked.

'Looks like someone's been throwing a few quoits, that's what,' explained Matt. 'All those cuts in the clay? They're from where the quoits land in it. There's no steel bar for them to hit as they're pulled out, that way the covers can be put on.'

Harry gave his head a scratch.

'So, someone's been out here having a game, have they?'

'Looks that way, yes. And it strikes me as a funny thing to be doing in the middle of the night, like.'

'Now that's something we don't know,' said Harry. 'All we do know is that Mandy had to kick the cover back over when she came out here in the morning. Could've been uncovered for a good while before, couldn't it?'

'Someone would've noticed, though, surely.'

Harry glanced behind him and up to the car park.

'There's no real reason to come and look down here, is there?'

'Probably best to just ask Mandy,' suggested Matt.

Harry stood up, took some photographs with his phone of the clay pit, then pulled the cover over again.

'Think I might get Sowerby over here again to have a look. Could be a connection.'

Having collected Smudge from the office at the community centre, Harry was leading Matt over to his vehicle, when the DS told him to wait for a couple of minutes and dashed off. Harry took the time to send a message to Sowerby about what they'd found on the quoits pitch, and received a frustrated and sweary message back as confirmation that she would be over to give it a look.

Matt opened the passenger door and slid into the vehicle.

'Something urgent?' Harry asked.

Matt pulled his seatbelt across his chest.

'Mandy's fairly sure that the clay pits were covered the day before,' he said. 'She can't be one hundred percent sure, but she was out there having a breather and enjoying the view in the afternoon and didn't notice anything.'

'Maybe she just didn't see it,' said Harry.

'That's exactly it, though, isn't it?' Matt replied. 'She'd have noticed if one of the pits were uncovered, because that would be different. However, if the pits were all still covered, she wouldn't. Or something.' Matt screwed up his face. 'Well, that all made more sense inside my head than when I said it out loud.'

Harry smiled, and started the engine.

'No, I get what you mean, and you're probably right.'

'Best we go chat with Mickey's pals, then, yes?'

From the back seat, a low woof answered Matt's question, and Harry pulled away.

When, just a few minutes later, they arrived at the house Mickey's friends were staying at, Harry rapped his knuckles against the door. The loud echo of bone against wood beat out in a jarring rhythm, echoing back at them from the house on the other side.

'How are you about Walker being here?' Matt asked, as they waited for one of the group to come and answer the door.

Harry wasn't sure how to answer. He'd been surprised to see the DSupt, that was true, and a little bit annoyed that she'd just landed on them without warning. But any misgivings he'd had about her presence had been quickly dispelled, not just because of what she had said, but how she'd acted.

'I'm good,' Harry said, because really there was little else to say beyond that.

'That's a relief,' sighed Matt, pretending to wipe sweat from his forehead, instead just clearing it of rain.

Harry frowned.

'Why?'

The look on Matt's face was enough.

'You saying I'm difficult to handle?'

'Wouldn't dare to,' smiled Matt. 'You're a pussycat, and you know it. Especially in situations sprung on you by people with hidden agendas ...'

Harry positively heard the ellipses at the end of that sentence.

'You think Walker has a hidden agenda?' he asked.

'No,' said Matt, shaking his head. 'But if she did? We'd all know just by looking at you, wouldn't we?'

Harry was trying to think of a response to that when the door opened and Eddie stood before them, his face drawn and pale, skin like a white plastic bag caught in the dead branches of a fallen tree. The day before, the man had seemed bigger, not just because he was built by a lot of time spent in a gymnasium, but Harry had wondered if he was in the middle of a bulking phase. He'd known bodybuilders in his time, their fluctuating weight between competition seasons, when they'd consume vast quantities of calories to allow them to really push their bodies. Then they would cut like mad, go into ketosis, restrict their diet to a horrifying degree to show off those muscles they'd worked so hard to build. Eddie, on the other hand, looked as though he'd done months of dieting overnight.

'Oh,' he said, eyes sunken. 'It's you.'

Harry caught the scent of the room then, a mix of wood ash and booze and something else, too, but then the stale reek of alcohol on Eddie's breath hit him, drawing his attention to a deeply unpleasant stain on the front of his black T-shirt. An attempt had obviously been made to wipe it away, but all that seemed to have done was make it worse. If indeed there was a way to make a large and unnecessarily lumpy vomit stain worse.

He waited to be invited in, but the rain forced his hand.

'Can we come in, Eddie?'

Eddie said nothing, just stepped back into the house and waited.

Harry led Matt inside, and Eddie closed the door behind them. They found themselves standing in a very comfy lounge, with two large sofas, a log burner, a television, and various bits of art on the walls, none of which looked expensive, but they gave the space a little bit of class.

'No one's up yet.'

'You are,' said Matt.

'Not been to bed. Couldn't sleep.'

'You mind giving them all a knock to let them know we're here?' Harry asked. 'I did say I would be around this morning, if you remember? Made it quite clear I'd be back for a chat, considering what's happened.'

'I guess,' said Eddie, and left the room through a door in the wall opposite to where they had come in.

'Shall we make ourselves comfy?' Matt asked.

Harry, who was really having to resist the urge to head after

Eddie, give him a slap, dunk him in a cold bath, then throw him at his housemates to wake them up, was looking around the room. He soon spotted things decorating it which jarred badly with the comfort the owners had clearly wanted it to express. Beer cans and wine bottles lay in dejected piles on the floor, half-full glasses sat on the coffee table caught in a frozen, drunken tango with opened bags of crisps, most of which were spewing their contents across the surface. By the side of the log burner, he saw an opened packet of cigarette tobacco, a lighter, and something wrapped in clingfilm.

'Thought so,' he said, going over to pick it up.

'What's that, then?' Matt asked.

'You can't smell it?'

Matt said, 'All I can smell is the aftermath of a night spent looking for solace in the bottom of too many cans and bottles. Absolutely understandable, but not exactly sensible. The hangovers these lads are going to have ...'

Shaking his head, he reached behind one of the sofas and revealed an empty whisky bottle.

'I'm guessing this isn't the only one hiding, either.'

Harry held up the clingfilm-wrapped object.

'Cannabis. Resin, actually, if you want to be specific. Not much here, but enough for a few joints. Thought I smelled something when we stepped inside. Turns out I did.'

'That word just sounds so odd coming out of your mouth,' said Matt.

'Joint, you mean? What other word do you want me to use? Spliff? Bone? Nail? Roach?'

Matt wasn't given a chance to answer. The door Eddie had disappeared through opened again and in walked Geoff.

'Bloody hell,' said Matt, and Harry had nothing to add.

Eddie had looked rough, but Geoff? He looked like he'd just been dug up.

'I've seen dead men with more life in them than you,' Harry said. 'Sit yourself down before you collapse.'

'I ... I can't ...' Geoff replied. 'I've been standing up all night.'

Harry and Matt both did a double take.

'What? Standing up all night? You can't have been! That's impossible!'

Harry saw a look of frightened horror in Geoff's eyes, as though he simply couldn't understand what his body had been doing, or how.

'You think I don't know that? If I sit or lie down, my head spins out and my stomach just empties itself. And there's nothing left in there to come up. In the end, I just stuffed a couple of chairs in the wardrobe in my bedroom, along with all the bedding from the bed, and jammed myself in so that I wouldn't fall down.'

'Did it work?' Matt asked.

'I don't remember. I just know I got into the wardrobe, and now I'm here, and I've not been sick. Not this morning, anyway. Last night, it was terrible. I couldn't stop, just fountains of the stuff. I was like a special effect from The Exorcist.'

'Are you going to be now?'

'I don't know.'

'I think we'd both prefer it if you could give us a more definitive answer,' said Matt.

The door opened again and in walked Chris, closely followed by Henry.

Harry shook his head in disbelief. Though he understood why they had all got themselves absolutely ruined on booze the night before, he was lacking a little in sympathy.

'I'm starting to feel like I'm on the set of The Walking Dead,' he muttered, as the three of them sat down in varying degrees of pain, and started to emit what sounded like death rattles. 'I'm hoping none of you are thinking you can drive today, because if you are, I'll be taking your keys.'

Eddie was last to arrive, and to Harry's amazement, he returned clasping an open can of beer in one hand, and a box of breakfast cereal in the other. He pushed through the others, tripped over a few feet, slumped into a sofa, took a deep swig of the beer, burped, then rammed his hand into the cereal box and stuffed what he'd found inside into his mouth.

Harry stared at Eddie for a moment, feeling for a second like a visitor at a zoo for extremely rare, and particularly disgusting, animals.

Realising Eddie wasn't going to stop feeding himself any time soon, Harry took a moment to survey the group, then asked, 'Have any of you actually eaten anything?'

Three pairs of eyes looked back at him with varying degrees of horror. Eddie was too busy eating cereal to respond.

'Matt?'

'Boss?'

'Tempted as I am to give them all a firm boot up their respective arses, I'm not sure such an approach would be entirely advantageous. Cathartic, yes, but that's about it. Instead, I think we need to cure some hangovers.'

'Very caring of you,' said Matt.

'Oh, I wouldn't go that far. You've not heard what I want to do, yet ...' Harry turned his eyes back to the group. 'We're going to have a little talk, as a group, and individually, but before we do, you all need to be human.' He held up a hand, and then counted off as he spoke, saying, 'That's going to involve water, very sweet tea, painkillers, bottles of Coke, and bacon and egg butties.'

'I ... I can't,' said Geoff. 'I really can't. I might die!'

'You won't die, that I promise,' said Harry. 'Anyway, you've zero option but to take the medicine I'm now prescribing. Your bodies need something to deal with beyond the booze and acid you've currently got swilling around inside you. You're dehydrated, you're hungry, and your brain is too drunk to know what's good for it. Luckily for you, I'm here, and I do.'

'Please, you don't understand,' said Chris. 'We're ... I mean ... Can you not just give us a while? Like, come back in the afternoon? We'll be better then, won't we? We have to be!'

'No, we bloody well can't come back this afternoon,' said Harry, then he looked again at Matt. 'Check their kitchen, see what they've got, if anything, then nip to the Spar and get what they haven't, understood?'

Matt gave a salute with an index finger, checked the kitchen, then pushed back out into the rain.

Harry sat down.

'Right then,' he said with a clap of his hands, 'by the time he gets back and has sorted you all breakfast, I want each of you showered and dressed, no excuses. And for the love of God, someone open a window ...'

EIGHTEEN

Driving Detective Superintendent Walker to meet with Sowerby and then Mickey's parents, Jen didn't want to admit it, or for it to show, but she was nervous. It was an emotion she rarely felt, except perhaps when she was taking part in a race. The nerves at the starting line, the build-up to crossing over it to try to run the kind of distances people only ever travelled in a car were something she was used to. She also embraced them, used them to get her going, to focus, to be absolutely in the moment, regardless of weather or terrain. This, however, was different.

For Jen, there was pressure enough as it was in having to handle such an emotionally charged and tragic situation as being with relatives identifying a loved one, but to do so with someone so senior certainly added to it considerably. Meeting with the pathologist would also be challenging. Not that she hadn't done that before, but something deep down made her feel as though she was back doing her police training with someone observing her. The weather wasn't helping either, the rain relentless, the wind twisting it into thick, watery knots, making visibility an issue and the road treacherous, as it whipped at the windscreen and lashed across the landscape.

The drive down the dale had been slow, with corners and dips in the road hiding numerous puddles. The rivers would be rising, and that had the potential to cause flooding. And when the Dales flooded, they could do so in quite a spectacular fashion.

'Lovely day for it,' said Walker. 'Might have to nip out later to have a look at Aysgarth Falls; I keep hearing how spectacular it is when the weather's like this. I just never seem to get a chance to go for a peek.'

'It's as terrifying as it is beautiful,' said Jen, navigating the car between puddles stretching out towards each other from both sides of the road. 'Gayle Beck will be quite something as well, especially under the bridge in Hawes. If it stays like this, there won't be a river or beck that isn't apocalyptic.'

'Where is it you live, then?' Walker asked. 'Have you been local all your life?'

'I have,' Jen answered. 'I'm in Middleham, with Steve.'

'The place with the castle, right?'

'That's it. I'm lucky to live there.'

'You are indeed. And who's Steve; your boyfriend?'

The laugh that burst from Jen came out before she had a chance to hold it back.

'God, no.' She smiled, shaking her head. 'He's, well, he's my pet.'

'You have a pet called Steve?'

'I do.'

'Cat? Dog?'

'Monitor lizard,' Jen corrected, and a quick glance at Walker confirmed the response she'd expected: a mixed look of shock and confusion, seasoned with a sprinkling of amusement.

'You're having me on.'

'Oh, I'm very much not,' said Jen. 'We can swing by on the way back if you want, introduce you?'

'My God, you're serious! You have an actual lizard? He's kept in a thing, though, isn't he? One of those glass boxes with warm lights and sticks, and he can't get out or anything?'

'He's too big,' Jen explained, giving Walker a quick description of Steve, his size, his love of the sofa, that he'd recently gone on walkabout, and how he and Jadyn, her actual boyfriend, had at long last started to accept each other.

'Does he bite?' Walker asked once Jen had stopped talking. 'I'm not even sure if that's a relevant question. I've never met anyone with a pet lizard. And he really just lounges about on the sofa?'

'He loves a bit of a cuddle in the evening,' said Jen. 'And if I get up and go to the kitchen, he likes to clamp himself onto me, either climbing up my leg to hang on, or going that bit further to sit on my shoulder. He's quite heavy, so I don't have him up there for long, but he's a real sweetie, honestly.'

'Did you really just describe a giant lizard as a sweetie?'

'Like I said, you'll have to meet him.'

Walker laughed.

'You know, I've never had a pet. Not even a goldfish. Not sure I'd ever have the time.'

'You sound like Harry used to,' said Jen. 'Smudge changed all that, though, and she's like his shadow now; where he goes, she'll be there, stuck to him like glue, staring up at him with those huge eyes of hers.'

'There's a surprisingly soft side to him, isn't there?' Walker said.

'There is,' agreed Jen. 'And a not-so-surprisingly hard one, if you get on the wrong side of him.'

'What's he like to work with?'

Jen thought about that for a moment.

'I'm not going to say easy,' she said, 'that would do him a disservice, because he's the opposite of a pushover. Neither is he so hard that everyone always feels like they're just being driven into the ground. I think I'd describe him as fair, you know? He's got this compass-like sense of right and wrong, doesn't cry over spilt milk, and I've never known anyone to have my back quite like him.'

Walker mulled that over, then asked, 'Do you think he misses the city life down south?'

'Probably in the beginning, when he first arrived, like, but not now. Not at all. He's still got that Somerset twang, but the Dales are in his blood now. He one of us. Sometimes more than I think even he realises. And seeing as he's moved in with Grace, I think that's sealed the deal.'

'Grace is his partner, not a lizard, correct?'

'Correct.' Jen laughed, then found herself wondering where Walker's questions were coming from exactly. 'Is something up?' she asked.

'With what?'

'I don't know,' Jen replied. 'It's just that you seem very interested in Harry, what he's like, his past. I can't imagine the team without him; I don't think any of us can.'

'Well, neither can I,' said Walker. 'Believe me.'

Somewhat relieved to hear that, Jen set her mind to getting them safely and without incident to their destination. She managed it, despite being overtaken by an idiot in an electric car, who she then caught up with at a junction, and with the aid of her blues and twos, pulled them over for a very wet talking to.

The driver expressed his unhappiness at being forced to stand in the rain. Jen expressed hers by ticketing him for dangerous driving.

Arriving at the mortuary, Jen parked as close as she could

to the main building, apologised for not having an umbrella, then led Walker to the main doors. Sowerby was waiting for them.

'Hi Jen,' she said, then looked at Walker. 'And ...?'

The DSupt introduced herself, offered her hand, and Sowerby shook it.

'Standing in for Grimm,' she added. 'Hope that's okay?'

'Rather you than me,' said Sowerby. 'He's going to pester you with questions, I promise.'

She then led them into the building, through to the mortuary, and sorted them out with overalls, boots, gloves, and face masks.

'There's not much for me to show you really,' she said, as she then led them into her workplace, a room of stainless still and chemical smells. 'But I think it's important you see what I've found anyway.'

Jen came to stand beside Walker as the pathologist swung around to the other side of a stainless-steel trolley. On top of the trolley, the body they'd come to see was hidden beneath a white sheet.

'Ready?' Sowerby asked.

She didn't wait for an answer, reached for the sheet, and slowly, respectfully, eased it downwards.

Jen stared as Mickey's face came into view, then his torso.

Sowerby rested the edge of the sheet at his waist.

'No point going any further,' she said. 'There's only one injury, and it's very clear to see, isn't it?'

And it certainly was. A thin, dark line circled Mickey's neck. The head was held in place with stitching so neat it was barely visible.

'Figured it was best to have him in one piece for his parents,' said Sowerby. 'I won't show them the wound, though; I'll rest the sheet just below his chin.'

'Very sensible,' said Walker. 'And sensitive, too, if you don't mind me saying so.'

'I know some people view what I do as ghoulish,' said Sowerby. 'I don't. I treat everyone who comes here as a person, not just a body. They had a life, a history, friends and family and experiences, loves and losses, favourite TV programmes ...'

'What is it you want to show us, then?' Jen asked, deciding to take the lead.

Sowerby pointed at the wound.

'That,' she said. 'The head was severed with four blows, all from the back. The first cut straight through the spine, killing him instantly. The next three blows cut it free completely.'

'That's not easy to do,' said Walker. 'You can't just cut someone's head off.'

'Depends,' said Sowerby.

'Does it? On what exactly?'

'Physical strength of the killer, for one. Then there's where the blows landed; if they struck bone, that's going to cause problems. The blade could get stuck, they'd have to yank it free. But if it somehow managed to miss the bone, cut straight between the vertebrae? Not so much of an issue. And then there's the weapon itself.'

'Which was?' Walker asked.

'That's why I wanted to see you,' said Sowerby. 'I've been doing a bit of research into beheadings ...'

Jen was pleased the mask on her face hid her look of horror.

'That can't have been pleasant,' she said.

'Obviously there's the guillotine, with its angled blade; slices through very quickly. In this country, we had the gibbet, which was a lot more primitive, just a huge axe blade attached to a hefty piece of wood. Still did the job, though.'

'Not the history lesson I was expecting,' said Walker. 'But go on ...'

'Beyond that, it's an axe or a sword, isn't it? The sword was preferred, because the axe could be a bit sloppy. It would have a straight blade, no point, and the condemned would kneel, rather than have their head on a block. More dignified that way, apparently.'

'You mean you think this was done by a sword?' Jen asked.

'In Saudia Arabia, public beheadings are still carried out,' continued Sowerby. 'The blade isn't straight, it's curved, and that gives a slightly different profile to the resulting wound.'

'But where would someone get such a blade in this country?' Walker asked.

'Not a clue,' Sowerby replied. 'Whatever was used to do this, it was definitely curved, but the angle of the blade was steeper, if that's the right way to explain it. More acute, perhaps? I'm not sure. Best image I can come up with is if you think of how you would draw a pirate's cutlass. Something like that.'

Jen sighed.

'Please don't tell me I have to report back to Harry that the murderer is a pirate.'

Sowerby took hold of the sheet and covered Mickey.

'It's an odd one, isn't it?' she said. 'Whatever they used, it was sharp, but not like a razor; a rough edge maybe, ground down with a file or something. It had enough weight and momentum to do what it did, and was just sharp enough to slice through flesh. A large knife just wouldn't have been heavy enough. I really don't know ...'

'Is there anything else?' Jen asked.

'You know about the condom, obviously,' said Sowerby.

Jen shook her head, and Sowerby told her and Walker what she had told Harry, adding how Harry had found a box of them on the steps down to the quoits pitch.

'Anything from his clothes?' asked Walker.

'Only that they're covered in his blood,' said Sowerby, 'and his shirt seemed more than a little on the large side for him, if you ask me, but maybe that's some kind of fashion thing.'

'And that's it?'

Sowerby reached for a clipboard.

'Right now, yes; I'm still waiting for an analysis of what was found in the wound. Probably just mud and dirt, but sometimes there's something traceable; hair, skin, that kind of thing..'

Jen asked, 'Do you know when the parents will be here?'

Sowerby glanced at a clock on the wall.

'Soon,' she said. 'I'll wheel him through to the viewing window, and get myself ready. The room is through the other door where you got changed. They'll be brought down by someone and let in through another entrance.' She braced herself against the trolley, then looked up at Jen and Walker. 'What you're about to do? It's the most difficult job of them all, isn't it? I know I do this, and it's quite intense, but breaking the news, being there with relatives as they identify the deceased? I've nothing but admiration and respect.'

'We'll see you from the other side of the glass, then,' said Walker, and with that, Jen followed her back to the outer room to remove their boots and overalls, and to prepare themselves to meet Mickey's parents.

NINETEEN

Harry had done a lot of strange and bizarre things in his life as a police officer. He'd dealt with the theft of a penguin by a toddler who had somehow managed to squirrel the creature away in his buggy without his parents noticing. He'd arrested someone after a burglary at a 7Eleven whose response to being found was to argue that no, he wasn't a burglar at all, but a shadow, and had refused to leave his hiding place under a car. He'd even, on one occasion, pulled into a service station to have a van driver in front of him send him a friendly wave, utterly oblivious to the fact that the fake numberplate he had stuck over his real one had just come loose.

What he had never done, though, not even once in all his years on the Force, was to help prepare breakfast for a group of grieving friends so hungover their collective moans sounded like Paul McCartney's Frog Chorus, played at half speed.

'Pretty sure this wasn't on the job description,' said Matt, heading through to the lounge with the last of the bacon butties.

'I don't know if you've noticed, but a lot of what we do isn't on the job description,' said Harry, deciding not to clear anything away, because that was a step too far. 'They're eating, yes?'

'Eddie is still really into that breakfast cereal,' said Matt. 'But yes, they're all eating. Even Geoff, and honestly, when he first came in, I thought he was seconds away from just dissolving in front of our eyes.'

Harry followed Matt through to the lounge. Geoff, Chris, Henry, and Eddie were occupying the sofas, all of them forcing themselves to eat, some with greater success than others, though that wasn't saying much.

'Don't avoid the water and the tea,' Harry advised. 'A hangover is dehydration, so get it down your neck.'

'I don't like sweet, milky tea,' said Henry, his goatee shiny with bacon grease.

'And I don't like having to walk around with a face that looks like I had an argument with a lawnmower, and yet here we are, all together in the same room, just getting on with our lives, aren't we, Henry?'

Henry didn't reach for his mug of tea.

'Henry?' Matt whispered, and pointed at the mug.

'I don't ...' Henry began, then saw Matt shaking his head very slowly.

He picked up the mug, took a sip.

'Good lad,' said Matt. 'Now, isn't that better?'

A groan was the only answer he received, but it was enough.

'Firstly, and ignoring how you all decided to deal with the news about Mickey,' Harry began, eyeballing each of them in turn, 'I really am genuinely sorry about your loss. And don't for one second think that I don't mean that, because I do. I've lost friends myself, and I do not say this lightly: I know what it's like, and it's horrendous.'

'I can't believe he's gone,' said Chris. 'You're sure it's him? Like absolutely sure?'

'His parents are identifying his body today,' said Harry, 'but yes, we're sure.'

'Why would someone kill him, though?' asked Geoff, who was now looking and sounding the most human of them all, not that that was saying much. 'It doesn't make any sense.'

'Sometimes, actually a lot of the time, you can't and won't ever make sense of it,' said Matt. 'But what you can do is help in trying to find out who was responsible.'

Harry's eyes turned to the member of the group still stuffing his face with fistfuls of breakfast cereal.

'Which brings me to the subject of the escort, Eddie,' he said. 'Last night, I forgot to ask where you found the number. My error. Can you tell me now?'

'Just off the internet,' Eddie replied. 'Some website I found, that's all.'

'Need you to be a little more specific than that,' said Harry. 'And I also need you to stop eating that cereal like a starved raccoon.'

Eddie's shoulders sagged.

'But I really like Coco Pops.'

'Everyone really likes Coco Pops,' said Matt. 'There's not a person on the whole planet who doesn't like Coco Pops. Just not dry by the handful, that's all, lad; so do as he says, like, okay? He's asked politely, and you can count yourself lucky with that.'

Eddie hesitated, Harry saw him consider eating more, but at last, he placed the box of breakfast cereal on the floor.

'So, this website, then,' said Harry, in an attempt to coax the information from Eddie.

'What about it? It's just a website, like I said.'

'Do you remember the site address? Its name?'

Eddie shook his head.

'But you used it to book her,' said Harry. 'How can you not remember?'

'I just don't, that's all,' Eddie replied.

'What about your phone history, then?' Matt asked.

Again, Eddie shook his head.

'I delete my history every day.'

Not suspicious at all, Harry thought, and asked why.

'It's nothing dodgy, I promise,' said Eddie. 'It really isn't.'

'Never said that it was.'

'I just don't like the idea of someone stealing my phone and finding out what I was up to.'

'So, there's no way we can get back to it, then?'

Eddie shook his head.

'That's not what I said.'

Harry's patience was thin at the best of times, but right now, it was a sopping wet sheet of tissue paper stretched over the barrel of a gun. He gave a warning glance at Matt.

The detective sergeant walked over and stood in front of the morose Eddie. Then he lowered himself down ever so slowly until they were eye to eye.

'If I were you, I'd be helpful and get to the point,' he whispered just loud enough for everyone to hear. 'If you don't, there's a very good chance you won't be enjoying the rest of your day.'

Eddie raised tired eyes at Matt, hearing the barely disguised threat in his words.

'What? How do you mean? What are you going to do? You can't hurt us. That's illegal!'

Harry's shadow stretched out across the floor as he walked over and joined Matt, casting the pathetic-looking man in darkness. His eyes stared out of it at Harry with the glare of a man trapped at the bottom of a well.

'It was you, Eddie, who contacted the escort,' Harry said, his voice deep, thick with contempt, and starting to burn at the edges with rage. 'You didn't tell anyone else in the group. You've conveniently lost the details of how you found her. She was the last person to see Mickey alive. Which means, right now, this is at best, obstructing police work, at worst—'

'This is the website!' Eddie blurted out, lifting his phone as he rapidly tapped his fingers on the screen. 'Here, just a sec, it's loading ... There! Look! That's where I found her number! That's it, there!'

Harry took the phone from Eddie's shaking hand and found himself staring at a website the design of which seemed trapped in the first few years of the birth of the internet. There was a very simple search facility, comprising little more than location and distance, beneath which were profiles of women in various stages of undress. He saw also a couple of other drop-down menus, one being 'filters,' the other 'gallery.' He avoided both.

'She's on here, then?' he asked.

'Yes,' said Eddie. 'Just type in Leyburn, and a distance of five miles, and you'll find her.'

Harry did exactly that and saw three profiles staring back at him, astonished to note they were all showing their faces, as well as everything else.

He flipped the phone around to Eddie.

'Which one's Candy?'

Eddie pointed at the second profile.

'That's her,' he said, tapping on the screen and opening her profile. A larger photo of Candy appeared on-screen. She was a young woman with red hair and a bright smile. 'Says she's 23, but they all say that, or younger; never are.'

Harry narrowed his eyes at Eddie.

'So, they all say that, do they, Eddie?'

Eddie's eyes went so wide it looked like his eyelids had fully retracted into his skull, never to be seen again.

'Don't judge me, okay?' Eddie countered, pushing himself back into the cushions of the sofa. 'It's not illegal to pay for an escort, and you know that, don't you? Of course you do, you're the bloody police! So, don't you go judging me, right? My life, and I'll do what I want with it.'

'You're right,' Harry agreed. 'I do indeed know that it's legal, Eddie. I also know, having had to deal with enough prime examples, that some of the men these girls end up having to entertain are less than considerate in how they go about getting what they want. I'm hoping, for your sake, you're not that kind of man.'

Fear drew dark lines appeared on Eddie's face, cracks in a cliff caused by an earthquake.

'How do you mean? What kind of man?'

Harry leaned over Eddie, his face close enough for him to feel the heat of the booze still sweating out of his skin. When he spoke, his voice was the low rumble of an approaching avalanche, and one Eddie hadn't a chance in hell of escaping.

'The kind of man who likes to ruin marriages. The kind of man who thinks women are objects to be bought and used. The kind of man who thinks his money is a way to kick open a door and get away with doing whatever he wants. The kind of man who doesn't know his own strength, who I've dragged out of bedrooms kicking and screaming, claiming, because he paid a few quid for her time, that *she was up for it* and that *it was consensual,* with half a mind to just throw them off a balcony or drop them into the sewers, because frankly, society doesn't need any more arseholes, does it, Eddie? Does it?' Harry hadn't blinked once as he'd spoken, and still didn't, staring at Eddie with an intensity that bordered on hatred. 'That kind of man, Eddie,' he said. 'That kind of man ...'

Tears formed in Eddie's eyes, and Harry had zero sympathy for him.

'No,' he whimpered, 'I'm not ... I'm not ... I've paid for escorts, but I've only ever been nice. I promise, okay? And that's why I thought it would be a good thing for Mickey. I didn't think anything like this would happen, did I? I didn't know that he'd end up—'

His voice caught in his throat.

Harry shook his head at the sorry state Eddie was in.

'Matt,' he said, showing the DS Eddie's phone. 'Pull this page up on your phone. I want those two other girls contacted, see if they know Candy. My guess is that they probably do, because in that business, they often stay in touch, supporting and protecting each other, sharing details of regulars, that kind of thing. If they don't, at least we know what she looks like.'

'I'll nip through to the kitchen, see what I can get. And we can use her photo to start asking around, see if anyone's spotted her.'

With Matt gone, Harry's attention turned to something he'd not yet touched on, simply because, with Mickey's murder, it had seemed somewhat less important.

'Your cars, then,' he said. 'Something about them being vandalised, yes? And by someone called Ian, another member of your group, who was enjoying himself so much, he buggered off early.'

'He needs to pay for what he's done,' said Chris. 'We were only taking the piss.'

'Not our fault if he's got a hangup about what he does, is it?' added Henry.

'I didn't see any vehicles parked outside,' said Harry. 'Where are they?'

'There's no parking here, so it's on-street only,' said Geoff. 'They're all in the car park, the one behind the primary school.'

'And what is it that your friend Ian has done, exactly?'

'Every bloody tyre, for a start!' hissed Chris. 'Not just let them down either, but stabbed them with something.'

'And shaving foam,' said Henry. 'Wrote stuff on the bonnets

of the cars and it was on long enough to dry before the rain washed it off.'

Harry had seen that done plenty of times before, shaving foam left long enough on car paint discoloured it for good.

'What did he write, exactly?'

'He drew stuff, too,' added Chris.

'Like what?'

Chris hesitated.

Harry waited.

'You know ... knobs ...'

Harry was able to keep a straight face because even when he smiled, he looked serious. He was also beginning to like this Ian, whoever he was, and was struggling to see how he could be connected to what had happened to Mickey. Someone who hacked off another person's head probably wasn't going to bother vandalising another friend's car with a picture of a penis.

Yes, that was an assumption, but a fair one, Harry thought. He still needed to speak to him, though, and if they still had no luck in finding him, then a phone call to his old friend, Kett, down in Norwich, would be his next step.

Matt entered the lounge.

'Well?' said Harry.

Matt shook his phone at Harry.

'I've spoken with both girls,' he said. 'Candy's real name is Tracey Boyes. They've not heard from her since Saturday night.'

'And they didn't think to phone us?'

'Candy—I mean Tracey—texted them both in the early hours, said everything was fine, and that was the last they heard.'

'What about where she lives? Do they know that?'

'Address in Leyburn. Easy to find. One of the girls has a spare key.'

'Really? Why?'

'In case of emergencies,' Matt said. 'You good to go?'

Harry paused, considering whether or not to go and have a look at Ian's artwork.

'Have any of you heard from Ian since you last saw him?'

Four heads shook in answer.

'Then we'll do our best to track him down so that he can be held responsible for the damage he's caused. Until then, however, my advice is to let the hangovers run their course, contact your insurance companies, and give Mike a call.' Harry jotted Mike the mechanic's number down in his notebook, tore out the piece of paper, and handed it to Geoff. 'He'll be able to sort out tyres, get you back on the road, and probably sell you a Land Rover and a tractor in the process. Once all of that's done, and you're heading back home, be aware that there's a very good chance we'll be in touch.'

Geoff, Harry noticed, looked visibly relieved.

'You mean you're not keeping us here?'

'Why the hell would we want to do that?' Harry asked. 'Ignoring the fact that you all reek like the last days of Sodom and Gomorrah, you're not under arrest. So, as surprising as it may seem to all of us gathered here, yes, you're free to go. But if we do call, make sure you answer. Agreed?'

The four men nodded, and Harry and Matt left them to the rest of their day.

Outside, and with their next port of call being Leyburn, Harry got his phone out of a pocket.

'Time to phone a friend,' he said, but as he went to pull up the number, the phone buzzed in his hand.

When he answered the call, the news he was given made his blood run cold.

TWENTY

Jim was behind the wheel of the old police Land Rover, Fly clipped into the back, Dave beside him They'd spent the morning going through the list Mandy had provided of people who had been in the pub on the night Mickey had been killed. It hadn't taken them all that long, with a good number of those contacted dealt with on the phone.

So far, nothing suspicious had come to light. The two locals who'd had a scuffle could barely remember what the argument was about, and the chef at the Fountain had just laughed when asked about the complaint. Currently, they were following up on what had happened during the disagreement over a flat cap, and they'd just pulled up to a house over in Hardraw, its cobbles glistening with rain.

'Who's this, then?' Dave asked.

'Mary Hick,' said Jim. 'Used to own a sweet shop in Hawes years ago.'

'Used to?'

'Retired a while back, like. Everyone was sad about it, especially the kids; everyone had grown up visiting Mary's little place. It was tiny, but every space was used.'

'No one bought it?'

'Oh, someone bought it alright,' said Jim. 'But not as a sweetshop. I think it was knocked through into part of another building, turned into a holiday cottage.'

Dave leaned forward to look out of the windscreen.

'And she lives here?'

Jim smiled at that. The house was a thing of grey stone, hunkered down against the elements, and hunched almost protectively over the yard they were now parked on. It didn't really say sweetshop owner, more someone who was a bit of an isolationist.

'She does,' he said. 'Her and about a dozen or so ferrets and polecats.'

Dave's expression turned to one of disbelief.

'You're having me on.'

Jim reached around to give Fly a quick chin scratch, then climbed out of the Land Rover.

'Come on,' he said. 'Let's go and say hello. Oh, and she plays quoits, so she's got a hell of a right hook on her.'

Striding across the yard with enough care to avoid slipping on the cobbles, Jim knocked on the door. He'd have called ahead, but Mary didn't have a phone.

'You sure she's in?'

'If she wasn't, that wouldn't be there,' Jim answered, pointing across the yard at an old bike to which was attached a number of rickety-looking wooden boxes with small, mesh windows.

'She's not answering,' said Dave.

Jim, though, knew to wait.

A moment or two later, he heard shuffling on the other side, then the sound of locks being opened and a latch pulled. The door was then yanked into the darkness of the small house beyond.

'Who's that, then?' came a voice from the gloom, and a small woman wearing a chequered shirt and a waxed gilet emerged into the daylight.

Jim introduced himself and Dave, and added, 'You need to come out to the farm soon with your ferrets, the rabbits are running riot again.'

'Jim!' Mary exclaimed, then turned her eyes on Dave. 'Bloody hell, lad, you've gone and brought Goliath with you! What the hell for? Been a long, long time since I've asked anyone to act out a Bible story, but we could give it a go, if you want? I'm sure you still remember it, and the song ... Now, how did it go ...' Mary started to swing her arm around above her head. 'Something about a sling ... Come on, now, young Jim, you can remember!'

Before he was roped into joining in, Jim said, 'We need to ask you a few questions, Mary.'

Mary dropped her arm.

'You do? What about?'

'You were at the Fountain a couple of nights back.'

'And you're standing out there in the rain, aren't you? Get yourselves inside, come on.'

Before Jim could reply, or explain further what he wanted to talk to Mary about, she swept them both into her house and hurried them along into a small lounge.

'Tea?'

Jim went to answer, but saw a startled expression on Dave's face.

'Ferrets,' said Dave.

In various places around the lounge, a number of ferrets were, for want of a better word, relaxing. Jim counted six, two of which were snuggled up in an empty fruit bowl on a small coffee table in front of a roaring fire. The other four were dotted here and there, on cushions, on the arms of sofas, and squeezed into a tiny space on a bookcase.

'Oh, don't you mind them,' said Mary. 'They're harmless.'

'Oh, I'm not worried at all,' said Dave. 'Honestly, I've been thinking of getting a couple myself ...'

Mary's face lit up.

'Really? You have?' She gave his thick arm a squeeze with her tiny hand. 'Then sit yourself down and we'll chat!'

Mary left the lounge.

'We're alright, we don't need tea,' Jim called after her, but knew it was hopeless. 'Best just sit down and wait,' he said.

Dave lowered himself onto a two-seater sofa. The ferret lounging on its arm opened its eyes to stare at him, then closed them again, clearly keen to get back to sleep.

Jim sat down on a small wooden stool by the bookcase, and was sure he could hear the ferret above him snoring.

When Mary came back into the room, the ferret on the sofa arm was on Dave's lap.

'You've made a friend there, then,' she said, placing a large tray down on top of a folding table pushed against a wall. 'That's Peter. The others are James, Matthew, Bartholomew, Thaddaeus, and Simon.'

'Good names,' said Jim. 'Disciples, right?'

Mary beamed, clapped her hands.

'You remembered!'

'Not all of them, but yes, you kind of drilled it into us!'

'You used to walk or bike all the way from your farm in Burtersett,' Mary said. 'Just to come to Sunday school.'

'Didn't have much choice,' Jim laughed. 'As Dad always said, he went, so I had to, too. Wanted me to have a good knowledge of the Bible. Said it would give me an appreciation of just how lucky we were to be here at all and to do what we did.'

'And he was right, too, wasn't he?' said Mary, though in such a way it was clear she wasn't expecting an answer.

She poured Dave and Jim tea, handed around a plate of homemade shortbread, then sat down, and said to Dave, 'So, about you wanting some ferrets ...'

Jim didn't give Dave a chance to speak.

'Can you tell us about that night at the Fountain?' he asked.

Mary's face turned serious, and she leaned forward conspiratorially.

'I've heard, you know, everyone has, about the body? Awful. Mandy's still in shock. Everyone is. And on the quoits pitch, too, of all places. No respect, some people, have they? Won't be wanting to play there again in a hurry, that's for sure. Though, it's not like I've much choice.'

News like that was bound to spread fast, Jim thought.

'We're trying to see if there's a link between anything that happened in the bar that night, and the, er, incident.'

Mary gasped.

'What? You think the killer was in the pub? I could've met them then, couldn't I? Spoken to them! God, that's awful!'

'Can you remember anything out of the ordinary?' Dave asked. 'Maybe the way someone behaved, an argument, perhaps; that kind of thing?'

'And there was something about a flat cap being taken, I think. Is that right?' Jim added.

'You mean that young idiot who stole Graham's cap?' Mary said.

'Perhaps you could just tell us what happened?' Jim said, encouraging Mary to continue.

'A few of us were sitting round that table in front of the bar,' Mary said. 'Then this big lad just comes over and stands in front of us. All muscle he was, built like a walking wall. Knew it, too, if you know what I mean? Proper show-off, if you ask me.'

Dave asked, 'What did he do?'

'Well, first off, he tried to talk Yorkshire in as insulting a way as possible, then he took Graham's cap off the table, plopped it on his head, and walked back to his friends, bold as brass, like! Never seen anything like it.'

'Graham?' asked Dave.

'Graham Suggitt,' Mary clarified. 'Works up at the Creamery. He's on the quoits team as well.'

'And what happened then?'

Mary didn't answer immediately.

'You think that's important, then, that this happened on the quoits pitch? Is that it?'

'It's just another line of inquiry,' Jim answered.

'We do get competitive, that's for sure, but I think this might be pushing it a bit, don't you? Was it someone local?'

'Back to the cap,' said Jim, avoiding Mary's question and instead getting the conversation back on track. 'What happened after it had been taken?'

'We went and got it back, that's what happened,' said Mary. 'Can't have folk just nabbing your hat like that, can you? Graham wasn't happy, I can tell you that for nowt!'

'Do you have Graham's contact details?' Jim asked. 'And the names of everyone else you were sitting with?'

'I can jot them down for you,' said Mary, and was again on her feet. 'Wasn't like there were many of us.' She dashed out of the lounge and returned with a pencil and an old envelope. 'Here you go,' she said, and scribbled names, telephone numbers and addresses on the envelope. 'That's me, Graham, Larry, and Ray. We're the quoits team. Well, Larry isn't, not after he lost his wife. She was the keen one anyway. So, it's just me, Graham, and Ray.'

'There's no one else?'

'No, just the three of us right now. Should be eight really, but it's a struggle to get people to play. Means we all have to double up when we play another team, you know, play against two players, sometimes three, instead of one? It's not really allowed, but I don't think anyone really minds. It's just a game after all, isn't it? Though don't go telling anyone I said that, will you? We don't take it as seriously as the darts teams do, but that's not to say it's not important now, is it?'

Jim was about to read what Mary had written and to ask for a description of the person who had taken the cap when his phone buzzed. It was Harry. Jim answered, but was given no time to speak.

'Where are you?'

'Just finished having a little chat with Mary,' said Jim. 'She was at the pub, and we've some other names now, too. All on the quoits team, too, as it happens.'

'Well, scrap all of that for the moment,' Harry said, urgency in his voice. 'I need everyone over to Hardraw Force immediately.'

'But that's where we are right now. Well, not at the waterfall, like, but just down the road.'

'Then I need you there right away,' said Harry.

'What? Why?'

There was a slight pause before Harry answered, and when he did, Jim had already guessed what he was going to say.

'They've found a body,' he said.

TWENTY-ONE

Harry arrived in the tiny village of Hardraw just after two in the afternoon. He pulled into the small car park around the back of the Green Dragon pub as a delivery van and a couple of cars headed back out and onto the lane, all of them heading in the direction of Sedbusk.

'Under better circumstances, I'd be asking if you fancied a pint and a pie for lunch,' said Matt, as they left the vehicle and headed up towards the entrance to the waterfall, leaving Smudge fast asleep in the back.

Harry remembered the last time he'd been there, though not to the pub.

'Not been here since Grace brought me,' he said, and despite the circumstances, the memory made him smile. 'Somehow, she managed to persuade me to go for a swim.'

Matt stopped mid-stride.

'You went for a swim here? Really? You're having a laugh.'

Harry shook his head.

'Not at all. Rather enjoyed it, too.' He laughed, and led Matt along to a stone building that housed the entrance to the waterfall itself.

'But you're not actually allowed to swim in the pool,' said Matt as they pushed through a door. 'There's even a little gate stopping you getting too close to the Force.'

'Added to the fun of it, I think,' Harry said with a wink. 'Though, obviously negotiating a wooden gate that barely came up to my knees was quite the obstacle.'

'And to think, you a detective chief inspector; shameful flaunting of the law there, if you ask me.'

Inside the building, which was half visitor centre, half café, Harry glanced around to get a feel for the place. The walls were decorated with numerous pictures of Hardraw Force, not just modern ones either, he noticed, some clearly decades old. He also spotted, displayed on an ancient, wooden table leaning drunkenly against a wall at the far end of the café, a collection of taxidermy. For the life of him, he couldn't think of a single reason as to why it was there and decided not to ask.

Jim came over from where he had been standing by the counter displaying various cakes and quite an exceptional selection of chocolate tiffin.

'Now then, Boss. Dave's up at the waterfall. Thought it best if one of us stayed here, just to make sure no one tried to get through or whatever.'

'You may as well be Scene Guard, then,' said Harry.

Jim pulled out his notebook.

'I've no clipboard, so this will have to do.'

'Who found the body?' Matt asked.

Jim pointed across to a grey-haired man standing behind a counter on the opposite side of the room.

'Best we go and have a chat, then,' he said, looking at Matt, and walked over to the counter. To the side, a turnstile led out of the building to allow access to the waterfall beyond.

'We're not open,' the man said, his voice shaky. 'There's ... there's been an incident. The police are, well, they're already here, as you can see, and—'

Harry showed his ID.

The man's shoulders sagged with relief.

'Oh, God,' he said. 'How could this have happened? How? In all the years I've worked here, there's never been an accident. We don't even allow people close to the pool now, never mind walking behind the waterfall itself. It doesn't make any sense!'

Harry kept quiet about his dip in the pool as Matt asked, 'You think it was an accident, then?'

'Can't think it would be anything else,' said the man. 'Maybe they were at the top and fell? That's all I can think it would be, really. We've had no visitors today, anyway. Really quiet, it's been, which is probably a good thing, isn't it, all things considered? I mean, can you imagine if someone had seen it, the body? Doesn't bear thinking about, does it? But it's all I can actually think about because it's so awful!'

Harry held up a hand in an attempt to calm the man down.

'Mind if we just take your name, please?' he asked.

'What? Why?'

'Just procedure, that's all,' said Matt. 'Nowt to worry about.'

'Paul,' the man said after a little hesitation. 'Paul Brown. I'm the manager of the centre. I don't own it or anything, I just work here. Don't want that kind of responsibility.'

'Which I'm assuming is where we are right now, yes?' said Harry.

Paul gave a nod.

'And was it you who found the body?'

Paul shook his head, and pointed to a woman sitting on a sofa in the café. She was so small, Harry hadn't even noticed her.

'I always do a walk round before we open,' Paul explained. 'Check the paths, see if there are any problems, check if there's been any rock falls, that kind of thing. Health and safety's so important, isn't it? Especially with a place like this. The drop is over a hundred foot, so you can't go exploring up top, peering over the edge, can you? I don't think people realise how dangerous the Force is. It is beautiful, though, especially when we've had a bit of rain, like right now; it looks spectacular. But we can't be held responsible for what people do, can we? All we can do is try and make sure they can enjoy their time here as safely as possible. The overhang, though? That's what worries me the most, all that rock above your head, just waiting for the wrong time to come loose and—' Paul clapped his hands together with a loud crack, then shuddered. 'Can you imagine? Awful.'

Harry was beginning to realise that Paul was someone who talked a lot when he was nervous and also aired on the side of drama somewhat.

'And you didn't see anything when you did your check?'

'I didn't see anything at all. Nothing! Obviously, I went up to check, you know, see that Elaine had got it right, because sometimes, even an old log can look like a body, can't it, tumbling around in the water?'

Harry said, 'Perhaps you and Elaine over there could show us?'

Paul's eyes went wide.

'What? You mean you want me to show you the body? You want me to take you up there and look at it again?'

Paul's voice crumbled with fear.

'I do, yes,' said Harry, and went to say more, but Paul's words were already tumbling out into the day like wheat from a burst sack.

'But I've already seen it! I don't need to see it again. I don't want to, either. And your other officer is already there, isn't he? I told him where to go. I'm sure he's found his way. It's not exactly difficult to find your way around, you just need to follow the path you see—'

'I'll have a word with Elaine, now. Anyway, Elaine saw it first, didn't she?'

Harry, sensing a pause in Paul's cascade of words, called Jim over.

'Would you mind having a chat with Paul while Matt and I head up to see what we're dealing with?' he said. 'Get a statement from him if you can.' He looked at Paul. 'Does that sound okay? PCSO Metcalf here will just ask you a few questions, jot down a few notes. That'll give me a chance to speak with Elaine.'

'A statement?' said Paul. 'You mean, like a confession? But I had nothing to do with whatever happened. I really didn't! I just found the body this morning, that's all. It was just lying there, and when I first saw it, I thought it was like a log or something, then I got closer, and thought it was maybe a deer, but then why would a deer wear clothes? It wouldn't, would it? And that's what I said to myself; I said, a deer wouldn't be wearing clothes, so what is it then? And—'

Jim said, 'Paul, would you be able to make us all some tea or something?'

'Tea? What? Yes, of course, no problem. I can do that right away.'

'Probably best if you let us through the turnstiles first, though,' said Matt.

Paul did exactly that, and as they pushed through, Harry turned to Jim.

'Well done on the tea request,' he smiled.

'No bother at all,' Jim replied. 'I think he needed distracting, that's all.'

'And you were right. You read the situation perfectly.'

'See you in a few minutes, then. Matt?' Harry pointed over to the woman called Elaine. 'Best we go have a little chat.'

TWENTY-TWO

Elaine, or as she preferred to be called, 'Mrs Elaine Spencer,' had very little to offer Harry other than some very clear indications that she had absolutely nothing whatsoever to do with the body at the Fountain, or the one here, other than finding this one and ignorance of the other.

Hailing as she did from Kent, and with enough years on her clock to make every day a surprise, she was there, as she had explained very clearly, 'To spend what little I've got, doing what I want.'

Harry had questioned her gently enough to understand that she had been in the area for a week now, staying in a caravan at a site just above Hawes, and was having a thoroughly good time exploring. It had taken quite some time for him to get her to tell him about what she had found, more intent was she on explaining to him just how beautiful the Dales were, and that he should really get out more.

With a statement taken, Harry had decided it was probably best to just walk up to see what Elaine had found for themselves, and had sent her on her way, informing her that someone would be in touch if they needed more information. The only odd thing she had mentioned was that she had heard a dog barking while up near the waterfall, but had seen no dog.

Matt had tried to suggest that perhaps she'd heard it from someone walking the fields close by. Elaine had shut that down with a hard stare, a tap on his knee to get him to listen, and then a repeated explanation of how there was no way the sound of the dog could have come from anywhere else. Elaine was very sure that her hearing was as good as it had been in her twenties, and that even though she was now eighty-three, that was no excuse to question her faculties.

With Elaine on her way back to her caravan, Harry and Matt made their way across the room to the turnstiles. As Harry opened the door, Matt turned back around and called over to Jim, who was still talking to Paul.

'If there's any cake going—' he said, half smiling at Harry.

Before Jim had a chance to answer, Harry had dragged Matt through the door.

WALKING OUTSIDE, Harry found himself once again stepping into the memory of his visit to Hardraw Force with Grace. What surprised him most, though, was that despite the reason for him being there now, the memory of walking the same path with Grace was so real, so bright in colour, that a warmth spread through him.

'You alright, there?' Matt asked.

Harry gave a nod, but decided to not verbalise an answer, lost as he was right then to an experience he was now realising was perhaps more special than he'd realised at first.

Looking around as they walked along the wet, gravel path, with trees reaching down towards them with sodden branches, like the expectant brushes of artists, he could remember nearly every step, every word, of that short trip with Grace. The place smelled the same, felt the same, the chill in the air from the deep cleft in the rock they were striding into biting the back of his throat.

'Something about this place, isn't there?' said Matt, his words interrupting Harry's recollection of walking along hand-in-hand with the woman he had fallen in love with.

'There is,' he replied.

'I've always found it to be a little on the creepy side,' Matt continued, as they passed a wooden bridge, following the thin path towards the growing thunder of the Force still hidden from sight. 'No, maybe creepy is the wrong word; haunting, perhaps? It's like, walking along here, you can almost sense everyone who's come here before, can't you? Does that make sense?'

In Harry's mind, he could hear Grace's laugh, teasing him gently enough to get him to take a plunge in the pool beneath the horse's tail of water falling from above.

'It does, actually,' he said. 'A place like this, it sort of holds its history, doesn't it? Like the cliffs and trees have somehow remembered it.'

Matt stopped, turning to look at Harry.

'That's exactly it,' he said. 'Shame it can't speak and tell us what's been going on, isn't it? Would make our lives a lot easier.'

Harry kept his eyes forward as they walked, waiting for the thin, white tail of water to reveal itself, and when it did, he felt a smile crease his scars deeply enough to open yet more hidden memories, fleeting moments lost between the cracks of the days lived since.

What hit Harry first was the spray of water in the air, thick clouds of it billowing from where Hardraw Force spewed out from its platform high above, to dive into a stony amphitheatre, and slam into the deep, dark pool below. He could taste stone in the drops that fell on his face, minerals collected by the water as it carved its way through the limestone of the hills and fells above.

'Impressive when it's like this, isn't it?' said Matt. 'Sometimes, in the summer, it'll dry up completely, but after the rain? It's something to behold for sure.'

Matt wasn't wrong, Harry thought. Last time he'd seen the Force, he'd been struck by its power, yes, but had probably been a little more distracted by Grace getting undressed and throwing herself into the pool's cold embrace. Now, though, it was impossible to ignore the raw power of nature announcing itself with such volume that the crash of the waterfall into the pool was deafening.

From out of the mist, a large figure approached.

'Now then, Dave,' Harry said. 'You're looking a bit wet.'

'Funny that,' Dave replied. 'Quite something though, isn't it? You know, I always think it's a shame that when the weather's like this, the Dales are the quietest. Folk come when it's sunny, don't they? Then either stay away, or hide in their cottages and caravans when it turns a bit rough. But to my mind, this is when the Dales really come alive. The colours are brighter, deeper, the smells more vibrant, and the waterfalls?' He turned back briefly to stare at the Force. 'I mean, you just can't find the words to describe it, can you?'

Harry had to agree, but said nothing, his eyes catching on something trapped in an eddy at the foot of the pool.

'What've we got, then?' he asked.

'Can't say as I rightly know,' Dave replied. 'It's a body, that's for sure. I've not had a close look or anything, just made sure I was in the way should anyone think it a good idea to come up for a gander.'

'But you can only get up here through the turnstiles, right?'

Dave shook his head.

'You can't fence something like this off, can you? Not really.

I mean, you can try, but there's always ways to get in, aren't there?'

'Like where?' Harry asked, looking around.

Matt pointed up to where the waterfall was chucking itself down with wild abandon.

'You've the dubs up top, like; deep pools carved out by the swirling water, and there's plenty of paths up there to go exploring, though you'd be a fool to get too close to the edge. You can swim in them further up, but you still need to be careful. And there's little to stop you nipping over a fence or a wall.'

With those words in mind, Harry stepped away from Matt and Dave and made his way further along the path to step over the small gate he'd ignored once before, though this time with no desire at all to throw himself into the pool.

As carefully as he could, and very aware of just how slippery the rocks and boulders were leading from the path down to the river, he clambered down just close enough to have a better look at what they were dealing with. The first thing that concerned him was just how angry the water was, bursting from the pool and careering down the twisting channel it had carved into the earth. One slip, one badly placed foot, and Harry knew there would be little chance of him surviving a tumble into the whitewater below. It would have him in its clutches and dash him against the rocks with little care.

The body was trapped between two large rocks, and the water was turning it over and over, the arms flailing around to smack back down into the churn, or against boulders, the head doing much the same, and echoing with the sound of a coconut being hit. Its clothes were dark from being sodden, but he could make out the greys and blues of the jacket zipped around the torso, deep pockets on the trousers, brown walking boots.

'There's something just over there as well,' Dave said, pointing to another eddy close to the body. 'Bit of rope, I think, and a roll of green plastic bags that have spooled out by the looks of it.'

Harry looked to where Dave was pointing, squinted, and recognised what he was looking at immediately. He also remembered what Elaine had been so insistent about having heard.

'Dog lead,' he said. 'And those bags? They're for picking up after your dog.'

Then, as Harry was about to pull himself back up to where Matt and Dave were, he spotted movement in the thick vegetation on the other side of the raging torrent A little too close to the edge for comfort.

'Matt? Dave? You see that?'

'See what?' said Matt.

Harry pointed directly opposite from where he was standing, then his left foot slipped and his heart leapt into his mouth.

'Here,' called Dave, 'grab on, Harry.'

Harry looked up to see a giant hand stretched out towards him. He grabbed it, and with relief, was soon back up on the path.

'You see anything?' he asked, looking back across the bubbling water.

Matt shook his head.

'Not a thing. What was it?'

Harry wasn't sure, but he wanted to know. Just a few metres away from where they were was another wooden bridge.

'Give me a minute,' he said, and headed down to the bridge and over to the other side, before making his way to where he had seen the movement.

'Well?' Matt called over. 'Anything?'

Harry didn't answer. He'd seen something, but wasn't sure what.

Leaning over, he reached out with his hands and parted the

thick fronds of bracken in front of him. Black eyes, riven with fear, stared back at him.

'Oh, you poor wee bugger,' he said, reaching down to retrieve the long-haired, scruffy-looking Jack Russell terrier, soaking wet and shivering from the cold.

'Well, it looks like we've got ourselves a witness,' he said, calling over to Matt and Dave, as the dog snuggled up under his arm. 'Just not so sure he's going to be much use.'

TWENTY-THREE

Back at the Rav, and already having called Margaret Shaw, and then Sowerby once again—this time to inform her that they had another crime scene to look at—Harry had introduced the Jack Russell to Smudge.

Both dogs had stared at each other for a moment or two, before Smudge started licking the smaller animal, her tail wagging as she did so. The Jack Russell, which was still clearly traumatised by what it had gone through, and cold, had simply snuggled down on the back seat, and allowed himself to be fussed over, cocooned by Smudge's considerably larger, warmer body. Harry had given him a bit of a rub down with a towel he kept in the back for Smudge, but after that, Smudge had taken over.

'She's properly mothering the little fella, isn't she?' said Matt, as they stared at both dogs. 'You ever thought of having puppies from her?'

'Can't say it's ever crossed my mind, no,' said Harry.

'Well, you should, because they'd be absolute crackers, I'm sure of it. And you'd have no bother selling them on, not round here, anyway; folk are always on the lookout for a decent gun dog.'

'My dad would have one, I'm sure,' said Jim, as he collected a load more cordon tape from Harry to take back up to where Dave was still standing guard over the body. 'You sure you don't want me here as Scene Guard?'

Harry shook his head.

'After what Dave and Matt said about how easy it is for people to get through to see the waterfall, I'd rather have you both up there until Sowerby's team arrives. As soon as they do, I'll let you know, and you can pop back. But until then, you're better use up there.'

Jim headed off, and Harry watched him go.

'Considering he's only half-time now, he's not lost any of his enthusiasm, has he?' said Matt.

'No, not a bit of it,' Harry agreed. 'No surprise really, though.'

'We'll lose him eventually, won't we?'

'We will, but that's to be expected. His heart and soul are on that farm, and we all know it.'

Movement caught Harry's eye, and he glanced across the car park to see Paul Brown approaching. He was carrying a tray on which he saw a large teapot and two mugs.

'Here you go,' he said, as he arrived. 'Tea, and some slices of tiffin.'

Harry pointed over at a couple of picnic benches at the edge of the car park.

'Let's pop ourselves over there,' he said.

Sitting down, Matt poured the tea, and Harry helped himself to the tiffin.

'I'd best get back,' said Paul.

'No need,' said Harry. 'Only visitors you'll be getting for a while will be us and the team we've called in to deal with what you found.'

Paul, Harry noticed, looked shocked.

'What? You mean we're closed for the rest of the day? But we'll lose our takings! The only visitor we've had today is Elaine, and I was hoping we'd make up for that this afternoon.'

Harry pointed to the space next to Matt.

'Grab yourself a seat, Paul,' he said.

Paul hesitated, made to leave, then relented and plonked down beside Matt.

'Paul,' Harry said, brushing crumbs from the corner of his mouth, 'has anyone come through today with our new little friend over there?'

Paul looked over at Harry's vehicle.

'No,' he said, shaking his head. 'We've had no one. I saw the body on my walk round before we opened, and called you straight away.'

'You're sure about that?'

'Of course I'm sure! Why would I lie?'

'Wasn't suggesting you were, just making sure.'

Harry took another bite of the tiffin, and Matt picked up a piece and did the same.

'Now that's good,' he said, holding up the slice in his hand as though appraising it. 'Joan makes this as well. Hasn't done so for a long time though. Think I might have to change that.'

'I'd like to say it's a family recipe, but it isn't,' said Paul, revealing the packaging he had clenched in his hands. 'It's a personal favourite, though, tastes homemade, I think. Do you know who it is? The body, I mean.'

Harry and Matt both shook their heads.

'No chance of knowing that until someone's managed to fish them out of the water,' Harry said. 'And that's not going to be easy. Hopefully, they'll have ID on them.'

'Maybe they fell?' Paul suggested. 'Plenty of people walk their dogs around here, and there's paths a plenty up top.'

Harry remembered Matt telling him the same.

'Maybe the dog ran off,' Matt suggested, 'ended up in the river, and whoever it is, they jumped in after them.'

The same thought had crossed Harry's mind. If not for the fact they already had one body, he would've taken it more seriously as a suggestion. Too much of a coincidence, and seeing as he had no time for them ...

'It would be a hell of a fall for that dog to survive,' he said. 'And not just that, but then managing to climb out of the water and get to safety.'

'Crazier things have happened,' said Matt, over the brim of his mug.

'Agreed,' said Harry, but decided it was probably best to not list all of the examples to the contrary that sprung to mind. 'So, if not that, then how did whoever it is get there?'

'And with his dog,' said Matt.

'We don't know that it's his dog.'

Harry's statement caused Matt to frown.

'Then whose is it?'

'I'm not saying he doesn't belong to whoever is in the river. I'm just saying that we can't assume that he does.'

A while later, and with the tea and tiffin replenished, Harry was standing over by the open door of his Rav, staring down at the Jack Russell, who was now snuggled up with Smudge, both of them fast asleep.

'You're a soft bugger,' he muttered, and reached out to stroke Smudge's head.

The Jack Russell jumped at the movement, his eyes on Harry.

'It's okay,' Harry said. 'You're safe.'

The dog shivered, then settled back down.

Knowing that Sowerby would soon arrive, Harry remembered a call he had tried to make earlier, but that he'd had to delay. So, he pulled out his phone and made the call. No sooner was it over, than the rumble of engines carried through the air and Harry looked up to see the less-than-happy face of Sowerby staring at him through the windscreen of a car, behind which followed two large, white vans. He gave a wave, and made his way over to where she was parking up.

'How're you doing?' he asked, as she climbed out of the driving seat to greet him.

'Oh, you know,' Sowerby replied. 'Another day, another death, same old, same old. No sooner had I finished with Jen and your DSupt, I got your call. And to think some people think the Dales is a quiet place. I was coming anyway, after your call about the quoits pitch, so I'll pop over and have a look at that once I'm done here. You're really getting your money's worth, you know that, don't you?'

'How were Jen and Walker?'

'I left them with the parents of the victim. Some people reckon my job is hard ...'

None of our jobs are easy, Harry thought, and asked, 'How's the tiredness?'

At that, Sowerby's eyebrows raised just a little.

'Didn't think you'd remember.'

'And why wouldn't I?'

Sowerby didn't answer that question, and just said, 'Insomnia's rubbish, isn't it?'

'Any idea what's bothering you?'

'I have, yes,' said Sowerby. 'And I'm dealing with it. Been here plenty of times before, much like yourself.'

That got Harry's attention.

'Nightmares?'

'I'm good most of the time, but then it all comes back to me.

And I don't just mean what happened all those years ago, either, I mean the things I've seen, that we've seen. It builds up, doesn't it?'

Harry couldn't remember all the details right then, and he wasn't about to go into them either. He could recall, however, that Sowerby had been out with a friend at university, that they had been attacked on the way home from a club, and that she had survived, but her friend hadn't. It was this awful, harrowing event that had caused her to change her degree to become a pathologist.

'It does,' he said. 'I'm assuming you have regular counselling, to help you decompress?'

'I also have my mum,' Sowerby smiled. 'She not here yet?'

Harry shook his head and realised Margaret should have been here before her daughter. He saw a flicker of concern in the pathologist's eyes as she pulled out her phone and pinned it to her ear, taking herself away from Harry for a moment.

'If she's fallen again ...'

As she waited for her mum to answer, another car arrived. The photographer. Harry tapped Matt on the leg, pointed at the car.

'You go deal with him,' he said.

'Do I have to?'

Harry's lack of response was response enough and Matt headed over as Sowerby came back to join him.

'Well? Everything okay?'

'She answered on hands-free. Just a couple of minutes away.'

'Any reason for the delay?'

Sowerby pursed her lips.

'You need to be sitting down for this.'

'Well, I'm not.'

'Your life ...' Sowerby took a deep breath in and out. 'She was ... she was trapped in her ... no, I can't say it.'

Harry folded his arms.

Sowerby rolled her eyes.

'Her choir gown,' she said, with a sigh. 'She was trapped in her choir gown.'

Harry wanted to laugh, but at that exact moment, Margaret arrived and parked her ridiculously huge Range Rover so sharply, the wheels sent gravel skittering across the car park like water on a red-hot skillet.

Margaret was out of the vehicle so quickly she practically threw herself into a fast march, slamming the door behind her, before shooting a wave over to Harry and her daughter.

'You get yourself ready,' Harry said, 'and we'll chat in a bit.'

As Harry headed off to meet Margaret, Sowerby caught his arm.

'I've just remembered,' she said. 'I got the analysis back on the wound. You know, what else we found in there, beyond the obvious.'

'Anything important?'

'Clay,' Sowerby said. 'Not just traces of it, either. There was quite a lot of it.'

'Clay?'

'That's exactly the look I had on my face when I read the report. Where the hell would clay be from?'

Harry wasn't listening. He was back at the quoits pitch behind the Fountain and staring at the marks in the pit at his feet.

'Quoits,' he said, eyes closed and rubbing his head, as though to do so would help him make sense of this new bit of information.

'What about them?' asked Sowerby.

'One of the clay pits on the pitch behind the Fountain;

they're usually covered, but Mandy found one uncovered when she went down that morning and found the body.'

'How did it get in the wound, though?'

'Exactly what I want to know,' Harry replied. Remembering something Jen had said, he gave her a call.

TWENTY-FOUR

After calling Jen to confirm, Harry had the briefest of chats with Margaret, then left everything in the capable hands of Matt. He secured the Jack Russell terrier in the back next to Smudge, then drove back to Hawes, and parked up behind the Fountain. With a cursory glance at the top of the steps, which led down to the quoits pitch, and leaving the two dogs snoozing, he marched past the community centre and around to the pub's main entrance.

Pushing through the main door to the public bar, Harry was greeted by the sight of a Great Dane spread across the floor at the feet of an elderly couple wearing walking gear. Their jackets and boots were so shiny, he guessed they'd only just been purchased. They were tucking into plates of pie, chips, peas, and gravy and the aroma made Harry realise he had, as so often happened, missed lunch.

Mandy, Harry noticed, was nowhere to be seen, then he spotted her beyond the bar, in the reception for the hotel, so made his way around.

'Here you go,' Mandy said, as Harry stood at the reception desk, and she lifted a large, steel ring for him to take. Its diameter was around the same as the span of his hand, but the weight of the thing took him by surprise.

'Bloody hell, Mandy ...'

'Heavy, aren't they, quoit rings? Now imagine throwing it!'

Throwing it wasn't what Harry was imagining at all.

He turned the quoit ring over in his hand, held it up for a closer look, checked its edge.

'This could do some serious damage.'

'Yes, if you dropped it on your foot.'

'Mind if I borrow this?'

'Not at all. Just bring it back when you're done; cost a small fortune, they do.'

Harry, with the ring in his hand, headed back the way he had come, but instead of walking through the public bar, took a left through a door into the function room at the back, where Ben and Liz's party had been held on the night of the murder. He then made his way through the kitchen, with a nod to the chef, and out the back door, into the car park.

A moment or two later, he was down on the quoits pitch, and had pulled the cover off two clay pits; the one he wanted Sowerby to have a look at, and the one next to it, which was untouched. That done, he walked to the other end of the pitch, and gave the ring a few practice swings. The thing certainly has some heft, he thought, and on the third or fourth swing, sent it flying.

The ring soared through the air with more ease than Harry had expected, shot right over the clay pit, and buried itself in the grass beyond, barely a foot away from a wall.

Harry jogged over and retrieved the ring, somewhat relieved he'd not sent it crashing into stone and damaging it.

Standing back where he had been for his first throw, he tried again, this time going a little more carefully. The ring fell short, so he picked it up again and went back for another go.

'Not easy, is it?'

Harry glanced up to where the voice had come from to see Mandy staring down at him.

Harry ignored her for a moment, gave the ring another heave-ho. It cut through the air with ease, and landed in the clay.

'You should join the team. They need a few new members.'

Harry retrieved the ring, and compared the mark it had made in the clay to the ones in the clay pit beside it.

When Mandy's voice came to Harry again, it was closer, and he looked up to see her sitting on the bench he'd perched himself on when he'd first come down to the pitch.

'Just taking in the view,' she said.

'Same,' said Harry, eyes still on the clay pits.

'Well, you'll not see it if you keep staring at the ground, will you?'

'Different view, that's all.'

Harry crouched down for a closer look. The mark left by the quoit Mandy had given him was smooth, like the edge of the quoit itself, which was rounded off and too blunt, as far as he could tell, to be used as anything other than a blunt force trauma weapon. He had no doubt it could cause nasty bruising, even break a bone or two, crack a skull, but cut through flesh? There was no chance of that. In the other pit, however, the marks were different. They were just as deep, but thinner, more ragged.

Harry stood up, recovered both pits, and went to sit beside Mandy.

'Hard to believe something so awful happened here, isn't it?' she said. 'And just a couple of days ago, too.'

Harry spun the ring between the palms of his hands.

'You said the team needed a few members.'

'I did. It's a popular game, like, but it's not indoors, is it, like the darts? Everyone wants to play that, but I think some folk see this as a bit odd. It's fits and starts, really; sometimes we'll have a good number on the team, other times not so much.'

'And now's one of the not-so-much times?'

'We've three, would you believe?' said Mandy. 'Not enough at all, but we manage, as we always do round here, because we have to.'

Harry held the ring out in front of him with his fingers wrapped around it in a strong grip. He then lifted it and swept it down through the air.

'What on earth are you doing?'

'Thinking,' said Harry, and did it again, this time bringing the ring down into the soft turf at his feet. The ring buried its edge easily into the grass.

Standing up, Harry went to hand the ring back to Mandy.

'You'll need to clean that up before I take it from you,' she said. 'Can't be storing it like that, can I? Anyway, you can carry it back up, and I'll follow.'

A few minutes later, and back in the reception, Harry handed Mandy the now-clean quoits ring.

'And that's the only pub set, is it?' he asked, as Mandy stowed the ring away with the others.'

'It is,' she said. 'And I keep them safe, too, because—'

'They're expensive?'

'They're just metal rings!' said Mandy. 'Honestly, when I found out how much ...'

Her voice faded with a disbelieving head shake.

'And they're the ones the team use?'

'Of course! Why else would I have them?'

Harry had no answer to that, said his farewells, and made his way back around to his vehicle.

Climbing behind the steering wheel, he pulled up Sowerby's number. He was expecting to have to leave a message, so was surprised when she answered.

'Where did you go?' Sowerby asked. 'You just disappeared.'

'I'm a man of mystery and intrigue,' Harry said. 'How's things going there?'

'Well, you'll be pleased to know that Mum confirmed death, so that's something, isn't it? Whoever she was, she's definitely expired.'

'So death and sex confirmed? That's something. Procedure can be a bit of an arse, though, can't it?'

'Can be? Is!'

'What else?'

'We had to get the body out quickly, what with the water rising.'

'But it's stopped raining.'

'Doesn't matter; there's been so much of it lately that everywhere's sodden, so there's loads more stored in the fells, filling the rivers; if we'd arrived much later, there'd have been a good chance of the body ending up either impossible to retrieve, or way off downstream, and in a considerably worse state.'

'Any idea of cause of death, or too early to tell?'

'Post-mortem will give more details, obviously, but we've a fair idea.'

'That being?'

'Massive trauma to the neck,' said Sowerby.

'The head's still there, though; I saw it myself, heard it too, as it ricocheted off the boulders.'

'It is,' Sowerby confirmed. 'However ...'

Harry did not like the way Sowerby left that word floating in midair.

'However, what?'

'Well,' Sowerby said, 'between you and me and everyone on

our teams, it's pretty damned clear someone had a bloody good try at removing it.'

TWENTY-FIVE

When evening came around, darkness was already pulling its thick blanket over the Dales, and clasped in its skeletal hands was a thick fog. The sounds Harry was so used to hearing in the fields around the house seemed eerily muffled by it, as though ghosts and other spectral figures were all that lay beyond the bend of light pushing into the gloom from the windows.

The bleats of sheep were quiet things, their sound cut off before they had a chance to echo across the fells. Car engines were little more than a distant rattle. It was as though the world had been covered in a layer of thick snow, yet no snow had fallen. The fog, though, Harry was sure, was growing thicker by the minute, a swirling eiderdown of silence, soft and suffocating and, in some strange way, oddly comforting.

'Not so much pea soup as leek and potato, isn't it?' said Grace, coming to join Harry outside their front door.

He was sitting on a low wall built of stone cleared from the ground before them to make way for a pasture. Little clouds of wool were drifting in and out of sight, unbothered by the approach of night, intent instead on seeking out fresh roots of grass.

Grace sat down beside Harry and handed him a glass of wine, the thick red liquid sending the aroma of rich blackcurrant and chocolate into his nose as he took a sip.

'Now that's a bit special,' he said, holding the glass up, as though having a closer look at what it contained would reveal some deeply hidden truth. 'Where'd you get it?'

'Elijah Allen's; they've a decent selection.'

'We going upmarket, then?'

Grace laughed.

'A little, but not too wild, not yet, anyway. Watch out, though; next thing you know, I'll be driving down dale to Campbells in Leyburn! Have you seen that room upstairs? Bottles as far as you can see, or so it seems. Some mad prices on some of them as well.'

Harry had never ventured upstairs there, but he'd heard plenty about it.

'There's a lot of money down there,' he said. 'All those racehorses, the owners, the stables. You know, I once had to park in Leyburn marketplace between a brand-new Ferrari, and a Land Rover so old the owner had to start it with a crank?'

They both laughed at that, sipped their wine.

'How's the week going, then?' Grace asked.

'From bad to worse,' said Harry, enjoying the way the taste of the wine lingered after he'd taken a mouthful. 'Nowt makes sense.'

Reaching out a hand to rest it on Grace's leg, he gave it a squeeze.

'You don't want me boring you with all that, though, do you?'

'Actually, yes, I do,' Grace replied. 'We laugh together, don't we? So, it seems to me a bit unfair if I only get to see that side of you.'

'That's not what I mean.'

'I know it's not. I'm just using it to support what I'm saying, that's all. If something is bothering you, tell me. It works both ways, so be warned of that, because as you know, I can't half go on if I need to, much like my dad! But don't go keeping things inside and getting all twisted up.'

Harry understood, and wished it was that easy.

'I can't tell you everything, though, can I?' he said. 'And with some of it, I'm not sure either of us would want me to, either.'

Grace rested her hand on top of Harry's.

'Out with it,' she said. 'As much as you can tell me, tell me. I'm a big girl. I can handle it.'

'Oh, I don't doubt that for one second.' Harry smiled.

For a moment or two, neither one spoke. Then two wet noses pushed between them, and they looked down to see the fluffy faces of Jess and Smudge looking up at them.

'You've an audience now,' Grace said. 'So, come on, get to it!'

Harry took a sip of wine, allowed it to play around in his mouth before swallowing. The last few days spun wildly in his head, finishing with Sowerby turning up at the quoits pitch to take casts of the marks in the clay pit Mandy had found uncovered.

'Nothing adds up,' he said at last. 'I can't say exactly why, but it just doesn't.'

'Well, what can you say?'

Harry frowned.

'You sure?'

Grace gave a firm nod.

'Both victims seem to have been killed in the same way,'

Harry explained, deciding to go straight in with the rough stuff, instead of beating around the bush. 'Or at least with either the same weapon, or similar weapons. The first victim is a young man from London, just months away from getting married. The second victim we were able to trace through the chip in her dog, a little Jack Russell. She's from a town no one's heard of in Suffolk.'

'Really? Where?'

'Stowmarket.'

'You're right, I've never heard of it.'

'First victim killed on a quoits pitch, second one found at Hardraw Force. Neither of them has anything to do with the Dales as far as we can tell. They're not connected to each other either. They're just ... well, they're just dead, aren't they? And it's my job to find out who did it, before—'

Harry stopped himself from saying any more.

'Before what?' Grace asked.

Harry sunk the last of his wine, had to think fast.

'The press,' he said. 'That's my main concern. They get wind of this, then we'll be inundated with all kinds of bollocks. Walker? She'll be forced to bring in loads of extra help. Either that, or everything will just get taken over by another team, and we'll be pushed into some backroom function, probably making coffee and picking up paperclips.'

'You can handle the press.'

'I can,' Harry agreed, standing up. 'But I've not got the grit I once had, you know? At least I don't think I have. I love it up here, and I know it's sanded off my rough edges, if that makes sense? But sometimes, I miss that part of me. I shouldn't, but I do.'

Grace stood up beside Harry, slipped her hand into his.

'What part of you do you miss exactly?'

'The part you've never seen,' Harry replied. 'That part. I'm not proud of it, or of some of the things it's done, but sometimes? Sometimes, it was bloody useful.'

Grace was quiet for a second or two. Then, as she went to speak, she moved herself to stand directly in front of Harry, still holding his hand.

'You're a different man, I know that,' she said. 'But you're also the same man. That dark part, it's still in there, it's just that maybe you know how to control it better now. You don't need to be afraid of it. I know I'm not.'

'Maybe we should be,' said Harry. 'Honestly, Grace, I—'

'I, nothing,' said Grace, cutting in. 'So what if the press finds out? All that matters is you, your team, and you all working together to get the job done. So, get it done, yes?'

Harry smiled, leaned forward, kissed her.

'You can be quite persuasive, you know that, don't you?'

'You're only saying that because I have a shotgun certificate.'

'You have two shotgun certificates,' Harry corrected.

'Exactly.'

Harry checked his watch. Evening was now night, and would soon be tomorrow. Before it arrived, he needed to rest. He also needed something else.

'Come on,' he said, turning towards the house, his hand still in Grace's. 'Bedtime, I think.'

'Tired?' Grace asked, but Harry saw a glint there that sent his pulse racing.

'Not yet,' he replied.

'Good,' said Grace, and with the dogs trotting on behind, they headed back into the house and closed the door on the night.

TWENTY-SIX

Harry woke to an empty bed and the smell of coffee. Reaching for his phone, he saw the time and knew that Grace had already gone to work, an earlier morning calling her out than the one that now invited him into its embrace.

A text message was waiting for him: *Got him. Now what?*

Harry yawned, sat up, saw his and Grace's clothes scattered across the floor, and with a smile, replied: *Just getting up. Will call in ten.*

No sooner had he sent the message than his phone buzzed.

'I said I'd call in ten.'

'The only thing I have ten of is Cadbury's Chocolate Fingers,' came the reply. 'They were a birthday present from one of my delightful offspring and I keep them in a locked drawer at work so no bugger can nab them.'

'Birthday? But that was ages ago.'

'You have no idea when my birthday is.'

'I have no idea when my own is, never mind yours.'

'You're a terrible human being.'

'From you, that's a compliment.'

Harry laughed, and heard the same sound come back at him down the line.

'Now then, Robbie,' he said.

'Now then? What kind of talk's *now then*? You've not gone all northern on me now, have you, Harry?'

Detective Chief Inspector Robert Kett was an old friend of Harry's, based in Norfolk. They'd met on a case further back in their careers than either of them cared to admit. Over the years, they'd kept in touch. Not so much as to call each other for a chat every week, or even to visit now and again to go for a pint or three. Yet just enough to know they could depend on each other should the need arise. And now, the need had arisen.

'Shut it, Norwich,' Harry growled, 'or I'll be posting you some cheese and cake.'

'That isn't a thing.'

'You try telling that to the whole of Yorkshire.'

'Happy to.'

With insults exchanged as the warmest of greetings, Harry pulled on a dressing gown and headed downstairs. He followed the scent of coffee and soon found himself sitting at the kitchen table, drinking a mug of it. Smudge stared at him from her bed, and thumped her tail twice in welcome at his arrival.

'So, this Ian bloke I've found,' Kett said. 'What is it you actually need me to do?'

'I don't need you to do anything,' said Harry. 'Not now that you've found him, anyway.'

'You sure?' Kett asked, and Harry heard disappointment in his voice. 'Can't I just scare him a bit?'

'Since when have you ever scared someone only a bit?'

'Says the man with a face like the four riders of the apocalypse all rolled into one.'

'I don't need him scared,' Harry said. 'I just need to talk to him for now, that's all.'

'You coming down, then?'

'And why would I want to do that?'

'To see me, obviously.'

'Your daughters, maybe. You? No.'

'You remember my daughters, right?'

Harry went silent for a moment.

'How many is it you have?' he asked. 'I always forget. I feel like it's somewhere in the teens.'

Kett laughed.

'Feels like that some days, that's for sure. Now, back to me scaring this Ian for you.'

Harry didn't take the bait.

'Where is he?'

'He's at the station, nice and comfortable. I had a couple of Uniforms keep an eye on his address, and when he eventually turned up, they went over, introduced him to the inside of their patrol car, and brought him in. Can't say he put up much of a struggle. Didn't seem entirely surprised by it either.'

'Has he said anything?'

'Only that they deserved it after what they did, not that I have any idea who they are, what they've done, or what he's done that he thinks they deserved.'

That sentence made Harry's brain hurt.

'I'll be down at the office in about an hour,' he said, 'and ready to speak to him in about an hour and a half. If you can have him ready for a little chat by then, that'd be great.'

'And you're sure you don't need me to scare him?'

'Robbie ...'

'Not even a little bit?'

Harry hung up.

Once breakfast was done, Harry was out in the fields with Smudge. The fog was still low, the sounds of the morning softened by it, but he sensed that the rain would not be returning.

He had no idea why, just that he'd spent long enough in the Dales to be able to feel it, as ridiculous as that sounded, especially to him.

He knew the smell of the rain now, how close it was, and was even able to guess from the way the wind was blowing through the fells what it would bring with it. Not that he was some kind of soothsaying reader of the seasons, more that the Dales were increasingly becoming a part of him, little bits of it connecting permanently to his DNA.

With Smudge walked, Harry clipped her into the back of his Rav, then headed into town. He'd usually walk, but with everything he and the team were dealing with, he wanted to have transportation to hand, just in case none of the other vehicles were available. And he wasn't about to jump on the motorbike Liz was so fond of. Not just because he didn't have a licence either, though that was obviously a good enough reason. It was more that even if he had a licence, he'd just never trust himself and was fairly sure his end would come up fast in the shape of a dry-stone wall on a corner he'd completely misjudged.

In the office, Harry was met by the team, all of them alert to what they were dealing with. Jadyn had tidied up the board, and Harry saw now that photographs from both crime scenes were dotted around it. Teas had been made, and someone—Harry guessed Matt—had already been to Cockett's for a few delicious morsels to get the day started.

'Right then, I want this to be quick, so let's run through everything sharpish, divvy up the jobs, and get cracking. Who wants to go first?'

'You do,' suggested Walker.

'I do?'

'Of course. You're bouncing on the spot like someone's just set fire to your feet.'

She has a point, Harry thought. He was certainly feeling fidgety.

Harry wasn't quite sure where to start, knowing that he would be speaking to Ian soon, and that afterwards, he'd head over to Leyburn to meet Tracey's friends, and hopefully see if anything could come from looking around her flat. So, he quickly ran through everything in his mind, including what he now believed to be the unlikely murder weapon, then picked something at random.

'Jen, anything from Mickey's parents?'

Jen shook her head.

'Only that they're broken,' she said. 'They have no idea why anyone would want to hurt their son, or who, for that matter. They've said they're happy to talk to you if necessary. They're also trying to support his fiancé, along with her parents. It's all beyond tragic and horrible, really. I can't begin to think what it'll be like for them when they find out what Mickey was up to when he was killed.'

'Then don't, not right now, anyway,' Harry advised. 'They'll be provided with the support they need. The best we can do for them is to try and find who was responsible. What about the postmortem?'

'Nothing to add to what you already know,' said Jen. 'Four blows to remove the head, and you've just mentioned the suspected weapon, which matches what Sowerby explained to us about her findings from the wounds. Only other thing she said was that the red shirt he was wearing was a little on the big size.'

With Jen finished, Harry turned to Jim, who was giving his dog, Fly, a head scratch.

'We did a door-knock,' he said. 'And we've spoken with Mary Hick. She was there when her teammate's hat was taken at the pub.'

Harry remembered that from what Jen had told him after her talk with Mandy.

'Do we know who the other party was?'

Jim checked his notebook.

'She didn't have a name, just a description. Big bloke apparently, there with a group of mates.'

Harry glanced at Matt; the DS was staring back at him.

'Are you thinking what I'm thinking?' he asked.

'Well, as this is one of those rare occasions where I'm not thinking about pies, then my guess is that yes, you are.'

'Eddie?'

'Eddie.'

'Who's Eddie?' asked Jim. 'Oh, and Mary gave us the names of the other two who are on the quoits team with her; Graham Suggitt, and Ray Allen. A Mr Bainbridge was also there, but he's not on the quoits team. It was Graham's cap that was taken.'

'By Eddie,' said Harry. 'He's a liability, isn't he?'

'A better description might be git,' said Matt. 'Or pillock. Or both, thinking about it. Looks like we'll be having another chat with him, doesn't it?'

'Sadly, yes,' Harry agreed. 'This Graham Suggitt, then, it was his cap that Eddie took? Did Mary say anything else about what happened?'

'No,' Jim replied, shaking his head. 'She might've done if we'd had longer, but you called about the goings on at Hardraw.'

'You're right, I did. Investigations have a habit of getting in their own way. You have the contact details of Mr Suggitt and Mr Allen?'

'Of course.'

Harry then explained what was known about victim number two.

'Thanks to our little Jack Russell friend, we now know that it was his owner found at Hardraw Force. A Ms Christine Judd, age forty-two, from Lincoln. Keen runner, up here for a week in a campervan. Last seen early yesterday morning, leaving the campsite with her dog, heading out on a run in the direction of Hardraw.'

'What happened with the dog?' Walker asked.

Jim gave a whistle, and from the corner of the room, where Fly's and Smudge's beds were stuffed beneath a radiator, a little ball of fluff shot across the floor and leapt up onto Jim's lap.

'He's a friendly one,' said Jim. 'We don't know his name, because those details aren't kept, just the owner's name and address, once you match the code from the chip to what's on the database. So, for now, I've been calling him Zip, on account of how he fairly zips along and has no other pace. He's either going full pelt, or fast asleep.'

'Poor wee thing, though,' said Walker. 'He'll be missing his owner.'

'He will,' said Jim. 'But Fly's keeping an eye on him, and so am I, and my mum and dad. Mum didn't want to let him come with me this morning, but I thought it was for the best.'

'The only other thing for now,' said Harry, 'is that we have a good idea of the weapon used in each attack. As mad as this may sound, it looks as though the killer used either a quoit or something very much like one.'

'But they're not sharp, are they?' asked Dave. 'I've thrown a few myself, and they're heavy, yes, but you couldn't use one to cut up cheese, never mind cut through someone's neck.'

'Sowerby's taken casts of some marks we found in one of the clay pits on the pitch,' Harry explained. 'She'll check those against what's found in the postmortem, maybe even come up with some idea as to just how much like a quoit the weapon used was.'

'That mean we have three suspects, then?' Walker asked,

looking now at Jim. 'Those names you mentioned; Graham, Mary, and Ray, yes?'

'No way Mary could've done it,' said Jim.

'And why not?'

'Because she was my Sunday School teacher, that's why!'

Harry smiled at that.

'Matt, I want you and Jen to interview Graham Suggitt and Ray Allen. I know Jim's already spoken with Mary Hick, but have another chat anyway. We need to know where they were, what they were up to, the usual. Not that any of that is ever watertight, especially in a place like Wensleydale where so many folk seem to just spend hours on their own out on the fells gathering sheep, dealing with cattle, or doing whatever job it is they do.'

'Will do,' said Matt.

'Walker, I need you over to Sowerby, see if we've got anything on what was found at the quoits pitch, anything from the second victim, just anything, really. Because we need something, a connection. These aren't random attacks. There's a reason behind it all, and we need to find it sharpish.'

'Not a problem,' Walker said.

Harry turned his attention to Jadyn, Jim, and Dave.

'Jadyn, you're to find out as much as you can about Christine Judd's last movements. Visit the campsite. Ask anyone and everyone if they saw anything, noticed if someone was following her, anything, understood? People don't just head out on a run with a dog, then end up at the bottom of a waterfall; someone must've seen something. Jim, Dave; you're doing the rounds with Tracey's photo, which Matt can give you. See if anyone recognises her, has seen her, anything, okay?'

Harry called Matt to the front.

'I have a call with the mysterious Ian now,' he said, picking up one of the office laptops. 'Can I leave you to get everyone gone?'

'Consider me the rocket up their backsides,' Matt grinned.

'An image I rather wish you hadn't conjured,' said Harry, and with that, he left the office and headed for the interview room at the end of the hall.

TWENTY-SEVEN

A voice from the main doors caught Harry short, not just because he wasn't expecting it, but also, and more disturbingly, because of who it belonged to.

He turned on his heels, snarled.

'Anderson.'

'Grimm.'

'DCI Grimm, to you,' Harry corrected.

The journalist laughed through a pencil-thin smile.

'I sometimes wonder if you throw that title around as easily as I suspect you've thrown those massive fists of yours.'

Harry ignored the jibe, not least because there was more truth in it than he was going to let Anderson take credit for. He stood his ground, and waited for the journalist to explain the reason for his visit.

Having had a run-in with him during his first few days in the Dales, and ever since enjoying what could best be described as a hate-hate relationship with the man, Harry expected it to be less than palatable.

Mind you, the last time they'd met, they'd actually

worked together. Somehow, they'd come to an agreement to handle dozens of celebrity-hunting journalists and fans who were in the Dales trying to track down a young couple who had disappeared. Amazingly, it had allowed them both to maintain their dislike for each other, but also make the best of the situation and develop a very, very thin layer of trust. Odd.

'Got a minute?'

'Not had one of those for years.'

'Busy, then?'

'Always.'

Anderson laughed.

'Wouldn't want to go losing your head over the day job though, eh?'

That comment alone was enough to make Harry want to throw Anderson out of the building, without bothering to open the doors first. The fact that his laughter had died so quickly, and that he hadn't smiled while saying it, though? That, Harry thought, was disturbing.

'One minute it is, then,' Harry said, and gestured for Anderson to follow him down the hall to the interview room. 'After which, you can crawl back under whatever rock you call home.'

'It's a bungalow, actually. You should visit.'

Harry opened the door, stepped through.

'No, I don't think I should.'

Anderson followed, and Harry closed the door.

'Sit.'

Anderson sat. Harry didn't, instead choosing to stand on the other side of the table and fold his arms.

'I mean it,' continued Anderson. 'Pop round sometime. I make a mean lemon drizzle cake.'

'I don't have your address.'

'You're a detective, so that's not really an issue, is it? At least I hope it isn't.'

Harry was growing more and more confused by the second. What the hell was going on? Was Anderson genuinely trying to offer some kind of olive branch?

'Moving on,' he said. 'By which I mean, you've now got thirty seconds. Don't waste them.'

Anderson leaned back in his chair, not to slouch, as Harry had expected, but to shove a hand into a pocket and retrieve a small, brown envelope.

'This arrived at the office for me this morning,' he said, sliding the envelope across the table. 'Someone pushed it through the door, so whoever it was, they were up with the lark.'

'What is it?'

'Probably best you open it,' suggested Anderson.

Harry took the bait, pulled on a pair of disposable rubber gloves from his pocket, and reached out for the envelope.

'The gloves are pretty pointless,' Anderson said. 'It'll have all kinds of DNA on it.'

'True, but I don't want it to have mine.'

The envelope was small, and Harry suddenly had a distant memory of his mother bringing similar home with her wage in it. It had never been much, but somehow she'd manage to make it stretch enough to feed the three of them.

Opening the envelope, Harry reached in a finger and slipped out a folded piece of lined notepaper.

'This had better not be a Christmas Cracker joke on here.'

'Oh, it's definitely no joke,' Anderson replied, and Harry heard something strange in the tone of the man's voice.

Was it fear? How was that even possible? Anderson fed off stories that involved people in pain, people having a very, very bad day; that was his bread and butter. So, just what the hell could this contain that would make the man so afraid?

'Open it,' Anderson said.

Harry set the envelope back on the table and opened the piece of paper.

The writing was spidery, a thin, jittery collection of blue lines etched into the surface with a ballpoint pen. Harry noticed that some of the lines were blurred, as though small drops of water had fallen on them. Tears perhaps, but kept that thought to himself.

'Any idea who sent this?'

'None. It was on my desk when I arrived.'

Harry remembered something Anderson had said a couple of minutes ago.

'I thought you were freelance? If that's the case, what's this office you mention, then?'

'Small place I rent in Richmond out on an industrial estate. It's new. One of those shared-office spaces where you can hot-desk, or rent a tiny little cubicle, that kind of thing.'

'How long have you been there?'

'A few months now. Got a bit tired of working in my lounge or on my dining table. Forces me to get out a bit more. Bit more social too, you know? Well, it would be if there was anyone else in the building. And the industrial estate isn't exactly picturesque; a garage, a couple of storage places for local businesses, a distribution centre for food for cafes and restaurants and whatnot, you get the picture.'

'Well, if it's working for you, then that's what matters, isn't it?'

Anderson didn't reply, just gave a noncommittal shrug.

Harry focussed again on the note. The writing was a little hard to decipher, and he had to hold the piece of paper at various angles until he was able to work out what the words were trying to say.

'As soon as I read it, I came here,' Anderson said. 'I know we've had our disagreements in the past, but—'

'You don't say,' interrupted Harry, but was unable to hide the wry smile on his face.

'Regardless,' Anderson continued, 'when I read that'—he jabbed a finger at the note in Harry's hand—'I figured the best thing was to come straight over.'

'You didn't think of ringing ahead?'

'Didn't want to waste time.'

Harry scanned the note, let the words sink in. As they did, he pulled a chair out from under the table, the weight of them forcing him to sit.

'Bloody hell ...'

Anderson laughed down his nose.

'Thought you might say that. Actually, no; I thought you'd say something considerably worse.'

Harry read the words again, only this time out loud.

'I am the lamb become the wolf. And I will keep these dark valleys safe from those who come here to destroy them.'

'Dramatic, isn't it?'

'Bollocks, more like,' said Harry, and lifted his eyes to narrow them at Anderson over the top of the piece of paper clasped in his hands. 'Do I need to check this against your handwriting?'

Anderson snorted, and stood up.

'Are you seriously suspecting me of ... Actually, I don't know what you suspect, because it can't be writing that and then bringing it over to you as some kind of prank, surely?'

'What do you know about what's been happening these last few days?' Harry asked.

Anderson walked to the door, gripped the handle, gave it a twist. Then, just as he was about to yank it open, he turned back to face Harry.

'Honestly? I didn't know a damned thing, not until I arrived here about half an hour ago. All I had was that note. Somewhere like Hawes, though? It's hard to keep a secret, isn't it? I just popped into a couple of shops, asked a few questions, and next thing I know, I've got a fairly good idea about what was found behind the Fountain.'

Harry read the note once more.

'Why bring this to me, though? Why would you think it had anything to do with this end of the Dale?'

Anderson hesitated at the door a moment longer, then came back over to the table and sat down.

'Believe it or not,' he said, 'and I know you're not going to believe it, but here it is anyway; I trust you.'

Harry balked at that, but Anderson held up a hand, not so much in protest, but as a request to be allowed to continue.

'You're a rare breed, Grimm. You never wanted to be here. You're a city cop with a dark, and I've no doubt, violent past, and yet here you are, settled into the Dales like you belong. And you don't belong here at all, you know that, don't you? Not in the slightest. But at the same time, you do. And do you know why?'

'Enlighten me.'

'You care,' Anderson said. 'For whatever reason, you've taken this area and its people under your protection. I was cynical about it, about you, at first, and I still am, if I'm honest, but less so now.' He leaned forward, stared. 'That's why I brought it to you. Something about it made me think that the best use of my time wasn't to turn it into a story, tempted though I was, but to turn it over to you. So, that's what I've done.'

Harry folded the piece of paper and slipped it back inside the small envelope.

'You know, this could be the start of a beautiful friendship,' he said.

Anderson laughed.

'No, I don't think it could.'

'Neither do I,' said Harry. 'But I'm hoping I can ask you to keep this to yourself for now. At least for a few days?'

Anderson drew pinched fingers across his mouth.

'My lips are sealed.'

'Ah, but you don't type with them, do you?' said Harry, and to his surprise, they both laughed.

TWENTY-EIGHT

With Anderson gone, Harry flipped open the screen of the laptop and sent a text message to Kett.

'Ready?'

'He is.'

A moment or two later, Kett appeared on the screen in front of him.

'Not exactly a sight for sore eyes, are you?' said Kett.

'Catch me in the wrong light, Robbie, and you'll go blind for days,' Harry replied.

'Which is why I always wear sunglasses whenever we meet.'

Harry laughed.

'Best you introduce me to your guest, then.'

Kett moved away from the screen and another figure appeared as he moved the laptop to face them. He was wearing a green jumper and a frown.

'Mr Ian Lancaster,' Harry said. 'Nice to make your acquaintance at last.'

'What's this about?' Ian replied. 'I've no idea why I'm here, why the police came to fetch me. No one's said anything at all!'

'You've been looked after, though, correct?'

'That's not the point.'

'If you knew that man in there with you as well as I do, then you'd know full well it is very much the point.'

Off-screen, a dark, menacing laugh slipped into the moment, and Harry watched the mask of bravado fall from Ian's face.

'What's this about?'

'You don't know?'

Ian gave a shrug.

'If it's about what I did to their cars, then I don't give a shit. They had it coming after what they did!'

'It was very creative,' said Harry, thinking back to what he had seen in the car park.

'Creative? Are you having a laugh?'

Harry was surprised at not just the shock, but the rage in Ian's voice. Then, before he could even think of what he wanted to say next, Ian was on his feet.

'You think this is creative, do you?'

Before Kett could respond, Ian had ripped off his jumper.

'Look at what they did! Look!'

Harry heard Kett swear, as Ian turned around to show his back to the screen.

'Bloody hell ...'

Ian's back was a latticework of cuts, some healing better than others, all of them red and ragged, a drunken patchwork of skin stitched together with weeping scabs.

Ian turned back around and sat down, remaining bare-chested.

'I woke up like that on Sunday morning,' he said. 'My hangover was enough to tell me that the two bottles of wine I'd drunk after leaving the pub had done little to numb the pain.'

'The window,' said Harry, remembering Mr Willis' antiques shop.

Ian rubbed his eyes, tiredness in them suddenly.

'I don't remember what happened,' he said. 'We were all in the pub and Mickey and his mates, they were acting like dicks. I'd had enough, especially when Eddie decided to nick that bloke's cap. So, I left early.'

Ian's words confirmed what Jim had shared earlier from Mary Hick, so Harry let him keep talking.

'I went for a bit of a walk, just to clear my head, decide what I was going to do, which was to leave first thing in the morning and never talk to any of them ever again. Next thing I know, there's footsteps, and I'm pushed, and I crash into something. I've remembered more of it over the last day or so, but it's still patchy. Whatever it was, it was obviously glass, because of how my back's so cut up. Hurts like hell.'

Kett asked, 'You didn't think of going to a hospital?'

Ian turned to look at Kett, who was still off screen.

'Too pissed off to think straight,' he said. 'Just wanted to get my own back. So, I cleaned myself up, did what I did to their vehicles, and laughed my arse off all the way home.'

Harry sighed.

'My guess is, from what you've said so far, that you've not spoken to any of them since leaving Hawes, am I right?'

Ian gave a snort.

'They've tried calling, but in the end, I just blocked them. Couldn't care less. They're arseholes. And Mickey's the worst. We used to be best mates, you know? Grew up together. He changed, though. I guess we both did. But that's no excuse, is it?'

'No excuse for what?'

Ian shook his head, folded his arms, and stared off-screen into a corner of the room Harry couldn't see.

'He's the only one who's not called. Can you believe that?

I've known him longer than anyone, and he can't even be bothered to pick up the phone and ask me what happened, why I left, why I did what I did. Says everything, really, doesn't it?'

'More than you know, clearly,' said Harry.

'How do you mean?'

Harry took a slow, deep breath, then exhaled, before making sure he had Ian's attention.

'I'm sorry to tell you, Ian, but Mickey's dead.'

Ian's first response was laughter.

'Sod off!'

'Ian ...'

Ian looked off-screen at Kett.

'Has he put you up to this? Bloody hell, he's got no shame, has he? I thought doing what I did to the cars would be enough, but obviously not. How much is he paying you? You're not even real police, are you? Unbelievable!'

'Ian,' Harry said once again, trying to get his attention.

'This is why he's not called, isn't it? All part of the joke. What a bastard!'

When Harry spoke again, all warmth was gone from his voice, and it was a cold wind blowing.

'The body of Michael "Mickey" Hadley was found behind the Fountain Inn and Pub in Hawes on Sunday morning. I've already spoken with the rest of the group. My understanding right now is that you left after Eddie took someone's cap. They made no mention of chasing after you or following you. Instead, they stayed till closing time and—'

'You're serious, aren't you?'

Harry saw the horror of realisation paint Ian's skin moon pale.

'He's rarely anything else,' said Kett.

'Mickey's dead?'

'He is,' said Harry. 'I'm sorry. And I know this is a shock, but I need to ask you some questions, if that's okay?'

Ian fell silent.

Harry gave him a moment or two, then said, 'Ian, believe me when I say I know how you feel, because I do. I've lost friends myself.'

'He wasn't really my friend,' Ian said, his voice sad, monotone. 'Not anymore. I think I agreed to go on his stag in the hope that maybe there was still something there, you know? Something of what it used to be? But there wasn't. He was no longer the Mickey I knew.'

'Regardless,' said Harry, 'it's still a shock. And I'm genuinely sorry.'

'Here,' said Kett, and a hand appeared on-screen with a glass of water.

Ian took it, lifted the glass to his mouth for a sip.

'Ian,' Harry said, 'I need to ask you a few questions, if that's okay? We—'

'Questions? Why? I left the pub early, so I've no idea what happened, have I? What did he do, get so pissed that he fell in front of a car or something?'

Harry closed his eyes for a moment, steeling himself to deliver more awful news, opened them, and said, 'Ian, Mickey was murdered.'

The glass fell from Ian's hand and crashed onto the table in front of him.

'What? He was ... What? How?'

He looked at Harry, at Kett, back at Harry.

'Murdered?'

Harry said, 'You left because Eddie took someone's cap, yes?'

Ian shook his head.

'No.'

Harry was confused.

'No? But that's what Eddie and the others said.'

'I left because Eddie poured beer over Mickey and me. That's why I left. The cap thing, that wasn't it, not really. Getting covered in beer and having no one care? That was me done, it just took a while for me to realise.'

Harry had no knowledge of beer being spilled by Eddie. No one had mentioned that to him.

'You did see Eddie take a cap, though?'

'Everyone in the bar saw Eddie take the cap!' said Ian. 'He just strode over and took it. God, it was embarrassing.'

'Was Mickey involved at all?'

Ian shook his head.

'Not really. I mean, Eddie put the cap on Mickey's head, but it wasn't like Mickey told him to or anything. He just sat there and let it happen to him really, but then no one argues with Eddie.'

Ian laughed then, and Harry thought the sound an odd one to hear, considering what they were discussing.

'Something funny?'

Ian shook his head, and Harry saw tears in his eyes.

'Eddie,' he said. 'You know, it's him I blame.? Mickey was in awe of him, would let him do anything, never challenged him.'

'How do you mean?'

'Well, for example, Eddie had just covered him in beer, right? And Mickey, he just sat there and let him pull his shirt off! He ended up sitting in the pub half-naked! Until Eddie gave him his shirt, that is. But I'm pretty sure he did that just so he could give us all a little gun show.'

'Gun show?'

Ian flexed his biceps.

'Eddie's shirt pretty much drowned Mickey,' he said. 'Looked like a kid wearing his Dad's clothes. Ridiculous.'

Harry was thinking back to Mickey's body on the quoits pitch, and to something someone had said in the office earlier.

'So, Mickey was wearing Eddie's shirt, then?'

'Massive red thing,' said Ian. 'It had been tight on Eddie, obviously, because everything was, but on Mickey? Honestly, it was embarrassing. The whole evening was. The spilled beer, Mickey being naked, the whole thing with the cap. Worst night ever.'

It had been Jen who'd said it, hadn't it? Harry thought. Something Sowerby had mentioned about the shirt Mickey had been wearing, that it had been a little on the large side. He'd thought nothing of it at the time, didn't seem important, but now? What if all of this was a case of mistaken identity? What if Eddie had been the intended victim all along? Was it the beer spilling or the cap incident that had set everything into motion? And what did it matter anyway? They had a second body already, and the strange note that had been delivered to Anderson's office. How the hell was he supposed to make any sense of any of it?

Harry turned to Ian once again.

'It's my understanding that three people had an issue with Eddie taking the cap. Is this correct?'

'Yes,' Ian replied.

'Can you describe them?'

Ian frowned, then did as Harry asked.

'Did you think any of them seemed particularly aggrieved about what had happened?'

'To be honest, they all looked equally pissed off. By which I mean everyone in the pub, not just those three.'

Harry sighed. For a moment there, he thought he was starting to get somewhere. That he might have found something to grasp onto, but no sooner had he reached for it, whatever it was, whoever it was, had turned to smoke and drifted away.

'Can you think of anyone from that evening, apart from the three we already know about, who you think might have wanted to go after either Mickey or Eddie?' he asked. 'Anyone at all?'

Ian gave a shrug, and the tears that had formed in his eyes started falling.

'I can't,' he said. 'And no one kills someone over a flat cap or spilled beer, do they? They just don't. It's ridiculous.'

'I honestly don't know, Ian,' Harry said. 'I honestly don't know at all.'

TWENTY-NINE

With nothing left to talk about regarding Mickey's murder, Harry had quickly touched on the damage Ian had done to the cars. As none of Mickey's friends had actually officially pressed charges yet, and with considerably more serious things to be dealt with, he had finished the chat by making sure Ian understood that what he had done was wrong, and that there was still a very good chance he'd end up in court because of it.

Ian, for his part, had seemed unconcerned, and all things considered, Harry had thought that was fair enough. He'd then finished off the call with Kett, both of them promising to stay in touch, and that was that.

Leaving Hawes, Harry made his way to Leyburn to meet with Tracey Boyes' friends outside where she lived. The rest of his team were busy, and doing their damnedest to find something that would help them identify who was responsible.

They had three suspects, true, but he wasn't convinced of any of them. True, he knew next to nothing about either Graham or Ray, but regardless, nothing seemed to sit right. Jim's comment about Mary had been as funny as it had been insightful, and although Harry had laughed, there was a lot more truth in what the PCSO had said than Harry had let on. Jim had spoken from his gut, and Harry had years ago lost count of the number of times his own had spoken with more honesty and truth than his head.

Regardless, Matt and Jen were on with meeting both Graham and Ray, and he could think of no one better to chat with them and find out what they'd been up to. Matt was the most disarming person Harry had ever met, never mind worked with, and he suspected that, given the opportunity to do so, he could've charmed the crown jewels off the queen. All he needed was a few minutes' spare, a mug of tea, and the offer of cake. Jen was the perfect person to have with him, her sharp mind lancing through Matt's softer approach. Harry had no doubt that together they would find out more than enough about the night in question and what Graham and Ray had been up to.

The rest of the team were on with doing what they could to find out about everything else. Walker was going over to visit Sowerby to see if there was anything from the second victim, Christine Judd. Really, all Harry wanted was confirmation that the killings were linked. At the same time, though, that was exactly what he didn't want, because that was horrifying, but that was the lot of a detective; sometimes you had to wish for the worst to make something right in the end.

Jadyn would hopefully come back with something from the campsite. Someone must've seen something, and right now, anything would be better than what little they had. Which pulled Harry's mind back to the reason Anderson had made the trip to Hawes in the first place: that note.

The words floated again to the forefront of his mind: *I am the lamb become the wolf. And I will keep these dark valleys safe from those who come here to destroy them.*

The lamb become the wolf? What kind of bollocks was

that? Someone with airs above their station, that was what, Harry thought. Or was it? Was there something in those words, telling him more than he realised? Was this someone who was weary of being looked down upon, perhaps, was that it? Or was it something else entirely? And what about that reference to dark valleys and people coming to destroy them? There was a poetry to those words, to the whole damned note, really, and Harry wasn't one for poetry.

Much better to just get to the point, say what you mean, than bugger around with clever metaphors for who knew what. But, if he were honest, and he was rarely anything else, it was that which worried Harry the most. Did this mean he was dealing with someone locally who had taken a dislike to tourists? Because if that was the case, he'd be hard pushed to narrow the number down from the entire population of the Dales ...

With those thoughts wrestling in his head, the journey from Hawes to Leyburn was already a distant memory the moment he arrived at his destination, but a whine from Smudge in the back had Harry pulling over to park up in the marketplace to give her a walk.

The town was busy, but he finally managed to find somewhere to park, opposite The Wonky Tree Bookshop, a place he had no doubt Gordy would've visited a few times, to grab something new to read. It had been a good while since Harry had tried to get into a book, and he made a mental note to pop in at some point during a rare bit of free time, to see if there was anything that grabbed him. He had no idea what that would be, though, which was always a problem.

Walking up through the marketplace, Harry headed down a thin, shadowy lane, and was soon walking along the narrow footpath of The Shawl, with the whole of Wensleydale before him.

God, it's glorious, he thought, as he let Smudge off her lead to trot off ahead, and perched himself on a bench to take in the view.

Penhill drew his focus, its silent slopes wearing a veil of fog, which hung around its feet, its edges whipped into torn feathers by the wind. Further on, he followed lanes and walls and streams, saw the path of the Ure, spotted tractors navigating their way through gates, and above him heard the mew of kites.

Smudge trotted back and sat with Harry and for a few minutes they enjoyed the silence and each other's company, then as Harry was about to take them back to the marketplace and on to visit Tracey's friends, his phone buzzed.

'Harry?'

Matt's voice pulled Harry out of his brief moment of contemplation with a sharp tug.

'Wasn't expecting a call.'

'Well, thought you'd like to know that we've had a good chat with Graham and Ray.'

'And?'

'They've both confirmed what happened in the pub the night before Mickey was found on the quoits pitch. It was Graham's cap that Eddie took. They were neither of them exactly full of praise for his behaviour, mentioned beer being spilled as well, and Eddie giving his shirt to Mickey. Apparently, he took a moment to show off his muscles.'

'Sounds like a very strange night.'

'Doesn't it, just?'

'So, what about afterwards?' Harry asked. 'What happened when they left the pub?'

'Solid alibis both,' said Matt. 'Graham was picked up by his wife, Helen; she'd spent the evening round at a friend's in Gayle, and drove him home to their farm in Widdale.'

'And Ray?'

'He went with them; he was staying over to head out for a bit of early morning rabbiting with Graham.'

'And this is all confirmed?'

'By Helen, yes.'

Harry had an urge to lob his phone off The Shawl and give up being a detective for good.

'What about Mary?'

'Heading there now. Just thought it was best to let you know.'

'Thanks, I think,' said Harry, and killed the call.

Stuffing his phone back into his pocket, Harry walked Smudge back to the Rav. He needed something to go on, because all they had right now were dead ends. And if Tracey's friends couldn't shed any light on things, then what?

THIRTY

Harry approached the woman with enough relaxed caution as he could muster. A huge part of him was now hardwired into finding who was responsible for the two murders, and what he didn't want was for that sharp edge to cut who he was meeting. He needed her to be relaxed, in the hope that she might have some information that would be useful. He had expected to find both of Tracey's friends waiting for him, but that was obviously not the case.

Harry introduced himself, showed his ID.

'Leah Tweedy?'

The woman nodded, smiled, though her body language gave Harry enough of a hint as to how relaxed and comfortable she really was, as she faced him, hugging herself tightly.

She was wearing jeans and a fleece jacket, and her thick, black hair was pulled back in a tight ponytail. Harry guessed she was in her early thirties. She was carrying a small canvas handbag, hung over her shoulder.

'Thanks for agreeing to meet me. Could your friend not make it?'

Leah shook her head, seemed to hug herself even tighter.

'Police make us nervous,' she said.

'You're not in trouble.'

Leah didn't reply.

'This is Tracey's place, then?'

Leah revealed a key in her left hand.

'I've not seen her since Saturday morning. I've tried calling, but there's no reply. I think her phone must be off.'

Harry saw the worry in Leah's eyes.

'She's okay with you letting yourself into her place?'

'We keep an eye on each other's things,' Leah said. 'Sometimes we crash at each other's flat as well. We've both got plants and they need watering, don't they? Tracey has a cat as well.'

Harry pointed at the door Leah was standing in front of.

'After you, then,' he said.

Leah slipped a key in the lock and pushed the door open, revealing a set of stairs leading upwards. At the top of the stairs, another locked door barred their way, and Leah used another key to open it.

As the door opened, Harry was gifted with a rich scent of lavender, and he stepped into a small, neat, well-furnished apartment.

'It's a lovely place, is this,' said Leah. 'I'm a bit jealous, to be honest. It's bigger than mine, for one thing, and Tracey's really good at finding nice bits of second-hand furniture and doing them up.'

Harry stepped past Leah and into the first room. He saw a comfortable-looking sofa, a small, fold-away dining table and chairs, and a television. A large window stared out over the rooftops of Leyburn and on towards the hills. The walls were covered with photos, and on closer inspection, he saw smiling faces staring back.

'That's Tracey,' said Leah, coming over to stand beside Harry, and pointing to a woman in the photos. 'Pretty, isn't she?'

Harry said nothing, just moved from photo to photo, smile to smile.

'You said you last saw her on Saturday morning?'

Leah sat down and a moment later, a cat appeared from wherever it had been hiding. It jumped up next to her and purred as it rubbed against her leg.

'Yes,' Leah replied, giving the cat a scratch. 'You hungry?'

Harry nearly said *yes*, then realised Leah was talking to the cat.

He watched her get back up out of the sofa, and walk through a door on the opposite side of the room, the cat in her arms. She returned with a pouch of cat food, which she opened into a bowl that was sitting on a plastic mat beneath the television.

'I best top that water up for you as well, hadn't I?'

Leah popped back through the same door and returned with a glass of water, which she poured into another bowl for the cat before sitting down again.

Harry pulled a chair out from under the dining table and sat.

'Did Tracey tell you anything about what she was doing Saturday evening?'

Leah leaned back, letting out a heavy sigh.

'Not really. I knew she was heading to Hawes. Something about a stag do, I think? Happens a lot, that, getting booked in to give someone a last night of fun.'

Harry noticed a sad tone in Leah's words.

'Did she have somewhere that she was going to meet them?'

'Whoever it was that booked her said he'd send her a message that evening and she could then take it from there.'

'How was she to be paid?'

'That had already been sorted; no one meets with a client without getting paid for it first. The money covers the meeting up, that's it. Anything else that happens afterwards is between the client and whoever it is meeting them.'

'What else does Tracey do?'

'Works at the co-op, does a bit of waitressing, just jobs that allow her a bit of flexibility with her life, really.'

'Did she give you a time that she would be back?'

Leah shook her head, and pulled out her phone.

'She sent me a text to let me know she was okay and was with the client. Here ...'

Harry took the phone.

'Those are her last messages.'

Harry scanned Tracey's words, quietly hoping for some revelation as to her whereabouts, but there was nothing. A lot of it was hard to decipher, littered as it was with emojis and acronyms he didn't understand.

'What's this mean?' he asked. '*I don't remember putting likes working outside on my CV.*'

Leah read the message, glanced up at Harry with an embarrassed giggle.

'Well?'

'I think she sent that while she was with the client, if you know what I mean? You know, while they were ... Anyway, I don't think they went back to his room ...'

Harry's mind cast itself back to the quoits pitch as he read the next message from Tracey out loud.

'Knees cold. Come on, hurry up! Should charge more if his mate's w—'

The number of emojis in this message outnumbered the words by at least ten to one, especially after *hurry up*.

'Don't think she got a chance to finish that one,' Leah said. 'He'd obviously, you know ... finished?'

'But what about that last word? If his mate's what?'

'My guess is watching?' Leah suggested. 'It happens. And she's right, she should've charged more.'

Harry looked at Tracey's final message. He noticed that the timestamp was just over an hour later.

'Everything is fine. See you soon,' he said, reading it out.

'Didn't though, did I?' said Leah.

Harry read the message to himself again, then handed Leah back her phone.

'Something's not right about that last message.'

Leah read it herself.

'Why? Just says she's ok, doesn't it?'

Harry held out his hand for the phone again, and Leah reluctantly handed it over.

It took a moment, but when he spotted it, the difference was glaring.

'No emojis.'

'What?'

Harry flipped the phone around so that Leah could see the screen.

'No emojis, Leah. Look ...' He then scrolled through the messages above. 'See? Every other message from Tracey contains emojis, don't they? It's how you communicate.'

'So?'

'So,' Harry said, 'why is it that in this final message there aren't any? Why wouldn't Tracey throw in at least one smiley face?'

Leah gave a shrug.

'How should I know? Maybe she was tired. It was late, wasn't it?'

'That message was sent an hour later,' Harry said. 'There are no emojis. And it's not exactly chatty, is it? Everything's fine. See you soon?'

Leah sat up, her eyes on Harry.

'What are you saying?'

'I'm saying, Leah, that I don't think Tracey sent that message at all.'

'Then who did?'

'Someone who knows where she is ...'

THIRTY-ONE

After meeting with Leah, and more concerned than ever for Tracey's safety, Harry stopped by Andy's Bakery. It was a favourite haunt of Matt's, and Harry had become a frequent customer as well, whenever he was in the area. He ate as he drove, heading back up the dale to see how the rest of the team were doing and to see if he could start pulling things together. What those things were, he hadn't the faintest idea, but as gruff as he was, he'd somehow always been more of a glass-half-full than half-empty kind of person.

Instead of parking in the marketplace, Harry drove down the small lane towards the Community Centre to park around back of the Fountain. That last message sent from Tracey's phone was bothering him, and he wondered if staring at the quoits pitch might help.

Walking over to the edge of the car park to stare down at the pitch, and with Smudge at his side, a raw cut of wind ripped into Harry, and he quickly decided that his thinking time would be much better spent inside the warm office than outside in the cold.

Leaving his Rav where it was, and fairly sure that if it was in the way, Mandy wouldn't hesitate to tell him to shift it, he left the quoits pitch behind, and was soon pushing through the Community Centre doors and into a comforting cloud of warmth.

Letting Smudge off her lead, Harry pushed the office door open and let the dog slouch in and across to her bed. When she got there, however, someone else was occupying it, and it wasn't Fly.

Smudge stared at Zip, the Jack Russell they'd found shivering at Hardraw Force, her tail almost wagging. Zip stared back, refusing to move from his cosy space. Smudge placed a foot into her bed, then another. Zip rolled onto his back. Then Smudge was in the bed with him, and the two of them were snuggled up together.

'That's one soppy dog,' said Jim from over in the small kitchen corner.

'Which one?' Harry replied. 'Where's Fly?'

On hearing his name, Fly padded over from where he had been hiding in the shadows behind Jim.

'He's been a bit funny these last couple of days,' Jim said. 'Dad's not feeling well, and Fly? Well, he won't leave him alone. Whenever we're home, he just sits with him, resting his head on his lap. He didn't want to come in today, but I couldn't have him doing nowt, could I? And Dad's got his own dog as it is.'

Harry gave Fly's head a scratch and could tell that the dog wasn't quite right. He was subdued, and his fur didn't seem to be as glossy as normal.

'You sure he's not ill himself?'

'I'm going to run him up to the vet in a bit, get him checked over, just to make sure,' Jim said.

'How's your day going?'

'Dave is still out with Tracey's photograph,' Jim explained.

'No luck so far, but you never know. I'm running off a load of flyers, so we can post them through doors, and if we need to, stick them around the place, telegraph poles, that kind of thing.'

'Anything from the others?'

Jim came over with a mug of tea. Harry caught the time on the wall clock and was stunned to see how little of the day was left.

'I had a chat with Jadyn about ten minutes ago. His report so far consisted mainly of how cold he is.'

'Not very useful.'

'Lots of people saw Christine Judd at the campsite and had spoken with her in the days before she was found. No reports of anything odd or of anyone following her. We do know that Zip over there's real name is actually Gandalf and that the last time she was seen was heading off for an early morning run with her dog.'

'How early?'

'I can actually give you a time,' said Jim, and pulled out his notebook. 'Just before six. Someone else at the campsite was out walking their dog at the same time. Said it was actually quite busy, with the site staff doing the rounds to check on bins, check off the morning delivery, clean the toilets and shower block before everyone was up, that kind of thing.'

'And that was the last time she was seen?'

'She headed out across the fields, up towards Sedbusk. Apparently, she was doing a loop, up over the tops, then back round to Hardraw.'

'Which is where she was found.'

Jim laughed.

'Not sure that's funny,' said Harry.

'Sorry, no, I wasn't laughing at that. I was laughing at Gandalf.'

Harry glanced over at the little dog, who was now lying across Smudge's back, fast asleep.

'He's a funny little bugger, isn't he?'

'Little bugger is the right description,' said Jim. 'Had a bit of a reputation on the campsite for escaping. Always seemed to be everywhere he shouldn't, helping himself to other people's tents and caravans. He's not a bad lad, I don't think, maybe just not that well trained?'

'And our Christine Judd took him running? Bit risky.'

'A little,' Jim agreed. 'A dog loose on a farm is at risk of getting shot.'

Gandalf let out a soft snore.

'Any idea what we're going to do with him?' Jim asked.

'My guess,' said Harry, 'is that a friend or a family member will take him. That's usually the case, anyway.'

The office door opened and in came Walker.

'Tea?' Jim asked.

Walker didn't answer, just sat down.

'That's a yes,' said Harry, with a wink at Jim, and walked over to sit next to the DSupt.

'How was Rebecca?'

'The pathologist?' Walker replied. 'Tired, but enthusiastic.'

Harry remembered his chat with Rebecca about how she wasn't sleeping.

'Enthusiastic's not the word I was expecting you to use.'

'The casts she took from the clay in the quoits pitch match the wounds or cuts, or whatever you want to call them, to the necks of both victims. Her conclusion is that the weapon used in both incidents was either something similar to a quoits ring, or a quoits ring, but not like the ones used by the Fountain's team. They're too thick, no sharp edge.'

Harry thought back to the feel of the quoits ring in his hand, the weight of it, and how it had felt to not only throw it through the air, but to bring it down into the ground at his feet.

'It's an odd choice of weapon, isn't it?' he said. 'Why would anyone be walking around with something like that, never mind have it in the first place?'

'The only person who can answer that is the person who's already used it twice.'

'And we're no closer to catching them before they use it again.'

'You think they will?'

Harry reached into his pocket and took out the small brown envelope Anderson had given him. He then quickly ran through Anderson's visit, and told Walker what was written on the note inside the envelope.

'You're kidding me, surely?'

'I'm going to assume that question is rhetorical.'

Jim came over with tea for Walker and she gripped the mug with both hands.

'I am the lamb become the wolf? What does that even mean?'

'Beats me,' said Harry. 'Never was one for poetry.'

Walker sipped her tea, Harry did the same.

The rest of the afternoon was lost to the rest of the team returning with no positive leads at all, and after a quick meeting, they all headed home. Harry took a moment alone in the office with the board and all the evidence they had collected so far. There was plenty of it, but what it was trying to tell him, he still didn't know.

The last to leave, he locked up behind him, gave a momentary thought to the Uniforms Walker had arranged to help out during the nights, then led Smudge back to his Rav. Turning around in the car park behind the fountain, Harry's mind was caught again by those words on the note Anderson had given him. There was something in them, he was sure of it, a clear link to the person who was claiming it was their job to keep these dark valleys safe.

Driving out into the marketplace, Harry knew that whoever they were, they could not have been more wrong, because if anyone was going to keep the dark valleys safe, it was him and his team.

THIRTY-TWO

Come the morning, Harry gathered the team at the office. They were all settled in, with mugs of tea and a few sweet delights from Cockett's, courtesy of Harry this time instead of Matt. Smudge and Fly were curled up by a radiator, with Gandalf somehow squished between them like a novelty hot water bottle. Fly seemed to look a little better, so Harry assumed Jim's trip with the dog to the vets had been worthwhile. The only member of the team who wasn't there, other than Liz, who was still away with Ben, was Jadyn, who was attending a call over at Aysgarth Falls.

A report had come in of someone playing the fool and hanging off the railings at one of the viewing platforms. The National Park staff had decided it was best to employ a bit of police presence to get whoever it was back onto the right side of the fence and away from danger.

The weather was clearer, but with the rain the dale had experienced over the last week the fields and fells were sodden, and thus still fed the streams and rivers to bursting point.

On his way back from Cockett's, Harry had taken a quick

detour to stand on the bridge over the river just beyond the cobbles, and simply allowed the thunderous roar of the waterfall to vibrate through him. Watching the chocolate brown torrent smash and tumble into a white froth, a thick mist soaking him where he stood, he had sent out the quickest of prayers, before wandering back to the office, ever hopeful that today would be the day they'd make a breakthrough.

Having run through the chat he'd had with Ian Lancaster, Harry told them about his trip to Leyburn and Tracey's flat, and the messages on her phone, and then gave them a summary of Anderson's visit, finishing with him reading the note.

'We've two victims and one misper,' he said. 'This is proving to be a busy week.'

'And who the hell says, "I am the lamb become the wolf"?'

Harry heard the treacle-thick disdain in Matt's voice as he repeated the words.

'Not the most comforting of sentiments, is it?' he said.

'This isn't even someone taking the law into their own hands either, is it?' said Jen. 'This is someone who has a grievance with anyone and everyone visiting the Dales.'

'How do you mean?' asked Jim. 'You think that's what this is about?'

'I'm inclined to agree,' said Harry. 'There's a clearly stated threat in the words, but it's not like our two victims were out vandalising the countryside, is it? We've got one having a fumble in the dark on the quoits pitch, and another going for a run with a dog.'

'You're right,' agreed Dave. 'There's plenty of other things for folk to get annoyed about.'

'Like what?' asked Walker.

Dave held up a hand and started to count things off.

'Caravans choking up the roads, bikers using the roads as a racetrack, the housing situation for locals with people buying second homes, walkers who leave their litter everywhere, people who don't clear up after their dogs, mountain bikers not sticking to the routes they can use and making a mess of those they shouldn't, backpackers lighting lovely little fires all over the place, Chinese lanterns lighting up the night sky then depositing wire all over the place for wildlife to get trapped in ...'

Harry held up a hand to stem Dave's tirade.

'I don't need to be worried, do I?' he asked. 'That's quite the list you just tripped off there.'

'I'm not saying I agree with them all,' said Dave, holding up his hands in a show of innocence, 'but what I am saying is that there's a lot of stuff that gets on people's wick, and none of it, that I can see, has anything to do with what happened to Mickey and Christine.'

'Can't say that I disagree,' said Harry. 'So, what does everyone else think?'

Harry's question was met with silence, broken only when Matt said, 'Well, whoever it is, they're not keeping the valleys safe, are they? Quite the opposite.'

'My guess,' said Harry, 'is that whoever delivered this note to Anderson hoped that he would have it in the papers sharpish. And, thanks to a surprising warmth in relations between everyone's favourite journalist and myself, that didn't happen. On one hand, I'm very pleased that's the case, because the last thing we need is panic. On the other, if the killer is expecting to see their words of warning printed in black and white in the papers, and that doesn't happen, what it'll do to their state of mind is unknown. And considering it's already very disturbed as it is, that's a worry.'

'The kind of worry that needs more tea, do you think?' Matt asked.

'Yes,' said Harry.

Matt stood up and headed over to the kitchen corner. As Harry drained his mug, his phone buzzed. He looked at the screen.

'Jadyn,' he said to no one in particular, and answered it. 'Now then, Constable, everything okay down at the falls?'

'No,' Jadyn replied, 'they're not.'

Harry's immediate thought was that whoever Jadyn had been sent over to have a word with had either fallen in the water, or simply run off, having had their fun.

'What's happened?'

Jadyn was silent for just long enough to drop a stone into the pit of Harry's stomach.

'Jadyn?'

'Harry,' the constable said, 'I think we've got another ...'

THIRTY-THREE

That had been a marked understatement, thought Harry, as he stood at the cordon tape, staring at the body hanging on the other side of the viewing platform. He'd arrived convinced he was going to find the missing Tracey waiting for them, but judging by the build of the individual, it very much wasn't.

'Did no one notice they're tied on?' he asked, pointing at the sharp ends of the length of rope he'd spotted, which had been used to make sure whoever this was didn't end up in the raging torrent below.

Jadyn, who had secured the crime scene, was standing at Harry's side.

'I don't think they got close enough. I spoke to both staff at the visitor centre up in the car park. Someone was down here walking their dog and reported it. They came down, but decided to not get too close. Can't blame them, really. And the rope isn't that easy to spot.'

'It is,' said Harry. 'It's bright yellow! It's positively glowing!'

Jadyn stayed quiet.

Harry allowed himself a second or two to calm down.

'You've done well,' he said. 'Called us, cordoned this all off, chatted with the staff. Ready to have a closer look?'

Jadyn frowned.

'You sure you don't want Matt or the DSupt with you for that?'

'Nope, just you, Constable. Come on.'

Harry gave Jadyn no time to back out, and lifted the cordon tape, stepping under, and keeping it up in the air for Jadyn to follow.

Approaching the body, the thing Harry noticed more than anything was the sound of the falls below. They were in the lower section, which was where a number of viewing platforms had been built, but it was still possible to get really close, even on to the falls themselves, if you wanted to. Not that it was advisable, especially when the water was as high as it was. In fact, "not advisable" didn't come close to describing how utterly suicidal it would be to even consider getting closer than where they were now.

Standing just a couple of metres away from the body, Harry could see the terrifying waters of the Ure as they raged through the rocky cleft carved deep over millennia into the fabric of Wensleydale. He'd thought the beck in Hawes had been impressive that morning, but it had nothing on this, and the power of it made him step back a little, even though he knew he was perfectly safe.

'It's properly scary, like, isn't it?' said Jadyn.

It was at that point that, to Harry's disbelief, he saw two objects higher up the river racing towards them, one red, one yellow.

'Kayakers,' he said, lifting a finger to point at the two figures in their tiny plastic boats.

In awe, they watched as the fragile boats danced on the rapids, bouncing between the waves, before shooting over the waterfalls to disappear into the swirling maelstrom beneath, popping up again further down, both of them miraculously still the right way up.

'Not for me, not for me at all,' said Harry. 'I've jumped out of planes more times than I can remember, been shot at, blown up, forced to like cheese and cake, but kayaking? That's where I draw the line.'

'You and me both,' Jadyn agreed.

With the kayakers well gone, Harry took in everything that he could about the crime scene. And it didn't take him long to realise it was giving him nothing. So, it was down to the basics; a description of the victim, and of the crime scene, and then just wait for Margaret, Rebecca, and the SOC team.

'Come on, Jadyn,' he said, 'why don't you go over what we've got? See if you can spot something that I can't.'

Jadyn took out his notebook and pencil and started by describing what the victim was wearing, which didn't take long, seeing as they weren't wearing much at all.

'Changing robe,' he said. 'Can't see what they're wearing under it, but that's about it, isn't it? Bare legs though, and sandals, so if they're wearing anything, it'll be shorts and maybe a top.'

'Changing robes are awful things, aren't they?' said Harry. 'I know they're good for what they're for, which is getting warmed up and changed after being in cold water for whatever reason, but why are people just wearing them out and about now like normal, everyday jackets?'

'Are they?'

'I've seen people walking their dogs in camo versions, others just popping down to the shop for bacon and eggs, and what are they wearing? Those awful things! Almost as bad as dressing gowns!'

Jadyn looked at Harry, confused.

'You've not seen that, either? People parking up, and then walking across town to get fish and chips or something, and they're in their dressing gown?'

Jadyn shook his head very slowly.

'I'm ranting, aren't I?' asked Harry.

'A little.'

'Sorry about that. Anyway, back to what we're on with; anything else?'

'The rope,' Jadyn said. 'Looks a bit weird.'

'You can't put that down in your notes, can you? What do you mean, exactly? Weird in what way?'

Jadyn tapped his pencil against his teeth, a sound that made Harry nearly rip it out of his hands and lob it over the fence and into the river.

'I don't think it's climbing rope. In fact, I know it isn't; it's too thin for a start, maybe five millimetres? And it's shiny.'

Harry narrowed his eyes at where Jadyn was looking.

'You're right about that. No way I'd want to be dangling off that from a cliff edge.'

'Can't see what knots have been used, though,' said Jadyn, 'so I've no idea if whoever did this had knowledge of them, or just lashed their victim to the fence haphazardly.'

'That's all very good,' Harry said. 'Well done. Now, just one final thing, yes? And then we're done and can step back and let the other professionals come and do what they do.'

'One final thing?'

'Yes, one final thing.'

'What?'

Harry folded his arms.

'Jadyn ...'

It took a second or two too long for Jadyn to understand what Harry was getting at.

'Oh, that,' he said. 'Right. Yes.'

'Well?'

'The, er, the head,' said Jadyn. 'There isn't one.'

THIRTY-FOUR

Harry was tired. The day wasn't even halfway through, and he was already finding it difficult to keep his focus. He was fairly sure that he was getting enough sleep, but sometimes, as he knew all too well, sleep just wasn't enough. If the mind was given too much to be on with, and over a sustained period of time, what it needed more than anything wasn't sleep so much as a time with nothing to think about at all.

Harry wondered for a moment what that would be like to spend time not thinking. He had no idea how that would work. Surely his mind would still be thinking, wouldn't it? And about all kinds of things, too, not just work. Though work would be right up there, he had no doubt.

He made a mental note to chat with Grace about it. Maybe they could go away? That would be ... unique. Yes, that was the best word to describe that idea. Harry didn't really understand holidays. He'd had time off, of course he had, but he'd always used it constructively, to do jobs around the house, to visit people, to look back over old cases ... But an actual, honest-to-God holiday? Had he ever even taken one?

'Harry?'

Hearing his name, Harry shook himself free of the nightmare image of being forced to lie on a beach in the sun somewhere and pretend to enjoy running in and out of the sea now and again.

Rebecca Sowerby was standing beside him.

'Hello,' he said. 'We really must stop meeting like this.'

'This is literally how we always meet.'

'There is that.'

'Mum's headed off, and the photographer's down with the body, and probably enjoying what he's doing far too much.'

'How long's he going to be?'

'Can't really say, but I don't think this is going to challenge him artistically, do you?'

'The light might bother him, what with all the trees and ... No, I can't even pretend to know what I'm talking about with all that.'

Sowerby smiled.

'Good attempt, though.'

'How's the tiredness?' Harry asked.

'Better, actually, thanks for asking. Had a good chat with Mum about it. I've promised her that I'll book in for a few counselling sessions again. Won't do me any harm, will it?'

'Quite the opposite, if you ask me.'

'What about you?'

'What about me?'

'You look ... frazzled.'

'Bit insensitive, isn't? You do remember that an IED did this to me, don't you?'

Sowerby rolled her eyes dramatically.

'You know what I mean.'

'I'm actually thinking about chatting to Grace about having a bit of a break.'

'You mean a holiday? Do you even know what one is?'

'Beaches and sunshine, isn't it? That kind of thing? I don't really like sand.'

Sowerby laughed.

'Who on earth ever says they don't like sand?'

'Me.'

'Why?'

'Gets everywhere, doesn't it? It's like Mother Nature's glitter; looks lovely, but it's really bloody annoying, and you're washing out of your car, your clothes, your bags for months. Gets in your food, too. That's never good.'

'Here's an idea, then,' Sowerby suggested. 'Don't go to a beach. It's a wild idea, I know, but it might just work.'

'Like I said, I'm going to chat to Grace about it.'

'Poor Grace.'

The photographer walked past with a wave and a cheery, 'All done! Nice to see a bit of sunshine, isn't it? Photographs should come out really well. Very dramatic.'

Harry acknowledged the man with little more than a nod.

'Either of you fancy a coffee? There's a café in the visitor centre by the car park. The cakes look amazing.'

Neither Harry nor Sowerby responded, and the photographer gave a shrug, said, 'Next time, then?' and walked off, whistling as he went.

Sowerby said, 'He's just so odd, isn't he?'

'He enjoys his work, that's all; don't knock it.'

'That's me up, then, I guess, isn't it? I'll go get the rest of the team. Anything I need to know?'

'Only that the head's completely missing this time. We've searched the area, but there's no sign of it, no blood trail either to suggest it's been carried away.'

'And it's not rained for hours,' added Sowerby, 'so you'd probably spot it. Unless it was carried off in a bag.'

'Hell of a souvenir. My guess? It's bobbing along in the Ure and is halfway to the North Sea.'

'What a happy thought.'

'Isn't it?'

And with that, Sowerby turned away from Harry, and rustled off in her white disposable overalls to join her team and deal with the crime scene.

Harry took a short walk back up the path to where the rest of the team was gathered, passing Jadyn on the way, who was armed with a clipboard as Scene Guard.

'Everything okay, Constable?' Harry asked, as he stepped under the cordon tape.

'The photographer's just gone. He's odd, Boss, isn't he?'

'Takes all sorts.'

'It does.'

Arriving back with Matt, Jen, Jim, and Dave, Harry took them all to one side.

'Well, you all know what we're dealing with; a headless body in a changing robe, tied to the fence of a lookout point for Aysgarth Falls. We've no idea who they are, not yet, anyway. But my thinking is if they're here in a dry robe, then they, for whatever reason, either were about to get in the water, or had recently been in it.'

'Swimming, you mean?' asked Dave.

'Not a chance of it,' said Harry. 'While I was down there with Jadyn, we saw two kayakers shoot the rapids, so maybe there are others. Could be that they're here as part of a group, but if they are, I think we'd have heard by now that they were missing. That leads me to the conclusion we have a solo explorer.'

'Maybe they were somewhere else, and the killer brought them here?' suggested Jim.

Harry wasn't so sure.

'I think we're better off concentrating our limited resources on where we are right now. Check the paths, the woods, the fields, the car parks. Whoever it is, they probably arrived by vehicle, especially if they're kayaking. Maybe they're wild camping. Could be they're in a camper. Maybe there's a tent somewhere. However they got here, and whatever they brought with them, I want it all found. Understood?'

A cough caused Harry to take his eyes off the team and look to his left. A small woman with bright eyes behind large glasses, and dressed in the uniform of the National Park, was standing there.

'Hi,' she said, her eyes going momentarily wide as she set them on Harry's face.

'Hello,' said Harry. 'Can I help?'

'I'm Maisie Jones. I work up at the visitor centre. I run the café mostly.'

Harry waited for Maisie to say more, to give some hint as to why she had come over, but when nothing came, he introduced himself as well, in the hope it might encourage her to keep talking.

'That's why I'm here,' Maisie said. 'Thought it best to speak to a police officer or detective, or whatever it is you are, or do. Look, the thing is, I think I've found something. Up in the car park. It's a stealth camper.'

Harry looked at the rest of the team, hoping that one of them would be able to enlighten him, but all he got back were blank faces.

'And what's one of those, then?' he asked.

'It's a camper than doesn't look like a camper,' said Maisie. 'Some people like their campers to be real statements, don't they? You'll have seen the ones I mean; amazing paintwork, expensive, low-profile tyres, or the offroad ones with a snorkel and big chunky tyres.'

'And stealth campers aren't that?'

'No. They usually just look like normal vans. Nothing about them to make you think that someone's sleeping inside.'

'And why would anyone want to do that?'

'To go on holiday and get away without paying for parking is one,' said Maisie. 'Some car parks will charge extra for a camper, and if it doesn't look like one, you save, don't you? You can also park up in a village or a town and no one's any the wiser that outside their house someone's happily cooking up a bit of bacon and having a kip.'

'Sounds absolutely bloody awful,' said Harry. 'And you say you've found one?'

'Yes.'

'And how do you know?'

'Because I thought I'd see if the doors were locked, and they weren't, and I had a look inside, that's how.'

Harry smiled at that.

'Best you take me to have a look then, don't you think?'

THIRTY-FIVE

What Harry was looking at was not his idea of a holiday, not by a long shot. Then again, neither was sand, sea, and sun, but this? Well, he wasn't quite sure what it was. There was a kayak strapped to the roof rack though so, assuming this van belonged to their victim, Harry had been right about that.

Staring into the rear of what looked like a Ford Transit van that had been badly abused by a builder, Harry remembered another van he had encountered. That one had been a small thing, parked up by the crossing of Gayle Beck. It had been owned and occupied by a photographer with the personal hygiene of a hyena. This, though, was not that.

Though the outside looked rusted and beaten up, the inside was borderline luxury. Harry saw beautifully built cabinets, with a sink, gas hobs, a fridge. There was a seating area at the end, with a small table, and he guessed by the configuration that it could be turned into a bed. The walls and the ceiling were all clad in wood, and the floor was a laminate that sparkled like the night sky.

'How long has this been here, then, Maisie?' Harry asked.

'Overnight I think. Stealth campers usually turn up late and leave early, just so they don't get spotted. I think that's what alerted me really, that it was here when I arrived, seeing as it hadn't been when I'd left, if that makes sense? Struck me as odd. I mean, don't get me wrong, I've not got a problem with people having a kip in their van, it's just we can't let it get out of hand. We're not a campsite, are we? We don't have the facilities.'

'You've toilets and a café,' said Harry. 'If I was in a van, I'd want to stay somewhere like this over a layby any day, that's for sure.'

'Yeah, you're right, we do. Never thought of it like that.'

'And there's the kayak on the roof,' Harry added. 'My guess is they weren't just here for a nap. Probably planned to head out on the water.'

'Rather them than me.'

'You and me both, Maisie.'

Harry slipped on a pair of disposable gloves and climbed inside.

'Are you allowed to do that?' Maisie asked.

'Not at all,' said Harry, his voice a whisper. 'But if you don't tell, I won't either. How's that sound?'

Now that he was inside the van, Harry could really appreciate the work that had gone into it. Not only in making it so comfortable inside, but also in making it look so rough on the outside.

He opened cupboards, and found supplies of dehydrated food, a couple of bottles of wine, a pack of cards. In a drawer, he found candles, a small, fold-flat barbeque, and a hand axe. Another cupboard revealed a couple of wetsuits, a helmet, and a life jacket.

'They've got everything,' he said.

Opening the fridge, there was milk, vegetables, cheese, and something sweeter he recognised from Hardraw Force.

'Now these,' he said, pulling out the packages containing millionaire's shortbread, 'are fantastic!'

'You're not wrong,' said Maisie. 'We stock them here, too, and they sell out fast. Can't have got them here though, I don't think, because like I said, they weren't here when we closed up.'

'I had one over at Hardraw,' said Harry.

'There you go then; the supplier we use probably delivers all over the dale.'

'I'm already wondering if they do home deliveries.'

Harry closed the fridge, stuffed his hands in his jacket pockets, as though doing so would somehow help him see something that he couldn't.

'No phone,' he said. 'I'll check the front.'

Clambering out of the rear of the van, Harry nipped around to the passenger door, yanked it open, and had a good rummage around. Finding nothing, he did the same on the driver's side.

'Yep, no phone at all,' he said, as though just confirming it for himself. 'Found this, though.'

Maisie came over.

'What is it?'

'Insurance documents. Which gives us a name of the owner, an address, all very useful.'

'Have you checked behind the sun visors?' Maisie asked, pointing at them over Harry's head.

Harry laughed.

'Real life isn't like the movies.'

'Even so ...'

Harry gave a shrug, checked the sun visor on the passenger side, and found nothing. Then he checked the one on the driver's side, and when he flipped it down, something fell out.

'Well, would you look at that ...'

'Driving licence?' said Maisie.

'Did you put it there, Maisie?' Harry asked.

Maisie's face seemed to fracture with shock.

'What? Why would I do that? What are you suggesting? Of course I didn't. I mean ... I ...'

Harry held up a hand in apology.

'Sorry, Maisie,' he said, 'just a badly timed attempt at humour. May seem inappropriate to most people, but in our line of work, it's often our sense of humour, our ability to laugh in the darkest moments, that keeps us sane.'

Judging by the look on Maisie's face, Harry wasn't so sure she agreed.

'Anyway,' he said, keen to move on, 'we now have a name, an address and, most amazingly of all ...' He held up the driving licence. 'A photograph!'

He decided not to say that with a headless corpse, there was really no way for them to do a quick check that the owner of the van and the body tied to the viewing platform were one and the same.

'So, what now?' Maisie asked.

'You're keen,' said Harry. 'I like that. Ever thought of joining the police?'

Maisie shook her head.

'Do I look mad?'

'Do I? Actually, don't answer that; I know exactly how I look.'

'About that, I didn't mean to stare, you know, earlier, when I came over to tell you about the van?'

Harry shrugged it off.

'Maisie, even I stare! Every time I catch my reflection, see myself in a mirror, I can't help but have a look. So, don't worry about it. And, before you ask, IED, Afghanistan, a very long time ago.'

Walking back to the team, Harry thought back to what he had found in the van.

'So, Maisie, do you have a nice supply of that millionaire's shortbread, then?'

'I do.'

'Then I don't suppose you'd do me a huge favour, would you?'

About fifteen minutes later, when Harry arrived back with the team, they all stared in disbelief.

'Harry, you're carrying a tray,' said Matt. 'With mugs and ... my God, is that—'

'Millionaire's shortbread?' said Harry, guessing Matt's question. 'Yes, it is.'

Like wasps to a can of pop, the team swarmed around Harry, freeing him of his burden of drinks and biscuits, leaving one for the person who was approaching them.

'Rebecca,' he said. 'Thought you might fancy a bit of a pick-me-up.'

Sowerby pulled off her gloves and reached for the remaining mug and piece of millionaire's shortbread.

'You thought right.'

'I think I can help you with the identity of the victim,' Harry said.

Sowerby answered that with a raise of her eyebrows, her mouth filled as it was with the shortbread.

Harry showed her the insurance documents and driving licence.

'Adam Carpenter, and we have an address as well. No phone, though. You?'

Sowerby shook her head.

'All he's got with him is the pair of boxer shorts he's wearing under his robe and the cigarettes and lighter in one of the pockets.'

'Maybe went out for a quick smoke and a walk before hitting the water,' said Harry.

'Would make sense; can't think of any other reason he'd be down here.'

Harry asked, 'You have anything to tell us yet?'

'No head, but you already know that.'

'We do. What about how he was tied to the viewing platform?'

'The rope, you mean? More like a washing line than rope. No idea why the killer used that.'

'Maybe it was all they had to hand,' said Harry.

'He wasn't going anywhere, that was for sure,' said Sowerby. 'Never seen so many half hitches in one place.'

'And there's nothing else at all?'

Sowerby shook her head.

'I'm afraid that's it. Obviously, I might find more during the postmortem, but I won't be able to get on with that till later. Actually, on that, is the ambulance here yet?'

'I didn't see it,' said Harry. 'Might have got caught up with something.'

'Most likely.'

For the next few minutes, everyone fell quiet as they finished their shortbread and drinks. Harry collected the empty mugs and wrappers and took them back to the café. Unable to resist, he bought himself half a dozen of the millionaire's shortbread, and dropped them into a jacket pocket. He wasn't about to eat them now, but later? Yes, later would be good. He might even save one for Grace.

THIRTY-SIX

With the body eventually taken by the ambulance, which had been delayed thanks to a perfect storm comprising a caravan with a tyre puncture, a tractor which had a blowout while towing a stock truck, and a section of road still carrying a lot of water, Harry and the team had finally left the crime scene.

Sowerby had headed off to see if she had time to fit in the postmortem before the end of the day, but hadn't been able to promise anything. Before going, she had reminded Harry that he'd said he would speak to Grace about taking a holiday, and in return he'd reminded her about her promise to get counselling.

Arriving back in Hawes, Harry had again swung the Rav around to the back of the Fountain, only to find his way blocked by a large van reversing out. With a little bit of nifty manoeuvring, both vehicles had managed to avoid any scratches, and with the parking area free, Harry had pulled in to be greeted by Mandy.

Climbing out into the dappled grey light of the afternoon, and with Smudge at his side, Harry walked over to say hi.

'All good?' he asked.

'No, not really, of course it isn't,' Mandy replied. 'How can it be? We've had a murder, haven't we? And word's already got round quicker than food poisoning on a cruise liner.'

'That speaking from experience?'

'Goodness no. Can't think of anything worse than being cooped up in a big, floating hotel, with thousands of strangers, can you?'

Well, Harry thought, that's another type of holiday off the list.

'People bothering you, then?' he asked.

Mandy sighed.

'It's not too bad, really, and they do buy drinks and meals while they're here, so that's something, isn't it? Just feels a bit, well, ghoulish, doesn't it? People visiting us from all over the dale because of what happened down there.'

She jabbed a finger across the car park to where, beyond its edge, lay the quoits pitch.

'Don't suppose you've caught who did it yet, have you? That's the kind of news we want, isn't it? Something positive.'

'I'm afraid I'm not really at liberty to say,' said Harry. 'The investigation is ongoing, let's put it that way.'

He certainly wasn't going to mention anything about the third body they'd had to deal with, never mind the second. Word would get around soon enough, just like Mandy had just said.

'What are you doing out here anyway?' Harry asked.

Mandy directed the finger she'd pointed towards the quoits pitch back out of the car park.

'Delivery,' she said. 'We never stop, you know, us pub owners. Always on the go, always something to do; cleaning, ordering food, more cleaning, sorting out the pumps, cleaning, dealing with customers, meeting with the breweries, trying their new beers, cleaning ... It's endless, Harry.'

'Ever thought of doing something else?'

'What do you think I am, mad? Of course not! This is home! And what else would I do, anyway? I'm as much a part of this pub as the sign that hangs outside it.'

'You get away much?'

Mandy shook her head.

'Not much different to owning a farm, really; a pub's not something you can leave for too long. Would be nice to have a holiday, though.'

'I'm beginning to think the same,' said Harry.

Mandy laughed.

'Now I've heard everything!' she said, and without another word, she turned on her heel and headed back into the pub.

Alone with Smudge, and knowing that the team would all be busy in the office, discussing the investigation, mulling things over, trying to make a few things connect, Harry decided to delay joining them for a while. Sometimes, the brain required peace, especially if you wanted to think something through. With that in mind, he strolled over to the steps to the quoits pitch and made his way down.

Weary, Harry decided that a good sit down would be the best thing to do, so he plonked himself down on the bench. Smudge came alongside and leaned in against him, her heavy, warm head resting on his leg.

Harry reached out a hand, gave the dog a scratch. Smudge nuzzled in, pushing against him a little, and he scratched a little harder.

The view before him was, as ever, utterly spectacular. The light wasn't great, the wind was cold, and in places, the tops of the fells were hidden from view by sulking cloud, but that, Harry thought, only added to it. In all weathers, the Dales excelled at being glorious, and he could think of no place he would rather be.

Leaning back, and letting out a contented sigh, Harry heard something rustle in his jacket pocket. Remembering the millionaire's shortbread, he pulled out a packet. He knew he shouldn't, that he'd had plenty already, but he couldn't help himself. With a swift rip of the packet, he soon had a delicious chunk of it in his mouth.

Pulling his eyes away from the fells, Harry cast them across the scene before him, trying to remember what he had seen that morning, and attempting to push back in time a little to see Mickey and Tracey, and to somehow work out what had happened, and how. As to the why and the who, the answers to those questions still evaded him. As ghosts from conversations with Sowerby and the team were given form and substance by what he had seen himself, Harry watched them dance in his mind's eye.

He saw Mickey, stumbling down the steps, laughing in the rain. Too much booze in his veins to get him to stop what he was doing, to realise the betrayal he would soon commit.

He saw Tracey, following on behind, her focus no doubt on the money she was making from the encounter, perhaps wondering if she was getting paid enough considering the weather.

Then he saw, in an imagined darkness, a set of eyes watching as Mickey and Tracey fumbled and tumbled to the ground, hands undoing buttons and zips, grasping. Eyes that turned from observer to killer, eyes that belonged to someone who had taken a quoits ring, and brought down its sharp edge with such fiery rage that it had nearly severed Mickey's head with one slash.

Harry bit again into the shortbread, hoping the sugar rush would somehow fuel a revelation.

Those eyes. He saw the killer bringing down their weapon again and again and again, until Mickey's head was free.

What had Tracey felt, what had she seen, where was she now? And why had what had happened here, led to so much more death?

Harry swallowed, stood up, walked around the quoits pitch, stood over the clay pit Mandy had found open, where he had discovered the markings matching the cut marks in Mickey's neck.

He wanted to sit down again, needed to, as the long week, everything that they had all been dealing with crashed over him, tumbling him like a surfer kicked off his board by a rogue wave.

The bench welcomed him, and Harry read the brass plaque, wondered who the shepherdess was, and who had thought so much of her that they had placed the bench there in her memory.

No, he thought, sitting down wasn't going to help, so he turned away and walked back to the steps, glancing up to the car park above, seeing nothing but the roof of the Fountain, and grey skies beyond.

As Harry placed his foot on the first of the steps, something forced him to stop. He frowned, remembering the condoms he had found just above where he now stood. He looked once again to the car park, the Fountain's roof, the sky. Something was bothering him, something about where he was, what he was seeing, or perhaps not seeing, but what? Just what the hell was it?

Harry stepped back, away from his route up, out of the quoits pitch, pushed the heels of his hands into his eyes till he saw sparks.

The words from the plaque on the bench drifted across his mind, driftwood caught in an eddy of thoughts.

For my Shepherdess ...

Why choose that word? And why the hell was it bothering

him that it had been etched into that bench, of all places? What did it matter?

A thought struck Harry.

What if the killer hadn't been following Mickey and Tracey? What if they had been waiting for them all along, down here, in the dark?

No, no ... It wasn't that ... It was something else. Another what if ...

What if the killer had been down here when Mickey and Tracey had arrived? Was that it? And if so, why? Why the hell would anyone be down here in the first place, in the gloom of the night, with a set of quoits? What did it mean? What were they doing? Why do what they did? What triggered it?

Harry's eyes fell on the bench once again, then drifted to the clay pits, then up to the car park, the grey skies, and he realised something: the Rav was parked up there, and he couldn't see it.

He couldn't see it, he couldn't bloody well see it! And then a name came to him, and with Smudge at his heels, Harry was bounding up the steps towards the Fountain.

THIRTY-SEVEN

Pulling up outside an address in Appersett given to him by Mandy, Harry glanced over at Matt, who was sitting beside him. In his mirror he saw two other vehicles pull up, the old police Land Rover, and an incident response vehicle, Jadyn driving the first, Jen behind the wheel of the second, and with them, Dave, Jim, and Walker.

'Ready?' Harry asked.

'I was born ready,' Matt replied.

'I don't think you were.'

'No, you're right, but let's get this over with, shall we?'

Harry reached for his door handle, hesitated.

'What if I'm wrong?'

'You're not, though, are you?'

'What makes you say that?'

Matt leaned closer to Harry.

'My guess is that you've already consulted your gut, like, am I right?'

'You are.'

'And what did it say? That you were talking bollocks, or that you're on the nail?'

Harry's answer was to open the door and step out into the late afternoon air, walk past a large van, and up to a nondescript white front door.

He gave the door a knock, the sound of it racing off into the house to track down the owner.

'No answer,' he said.

'Give it a moment,' said Matt.

Harry did just that, then raised his fist and knocked again, this time loud enough to let the neighbours know that someone was growing very impatient very quickly.

Footsteps ...

'You hear those?' he asked.

'I do,' said Matt.

A rattle of chains, and the door opened to reveal a small man with a balding head.

'Mr Bainbridge?' Harry said.

'Yes?'

'Mr Larry Bainbridge?'

'What do you want?'

'I wonder if we could come in?'

Larry squinted up at Harry, then at Matt.

'Doesn't look like I've got much choice, now, does it?'

'Not really, no,' said Harry. 'May we?'

He gestured into the house beyond with a wave of a hand.

Larry stepped back to allow them inside.

'After you, if you don't mind,' said Harry, and with Matt following on behind, he stepped into the house.

Following Larry down a short corridor, Harry noticed that the walls were dotted with photographs of him and a woman. There seemed to be no plan to how they had been hung, no real thought to occasion or time or place. Instead, they were dotted all around, a dot-to-dot of memories through the years, where perhaps only Larry could see the lines that joined them together.

'Through here, then,' Larry said, and Harry and Matt followed him into a kitchen.

'Tea?'

'We're okay, thank you,' said Harry.

'Not sure I am,' Larry said, and proceeded to fill a kettle. 'May as well sit down.'

A small farmhouse dining table and chairs sat against the wall, and Harry and Matt each pulled up a chair.

'The pictures in the hall,' Harry said, as Larry waited for the kettle to boil, using the time to collect a mug, a tea bag, and some milk from the fridge.

'My wife,' Larry said. 'Angela. Gone three years now, you know? Only seems like yesterday she was sitting where you are now. I do miss her something terrible, like.'

Harry heard the grief crack his words and crush their edges.

'I'm sorry,' he said. 'Losing someone, it's hard. And I don't think time does really heal, do you?'

Larry, his tea now made, walked over to the table and sat down between Matt and Harry.

'Not a chance of it,' he said. 'I still talk to her, you know? Every damned day. I reckon people think I'm mad, but I'm not. It's just that I've spent so much of my life with the woman I loved that I can't seem to go on without her.' He tapped a hand against his chest. 'She's still here, in me, you see? I can feel her, smell her sometimes, too. Is that strange? Mornings mostly, when I get up and walk through to the bathroom, then downstairs; it's like she's waiting for me on the stairs, and I get to walk through her. It used to scare me, but I look forward to it now. It's my favourite part of the day.'

'I need to ask you some questions,' Harry said. 'Is that okay, Larry?'

'Of course it is, ask away. I've nothing to hide.'

Harry wondered about that.

'Saturday night gone; can I ask where you were?'

Larry smiled.

'Oh, I think you know, don't you? Otherwise, why would you be here?'

'Just answer the question, Larry,' Harry said.

'I was at the Fountain, as you well know. Met up with Angela's old quoits team, as we do a couple of times every month. I don't always go, because I'm not always in the mood, but mostly I make the effort. Angela loved it, you see, throwing the quoits. I even made her her own set, you know, to help her practice? For when she fell ill, like, not before that. She was a hell of player, could drop an apple into a bucket at fifty yards! Never seen anything like it.'

'You made Angela her own set?'

'Do you want to see them?'

Harry wasn't sure that he did, but he knew he had to, and gave a nod.

Larry stood up, and popped out into the hall, returning with what looked to be a handmade green canvas satchel. He rested it reverently on the table.

'The illness, it made her weak, you see? But she still loved to throw. With the regulation quoits too heavy in the end, I made her this set, and we'd go and play together on the quoits pitch behind the Fountain. I was hopeless, always have been. But Angela? Like I said, an apple into a bucket at fifty yards. She was a dead shot.'

'Is that what you were doing Saturday night?'

'I left the pub early,' said Larry. 'I was tired, and it was getting a bit rowdy. Then some young idiot spilled his beer, and that was it for me. So, I headed off, but when I got back here, I wasn't in the mood to go to bed. I'd not had anything to drink, hardly touch the stuff, really, so I decided the best thing I could do was to talk to Angela down at the quoits pitch, so that's what I did.' He leaned forward, gave Harry a wink, then added, 'She's helping me improve my game, you see? I'm actually doing rather well!'

'You were down on the quoits pitch that evening, then?'

'I was, and I had these with me.'

Before Harry could stop him, Larry had pulled the quoits out of the bag.

'They're a bit dirty, I'm afraid. Sorry about that.'

He handed one to Harry.

'See? They're a lot lighter than the ones the Fountain has, aren't they? Like I said, made them myself. Angela needed light ones, so I did my best, using an old angle grinder to shave off as much weight as I could, but without making them weak. They're a bit thin in places ... sharp.'

Harry saw dark marks and grey clay on the quoit in his hand.

'Can you tell me what happened then? After you'd thrown a few quoits?'

'I sat down on our bench,' said Larry. 'I had it put there in memory of Angela, but also so that I'd have somewhere I could always go and just sit and talk to her.'

'She was your shepherdess,' said Matt.

'That was my nickname for her, yes.'

'Why? You weren't farmers, were you?'

At that, Larry laughed almost too loudly, the sound of it twisted with nerves and fear.

'No, we were never farmers. Owned a little hardware shop in town. It's an antiques place now, isn't it? Trade dropped, couldn't make a living from it, and the stress of that just made Angela more ill, especially when we had to sell up and I took up being a delivery driver.'

Harry realised then that Pique Antiques was Larry's old shop.

'Did you push someone into the window of your old shop that night?'

Larry gave a shrug.

'It was one of the lads from that group, wasn't it? I'd been walking around Hawes after leaving the pub, getting more and more angry about what I'd seen, not really sure what I should do, or why I was so angry. I decided I needed to talk to my Angela because she'd help me make sense of things, wouldn't she? Help me decide what I should do. I couldn't get home quick enough, to grab the quoits you see? So, I ran back to my vehicle, which I'd parked behind the chippy, and I think I do remember knocking into someone on the way. Sorry about that.'

'What was wrong with your wife?' Matt asked.

'Not sure we ever really worked that out, if I'm honest,' Larry explained. 'Always struggled a bit with her mental health. She'd be anxious a lot, get stressed. The loss of the shop made it worse. She stopped eating, hid away, really. Got weaker and weaker. Then, one winter, the flu took her. I miss her, you know? I do miss her terribly.'

In those words, Harry heard Larry's heart breaking.

'But the nickname,' he pressed, following up Matt's question. 'Why Shepherdess?'

Larry said, 'From the moment I first met Angela, all those years ago, she always called me her lamb. Larry the Lamb, you see? That old kids' television show? My name's Laurence, but Larry's what everyone calls me. Anyway, I couldn't be the only one of us with a nickname, could I? I had to come up with one for her that matched. And all because of a poem by Alice Meynell. It's actually on the wall beside you, if you look.'

Larry pointed behind Harry and Matt, and they both turned in unison. There, in elaborate and quite beautiful calligraphy, was indeed a poem, framed, and hung on the wall.

'It's called The Lady of the Lambs. The first two lines say it all, I think: *She walks, the lady of my delight, a shepherdess of sheep.*'

'Then Mickey and Tracey arrived,' said Harry.

Larry sipped his tea, and as he did so, Harry saw a shake in the man's hands, which caused the surface of the liquid to ripple.

'That place, it's ours, you see?' he said. 'It's special. And what they did? It was ... it was just so wrong! There was no respect there at all! Not for me, not for Angela, not for the Dales. I had to do something to stop them, didn't I? Surely you can see that?'

'You struck Mickey with a quoit.'

'It was all I had,' Larry replied. 'I thought it would just bounce off. But it didn't, and I didn't really realise until after, until ... Well, you know ...'

Harry was about to ask another question when Larry said, 'Anyway, how do you know all this? How? I've been so careful, doing my work ...'

'You told Mandy you saw the body from your van. I realised today that was impossible; you can't see the quoits pitch from any vehicle, no matter where you park. In fact, if you stand down on the quoits pitch yourself and look up, all you'll see is the Fountain's roof and some sky. There's just no way you could've seen someone was down there if you hadn't already known. And if you'd walked over to the edge and looked down and seen him, then I think you'd have just said that, wouldn't you, instead of making something up about the van?'

'Well, that is annoying,' said Larry. 'Looks like you've got me. Is this where you arrest me?'

Harry was astonished by just how calm Larry was.

'We've a few more questions, Larry, if that's okay,' he said. 'Can you tell me where the girl is?'

'You mean Tracey?' said Larry. 'Of course; she's upstairs!'

THIRTY-EIGHT

Harry was more confused than he had been about anything in his entire life, because Tracey was sitting opposite him, and she seemed absolutely fine.

'Can you run that by us again, please, Tracey, if you don't mind?' Harry requested.

Tracey shrugged.

'Of course not. I don't see what the trouble is, really.'

'Just ... just entertain us, please,' said Matt.

Tracey smiled at Larry, who returned the same.

'I arranged to meet with Mickey through a friend of his. Mickey seemed okay, like really nice, but then, as we talked about what we were going to do, he said he didn't want to go to his room, he wanted to stay out. I said that wasn't what I was into, but he was very persuasive—'

'By which you mean he offered you more money,' said Harry.

'Yes, exactly that. So, we went behind the pub, and then down to that bit of grass, and we started having sex.'

'And then?'

'And then Mickey started to get really violent with it all. He was fine to begin with, it was fun, but then it wasn't and I wanted it to stop and he didn't and he wasn't listening. He started slapping me, gripping me really tightly, it was horrible, and it hurt.'

'You screamed out,' said Matt.

'Couldn't help myself,' said Tracey. 'I wanted someone to hear me and come help. I thought his mates might have followed, just to watch, but I've no idea where they went after we left them up at that children's playground. Anyway, Larry was there, wasn't he? And he knocked Mickey out, dragged him off me, and brought me here to clean me up.'

Harry thought about what Larry had actually done to Mickey.

'How did he clean you up?' Matt asked.

'I didn't really know how dirty I was, how messy, but Larry helped me. I was cold, really cold, so he insisted I take off my jacket and top and put on his instead, just to keep dry until we got to his car.'

'You were very trusting,' said Harry.

'Larry is a kind man,' said Tracey. 'I knew that straight away. Anyway, we did that, and when we got here, he put all my clothes in the wash and gave me some of his wife's just to tide me over. He even popped into Hawes to pick me some new things up, so that I didn't feel weird about it. I mean, none of it's what I'd choose, but it's comfy and clean, and I can't really go walking around in what I'd wear when meeting a client, can I?'

'And you've been here ever since?'

'Yes.'

Harry remembered something from meeting with Leah.

'Did you let Leah know you were okay?'

'I wanted to, but my phone was ruined by the mud and the

rain. I dropped it while I was with Mickey. It was Larry who found it.'

So, that last message had been sent by Larry, and not Tracey, then, Harry realised.

'Leah's really worried,' Harry said. 'And what about your cat?'

Tracey gave a shrug.

'Leah's fine, she'll just be enjoying looking after my cat. And Larry has been really kind to me. He's looked after me, cooked me some amazing food, put me up in the spare room. It's like a little holiday, really. Honestly, he's such a sweetheart!'

Harry shook his head, not only in disbelief, but also in some attempt to dislodge the memories he was making in these very moments, in the hope that they would just float away for good.

'And you're sure you're okay? Larry hasn't got you here under duress?'

Tracey laughed.

'Little Larry is the sweetest lamb, of course he hasn't!'

Harry decided it was best to send Tracey on her way, and she headed back upstairs to the bedroom she had been staying in all this time.

'Maybe we should get on with the rest of what's been going on,' Harry said. 'But, before we do, and as weird as this feels to say, thank you for looking after Tracey.'

'It's been a pleasure,' said Larry. 'I was a little worried that what happened might've damaged her, but I don't think she saw any of it. Well, I know she didn't, because I'd been watching, hadn't I?'

'Hardraw,' said Matt. 'And Aysgarth Falls.'

'The link is that you deliver food from a warehouse in Richmond,' Harry explained. 'It's on the same estate that Anderson has an office, which is how you knew where to post your note, and that you could do so without drawing any attention to yourself. That's how you chose your victims, wasn't it? While you were driving around? It was millionaire's shortbread that gave it away, you know. I realised I'd had it at both Hardraw and Aysgarth. It was just another piece of the puzzle; didn't make much sense on its own, but when it clicked into its rightful place, everything became clear. The little details, you see? They're the things that always matter.'

'I didn't mean to kill that young man,' Larry said. 'But it's no loss, is it? The way he treated the place, the way his friends were so awful in the pub. I didn't see it all, but I heard about it.'

'That doesn't explain Hardraw or Aysgarth,' said Harry. 'Not in the slightest.'

Larry's voice became quieter, and for the first time since arriving, Harry heard menace in it.

'You wouldn't understand.'

'Try me.'

'You mean you don't know? What about my note? Was that not enough?'

'I don't like poetry,' said Harry.

'I do,' said Matt, 'but that wasn't it, not by a long shot.'

Larry bristled.

'They're destroying it, though, aren't they?' he said. 'All of them, all the people who come here, to get drunk with their friends, to let their dogs shit everywhere or chase sheep, to not even pay to be here, freeloading off the goodness of the people who actually live here. It has to stop! Before everything is ruined, by people like them, people who aren't from round here!'

'And that's what it's all about?' asked Harry. 'Really, Larry? It's just you with a grievance against tourists?'

'They're not tourists, they're vermin!' Larry spat back, now on his feet, thrusting his chin forward in some vain attempt to make himself look important, powerful even. 'I am the lamb become the wolf! And I will keep these dark valleys safe from those who come here to destroy them! I will! It's what I have to do! For Angela! Can't you see that? Can't you?'

Harry stood up.

'Sorry, Larry,' he said, towering over the man. 'No, I can't.'

Matt rose to his feet and revealed a set of handcuffs.

'Larry Bainbridge, I am arresting you for the murders of Mickey Lancaster and Christina Judd. You do not have to say anything. But it may harm your defence if you do not mention when questioned something that you later rely on in court. Anything you do say may be given in evidence.'

Harry watched Matt lead Larry into the blue flashing lights, waiting for him outside his front door. There was the third victim still to add to that list, but with only a driving licence, and nothing confirmed as yet from the postmortem, a positive ID had not yet been made. But when it was, Larry would be charged with that, too. Then he made his way to the stairs, and slowly, wearily, started to climb them to collect Tracey and take her home.

THIRTY-NINE

A couple of weeks had passed since Larry's arrest, and Harry was, out of choice, sitting the closest he'd ever been to a murder scene, to have a drink. There was only so much paperwork and admin he could cope with before wanting to burn the Community Centre to the ground, so having finished late, he'd sent a message to Grace to meet him at the Fountain, and made it the short distance around to the public bar.

Huddled up in his favourite spot, sitting in the old wingback chair in the corner near the fire, he thought back over everything that had happened since Ben and Liz's engagement party.

The most important development since Larry's arrest was that Sowerby had ID'd the third victim. Larry had been more than a little aggrieved that no one could understand why he'd done what he'd done, and had spent an awful lot of time ranting about the loss of his old business, tourists, and for some reason, the cost of a tin of beans, as though that was some kind of yardstick against which to measure the downfall of society. Overall, though, he'd been generally compliant during the interview.

Tracey had returned home to Leyburn, and was being

provided support by Jen to help her come to terms with the reality of what she had experienced as opposed to the fantasy which Larry had spun for her.

Next of kin of all the victims were also being supported, and once again Harry was struck by how far-reaching such appalling crimes were, the echoes of which he had no doubt would roll on for years and through generations.

Reaching for his pint of Gamekeeper, a beer which Matt was firmly of the opinion was the best ale in the world, and if drunk at the Fountain, the best poured, Harry took a deep, deep draught. He went to take another, and possibly finish it, thus making a trip to the bar before Grace arrived necessary, when his phone buzzed. Too weary to think, he answered before he'd realised what he was doing.

'Harry.'

Harry almost took his phone away from his ear to stare at it.

'Margaret?'

'I've been meaning to call you.'

'About what?'

Harry was confused, and decided to take that next glug of beer. Why on earth would Margaret Shaw be calling him after work? Had something happened? Was it Rebecca? Was she okay? She'd been complaining about not being able to sleep... He understood all about PTSD, and as Sowerby had suffered from that herself, then perhaps—

'It's about you and why you're being such an idiot, that's what.'

That unexpected reply caught Harry sharp.

'Margaret, I'm tired,' he said. 'If there's something you want to talk about, perhaps you could pop down to the office tomorrow?'

'No need, this will be fine. Won't take long, I'm sure.'

Harry braced himself for a broadside.

'Have you decided what you're going to do about Grace?'

That question baffled Harry.

'Do about her? I'm not going to do anything about her. We've just bought a house together, in case you hadn't noticed, and I think everything's going fine.'

'And that's it, is it? You've bought a house and there's nothing else that's on your mind, or should be?'

'Not as I'm aware, no. There's a bit of decorating to do, and we probably need to get some decent furniture to replace the mismatched stuff we've got now, but that's about it, I think.'

'Harry, if I could reach my hand down this phone, I'd give you such a slap.'

Harry laughed.

'Look, Margaret, I've no idea what's rattled your cage, but you've already interrupted a quiet pint, and I've Grace on her way now, so I'd rather you didn't interrupt that as well. So, if it's all the same with you, what say we—'

'Are you going to marry the girl or not?'

The question slammed into Harry like a runaway train.

'Marry? As in Grace?'

'Yes, marry as in Grace. Who on earth else could I be talking about you marrying, Harry? Well, are you?'

'People don't have to get married, you know,' Harry said. 'They can just live together and be happy ever after.'

There was a pause from Margaret's side of the conversation, and it only served to unnerve Harry.

'No, they don't have to. You're absolutely correct on that,' Margaret eventually said, 'but there's a difference between being correct and right, isn't there? Call me a bit old-fashioned —'

'I wouldn't dare!'

'—but my thinking is that there's always more to be said about being married than not. There's a commitment to it that nothing else comes close to. Yes, you can stay living together if you want, and never get married. You need to ask yourself, though, why you wouldn't take the next step.'

'Margaret,' Harry said, 'I'm not sure we know each other well enough to be having this conversation.'

'And I think we do,' Margaret replied. 'Living together is a first step, but true love, true commitment? That's something else, I promise you. That's marriage.'

There was another pause.

'You finished now?' Harry asked.

'I am.'

'You're sure?'

'Very.'

'Good,' said Harry, and hung up, then turned his phone off.

Still a little stunned by Margaret's call, Harry got up to go fetch another drink, and get one for Grace at the same time, when Grace pushed in through the main door and gave him a wave.

'Same again?'

Harry mouthed a yes, and a couple of minutes later Grace was sitting beside him on a stool.

'You look a bit frazzled,' she said, lifting her pint of Gamekeeper to Harry before taking a gulp.

'What? Oh, yes, I mean, you know, just a bit weary, that's all. Dogs okay?'

Grace rolled her eyes.

'Well, Gandalf seems to be settling in okay.'

'We're not keeping him,' Harry said. 'We're not.'

Jim had looked after the dog they'd found at Hardraw until a couple of days ago when Harry and Grace had taken over, the aim being to share him around until one of his owner's friends took him on. So far, however, no one had come forward and offered.

'But he's so lovely,' Grace smiled. 'It would be fun.'

'No, it wouldn't,' Harry replied.

'We could give him to Ben and Liz, then,' Grace suggested. 'They'd love a dog.'

'You've asked them, then?'

'No, but I could. Well, you could, anyway. He could be an early wedding present.'

That word had Harry thinking back to Margaret's phone call. It also spurred something along in his own mind, because the subject of the phone call, and the question he would have to ask, had been on his mind now for longer than he would ever have dared to admit.

'Grace,' Harry said, 'there's something I've been meaning to ask you for a while now.'

Grace rested her glass on the table.

'Really? What? You look very serious, by the way. Are you okay? Is something the matter? What's happened?'

'No, nothing's the matter. Nothing's happened,' Harry said. 'In fact, to be honest, everything's bloody marvellous, isn't it? So, I just wondered ...'

The question floated to the top of his mind. He could read the words, he just had to say them.

'Wondered what?'

'If you would ...'

Just say the words, Harry, come on, just say them!

Grace cocked her head to one side, and smiled.

'Cat got your tongue?'

'... like to go on holiday?' Harry asked. 'Nothing too fancy, and we don't have to go far. Certainly not a cruise or anything like that. And I know it's difficult to arrange time off work, but —'

'I'd love to!' Grace replied. 'Not been on a proper holiday in years! Where do you want to go? Abroad? I'd love to go to Italy. Tuscany, how does that sound?'

'Er, it sounds good?' Harry replied. 'So, you fancy it, then? A bit of time away?'

'It's a wonderful idea,' said Grace, then sat back and added, 'You sure there wasn't something else?'

Harry picked up his glass.

'How do you mean?'

'It's just that you looked rather serious, and then you asked me about going on holiday, and that doesn't really make much sense, does it?'

Harry shook his head.

'No, not really. Just wasn't sure what you'd say.'

'I'd say yes,' Grace replied. 'Why would I say anything else?'

And for the briefest moment, Harry saw a glint in Grace's eye, and the hint of a smile on her lips, both so bright, so filled with love and humour, that he was pleased he'd not asked the question he'd really wanted to. Not because he was afraid, not because he wasn't sure, but because he wanted to do it right. And if he was going to do that, he would need a ring.

WANT TO KNOW if Harry is brave enough to pop the question while facing another deadly killer in the Dales? Scan the QR code on the next page to secure your copy of Book 20 in the DCI Harry Grimm series.

You'll also get a free Harry Grimm short story, *New Beginnings*, and be able to sign up for my VIP Club and newsletter.

ABOUT DAVID J. GATWARD

David had his first book published when he was 18 and still can't believe this is what he does for a living. Author of the long-running DCI Harry Grimm series, David was nominated for the Amazon Kindle Storyteller Award in 2023. He lives in Somerset with his two boys. Blood Fountain is his nineteenth DCI Harry Grimm crime thriller.

Visit David's website at www.davidjgatward.com to find out more about him and the DCI Harry Grimm books.

facebook.com/davidjgatwardauthor

Printed in Great Britain
by Amazon